Hollow:
A parable from Timberline County

by

Leland McBride

Table of Contents

to clan… everywhere

"The holler is a colloquialism for a hollow, a V-shaped ravine or valley between mountains or a long depression in the surface of the land that usually contains a river." (American Heritage Dictionary of the English Language, Fifth Edition. Copyright © 2016 by Houghton Mifflin Harcourt Publishing Company)

FOREWORD

In the current political climate, I believe it is advantageous and necessary to add my novel to the dialogue regarding contemporary Appalachia. This submission is in partial response to *Hillbilly Elegy*, the semi-biographical novel of Vice-Presidential candidate J.D. Vance. It is marketable, timely, and has literary value as well. Hollow: A Parable from Timberline County is based on the actual dynamics of how some families struggled and survived, amidst the odds, to survive the onslaught of the political and economic systems that exploited their land and resources through the coming of the roads into the hills and hollows of Appalachia.

In the late nineteenth century, business moguls and politicians constructed roadways that brought them into the holler settlements. They penetrated the pristine environment with their grandiose schemes toward economic gain for the national security of the country: the coal and timber industry. Due to the economic plight of the region, many landowners were persuaded to abdicate property and resource rights—albeit for a pittance of what their land was worth. It was, at best, a temporary economic upswing. The distribution of coal as a main source of energy in this country and in other parts of the world was a booming yet momentary groundswell of economic gain. While many moguls and politicians garnished a fortune during this time, their relentless exploitation of the ill-informed landowners, along with their reckless ravaging of the land, eventually plundered the region into what SE Kentucky Senator Harry Caudill called "a wasteland of refuse-clogged streams and sterile hillsides," with the people of the hollers left discouraged, desperate, and grim.

Hilltops and homesteads were gutted or leveled. Without proper drainage, streams were contaminated by toxins from the runoff from strip mining and roads that connected the outside world to the coal fields. The once-fertile soil was tainted by the flow of toxins in its veins. Often, the landowners had to face the dissolution of their land from farming. Without an initiative for reforestation, the rapacious demand for timber decimated the environment and perpetuated the disruption to the natural ecosystem of the region.

As the coal industry waned, the economic repercussions in the hollers became more desperate. In short, the economic boom that offered so much promise in the late eighteenth and early nineteenth centuries, by the 1960s, emerged as destructive in its fallout. The well-being of the people in the hollers would be of grave concern for years. Health issues such as black lung and chronic heart, respiratory, and kidney disease reflected exposure to coal ash or other toxic agents present in coal, released in its mining, processing, and inhaling.

Dangerous conditions, explosions, and slides within the mines themselves proved to be a constant danger and threat to the safety of people in the hollers as well.

Coal brought the outside world into the hollows, meadows, and mountains. Corporations pursued the extraction of coal, oil, ores, timber, natural gas, and saltpeter for generations. With the industry came the revenue that established a labyrinth of roads and brought railroads and truck shipping routes that challenged the poverty of the region. Other ventures flourished on the coattails of coal. Small towns grew economically with fishing and tackle stores, libraries and schools, local cafes and restaurants, and car repair garages. But when the coal industry waned in the 1970s, so did the desperation for survival of the fittest.

Jobs were scarce. Life was difficult to sustain. Yet, persons in the hollers, like the family of Aidan and Eva Kilbride, who refused to become dependent upon taking a government "draw," found their way through escaping out of the hills: seeking a formal education or by joining the military. Some sold moonshine—and later marijuana or methamphetamine. Others would play mountain music in any venue they could find. Many just succumbed to the local Wal-Mart.

The youngest son of Aidan and Eva, Marcus Kilbride, sought his path for survival his way. This is his story—and the story of the Kilbride family—during the fallout years of the 1980s in Timberline County. In keeping with the insistence on family and tradition, there often arose a dichotomy between making a decent living and living within the embrace of "Holler Law." The nobility in the hills regarded a devotion to family tradition with the wisdom of their ancestors. This story is one of many of how persons in the hollers most often survived and crafted a trail toward well-being.

The story unfolds through the life of Marcus Kilbride, the youngest son of Aidan and Eva. He is considered the "runt of the litter" by his older siblings. In his twenties, he has already experienced the fallout of the exploitation in the region. The first chapter opens with a drug deal "gone wrong." While this is fiction, it is based on real accounts in an area of the country that is often misunderstood and ignored. It is in this reality of that exploitation that Marcus and others seek to discover a path toward happiness in the hollers.

As the story unfolds through the interconnection of residents in Timberline County, the truth of the core issues that prompted much of the behavior criticized by Vance in his book is revealed— through a fictional account but exposed just the same through actual excerpts from historical documents, poetry, commentary from the area, and song lyrics. In that sense, *Hollow* transcends the work of another novel into the venue of historical fiction.

While this is my first novel, I have authored several plays, essays, homilies, and editorials. Having studied at Bellarmine University, Cumberland College, and Oxford University, my training has been in the areas of philosophy, theology, spirituality, and contemporary issues. *Hollow* brings much of that experience into its content with literary symbols and an understanding of human behavior. This educational tenure, along with my residential and family connections to Appalachia, has enabled this project.

While this story unfolds from Appalachia, it is more an epiphany to illustrate the human condition that may be revealed as the continuing result of the fall of Adam and Eve.

Respectfully,
Brian Shoemaker
Author, *Beyond Believing: BE-living in a Wonderful World Gone Wonky*
Louisville, Kentucky
Summer, 2024

Hollow: A Parable of Timberline County

"Let us here resolve that we shall never forget, even for one moment, the common welfare of the great people of Kentucky, who look to us for a faithful discharge of the sacred trust they have placed in our hands."

(Governor Simeon Willis, *Public Papers*, 1947)

"…in the hills and hollers of the Appalachians…a proud land and these are proud men, who have rallied to the nation's flag at every hour of danger. But the deep mines are closing, and the jobs have gone, leaving men without work, many of them crippled by the accidents and disease that lurks 'down in the mines,' their land a ruin of strip mines and stinking creeks…when another child is born, 'we just add a little water to the gravy.'"

(Attorney General Robert F. Kennedy, *Speech*, September 8, 1967)

"Once again, after the onslaught of the coal industry, we have seen the gnashed land struggle to heal itself with new growth. But the stillness that lay over it now seemed to portend, this time, a different fate."

(Senator Harry Caudill, *My Land is Dying*, 1971)

Preface

The raw nobility of the Appalachian regions provided early immigrants to this country with the promise of a new existence. Familiar, time-tested traditions, along with engaging in the trials that accompany human adaptation to ecological challenges, enabled clans to find a way to survive in an often unfriendly and often perilous environment. Early settlers had to traverse twisting valleys of rich bottomland, treacherous mountain terrain, and gullies; to contend with happenstance weather patterns and flash flooding, the displacement of wild animals, venomous snakes, and onery kin, and generally, hope for God's favor and/or the survival of the fittest.

Throughout the nineteenth century, the people of the hollers survived by their cunning and thrived through their devotion to the clan, traditional values, and "holler law." The constancy of their way of life through farming, hunting, mining, and moonshining allowed them to shun the influences of the encroaching outside world. While occasional disputes over land ownership or divided loyalties from the Civil War left a legacy of hate that often erupted into feuds among rival families, somehow, the communities in the Appalachian Mountains learned how to create a community living in sync with the environment.

Clans adapted to the ecosystem of the hills and hollers, the top and bottomlands. Their primitive remedies offered noble wisdom through which to make a good life. This existence was balanced within the spectrum of the pristine environment in which they co-existed with wild thistles, fertile and undeveloped soil, rocky ravines, birds of prey, and wildlife. There was the beauty of chestnut trees, white oak, and dogwood, along with the blaze of autumn leaves. This was a place where the changing of the seasons was planned and celebrated.

Both the scent of moonshine and the savor of music were provisions in the hollers. There was freedom in the making of both.

Life in the hollers was often harsh. An appreciation for life was a necessity for survival. The freedom of living without interference from the political world beyond the mountains was mostly invigorating. A community of clans celebrated births, childhood, churchgoing, hoeing fields and shucking beans, marriage and children, old age and storytelling, and singing a loved one into eternity as living the fullness of life.

According to folk-songstress Jean Ritchie, "Travelers from the level lands always complained that they felt hemmed in my hills…cut off from the rest of the world. For us, it was hard to believe there was any 'rest of the world.' We trusted in the mountains to protect us from it."

In the late nineteenth century, business moguls and politicians constructed roadways that brought them into the holler settlements. They penetrated the pristine environment with their grandiose schemes toward economic gain for the national security of the country: the coal and timber industry. Due to the economic plight of the region, many landowners were persuaded to abdicate property and resource rights—albeit for a pittance of what their land was worth.

It was, at best, a temporary economic upswing. The distribution of coal as a main source of energy in this country and other parts of the world was a booming yet momentary groundswell of economic gain. While many moguls and politicians garnished a fortune during this time, their relentless exploitation of the ill-informed landowners, along with their reckless ravaging of the land, eventually plundered the region into what SE Kentucky Senator Harry Caudill called "a wasteland of refuse-clogged streams and sterile hillsides," with the people of the hollers left discouraged, desperate and grim.

Hilltops and homesteads were gutted or leveled. Without proper drainage, streams were contaminated by toxins from the runoff from strip mining and roads that connected the outside world to the coal fields. The once fertile soil was tainted by the flow of toxins in its veins. Often, the landowners had to face the dissolution of their land from farming. Without an initiative for reforestation, the rapacious demand for timber decimated the environment and perpetuated the disruption to the natural ecosystem of the region.

As the coal industry waned, the economic repercussions in the hollers became more desperate. In short, the economic boom that offered so much promise in the late eighteenth and early nineteenth centuries, by the 1960s, emerged as destructive in its fallout. The well-being of the people in the hollers would be of grave concern for years. Health issues such as black lung and chronic heart, respiratory, and kidney disease reflected exposure to coal ash or other toxic agents present in coal, released in its mining, processing, and inhaling. Dangerous conditions, explosions, and slides within the mines themselves proved to be a constant danger and threat to the safety of persons in the hollers as well.

Coal brought the outside world into the hollows, meadows, and mountains. Corporations pursued the extraction of coal, oil, ores, timber, natural gas, and salt petre for generations. With the industry came the revenue that established a labyrinth of roads and brought railroads and truck shipping routes that challenged the poverty of the region. Other ventures flourished on the coattails of coal. Small towns grew economically with fishing and tackle stores, libraries and schools, local cafes and restaurants, and car repair garages. But when the coal industry waned in the nineteen seventies, so did the desperation for survival of the fittest and devotion of the faithful.

*

"In Appalachia, exploitation goes hidden under the rhetoric of economic development. People are forced out of their homes and from their farms because it is more profitable to let mud slide into their living rooms and across cornfields than it is to mine coal with care. Little thought is given to farmlands, which would have fed families for generations to come. People find that there are no jobs in the mountains because a cheap and ruthless method of mining requires few laborers. People are forced to take mining jobs, which destroy their homes and the entire economic base of the region, or else move away to migrant cities…Miners are injured and die because it is more profitable to mine coal in unsafe conditions than to run safe mines."(Harry Caudill, Mountain Life and Work, June-July 1972, 22)

The following is a story based on many of the dynamics I have described above.It is a novel, but it is based upon true stories, of life in the hollers during and after the sagging coal industry. The mines were shutting down. Jobs were scarce.Life was difficult to sustain.Yet, persons in the hollers who did not want to be subjected to taking a government "draw" found their way through escaping out of the hills: seeking a formal education or joining the military. Some sold moonshine—and later marijuana or meth. Others would play mountain music in any venue they could find. Many just succumbed to gasping and groveling for a minimum wage at the local Wal-Mart.

In keeping with the insistence on family and tradition, there often arose a dichotomy between making a decent living and living within the embrace of home-in-the-holler. The nobility in the hills highly regards a devotion to family. Family tradition with the wisdom of their ancestors is how persons in the hollers most often survived and crafted a trail toward well-being. This is the story of the struggle of one family to find their way on that trail amidst the seasons of change and influences of the outside world that would implode them.

In the late nineteenth century, business moguls and politicians constructed roadways that brought a promise of prosperity into the hollers of Appalachia. The coal industry penetrated the pristine environment with its grandiose schemes with the promise of economic gain for one and all. Due to the economic plight of the region, many landowners were persuaded to abdicate property and resource rights—albeit for a pittance--of what their land was worth.

It was, at best, a temporary economic upswing. The distribution of coal as a main source of energy in this country and in other parts of the world was a booming yet momentary groundswell of economic gain. While many moguls and politicians garnished a fortune during this time, their relentless exploitation of the ill-informed landowners, along with their reckless ravaging of the mountains, eventually plundered the region into what SE Kentucky Senator Harry Caudill called "a wasteland of refuse-clogged streams and sterile hillsides," with the people of the hollers left discouraged, desperate, and grim.

Hilltops and homesteads were gutted or leveled. Without proper drainage, streams were contaminated by toxins from the runoff and residue from strip mining from the coming of the roads that connected the outside world to the rich coal and timberland in the hollers. The once fertile soil in the bottomland was tainted by the downstream flow of toxins in its circulation. Often, the landowners faced the dissolution of their land from farming. Without a restoration or remedial plan, the rapacious demand for coal and timber decimated the environment and perpetuated the disruption of a natural and healthy ecosystem in the region.

As the coal industry waned, the economic repercussions in the hollers became more desperate. In short, the economic boom that offered so much promise in the late eighteenth and early nineteenth centuries, by the 1980s, all but collapsed, leaving much of the tenets in despair and dependent upon government handouts. The well-being of the people in the hollers would be of grave concern for years. Health issues such as black lung and chronic heart, respiratory, and kidney disease reflected exposure to coal ash and other toxic agents present through unsafe processes and less-than-satisfactory supervisory practices in the mining of coal. Moreover, hazardous conditions, explosions, and unsafe working conditions within the mines themselves proved to be a constant danger and threat to the safety of miners.

The highways and byways to and from the hollers ignited business and political visionaries with a fervor for economic profit and political influence. Corporations pursued the extraction of coal, oil, ores, timber, natural gas, and saltpeter. With the industry came

14

the revenue that established a labyrinth of roads and brought railroads and truck shipping routes that challenged the poverty of the region. Other ventures flourished on the coattails of the coal industry. Small towns grew economically with fishing and tackle stores, libraries and schools, local cafes and restaurants, and car repair garages. But when the coal industry waned in the nineteen seventies, so did the desperation for the survival of the fittest.

In keeping with the insistence on family and tradition, there often arose a dichotomy between making a decent existence for survival versus living life well at home in the holler. The nobility of life in the hollers regarded a devotion to family and tending well the land. In better days in Appalachia, there was little to no dependence on the government draw or making a living through desperate means. There was cooperation between the well-being of the clans with the company's stewardship of the land. After generations of what came to be a dependence on the coal industry, with the closing of the mines, this tradition of in the hollers became challenged, if not a fleeting memory. This is the story of the struggle of one family in the post-coal years of the 1980s who were challenged to find their way amidst a season of change and influences of the outside world that would implode them.

This is a novel, but it is based on several real stories of life in the hollers during and after the sagging coal industry. The mines were shutting down. Jobs were scarce. Life was difficult to sustain. Yet, persons in the hollers, like the clan of Aidan and Eva Kilbride who refused to settle for taking a government "draw," found ways of survival. They made their way to the last days of the coal mines and sold moonshine—and later marijuana or methamphetamine. At times, the elder Aidan Kilbride resorted to "whatever he had to do" to make a living for his clan. All the while, their youngest son, Marcus, sought his own path to survival his way.His story reflects the narratives of "holler law" for survival during the coal crisis years of the 1980s in Timberline County… where myths become sacred truths and family secrets are never spoken.

Chapter One:
Backroads and By-passes

"Once I had you and the wildwood
Now it's just dusty roads
And I can't help but blamin' your goin'
On the coming of the roads." (Billy Edd Wheeler, "The Coming of
the Roads," 1979)

"We cannot lower basic standards by building highways that will not stand up under the anticipated traffic. This would be foolish." (Kentucky Governor Bert T. Combs Public Papers, 1961)

"The demand for coal is at an all-time high in recent years. New uses for coal are being discovered almost daily. New equipment to recover coal is being designed and perfected. Shorter, more economical avenues of transportation are being opened for the shipment of your product. What does the future hold for your industry? Clearly, great problems lie ahead, problems that will test man's ingenuity and determination." (Kentucky Governor Louie B. Nunn, Public Papers, 1969)

1983. The "Good Road" initiative interconnecting major towns in Appalachia was a godsend for the time. Locals could escape from their homeplaces when necessary to the bigger cities. Drivers from the finer, urban places could drive by the picturesque scenery of the mystical mountains on paved expressways with sporadic guard rails without having to risk getting lost with any wrong-turn or disappearing off some misbegotten hillside. This was the era of the "good road" for the curious outsider who wanted to peruse the region and for the indigenous few who wanted to escape it.

Strategic road projects enhanced the opportunity for outside spectators to enjoy the pristine wilderness by automobile without the threat of being accosted by the primitive living conditions of some unfortunate residents. The bypasses were advantageously popular and politically correct. Signs of the era included billboard advertisements for motels, wildlife zoos, chewing tobacco, and pecan rolls, among many other attractions in the area. Some roads promised opportunities for employment for persons in the hollers in the wake of the dying coal industry.

It came to pass in the post-coal bust, as the coal and timber moguls made their strategic and lucrative pillaging of the land and subsequent departure of the region, that other opportunities emerged for the miners left behind. Replacing their precarious but lucrative hire in the mining and timber industries came the *quick fixes* for those who took umbrage at their plight. Umbrageous politicians showcased their promises for the re-development of the region. The clans had learned to trust alternative means for survival:moonshine, music, and ministry, and with the coming of roads, nominal-paying jobs at shopping marts in the larger towns nearby.

Over generations, seclusion in the hollers served the clans as a sheltering cocoon from both the blessings and curses of the outside world. Some feared the influences of the "civilized" world outside the mountains, believing "civilization ain't all it's cracked up to be." Others simply *had* to live there. While others *chose* to live where they could trust the clan community to provide the essentials for living not wealthily but well. Still, others broke free from the cocoon and learned to fly elsewhere. Even so, most never abandoned their reverence for the hollers from which they were nestled and nurtured.

The consequences of the booming years of mining and timber industries left much of the land bereft of good farming soil. Families learned to survive day-to-day by just doing the best they could do— some in reminiscing what life was like before the coal rush. Others looked for roads out of the hollers and home. Many locals looked for ways not only to make a living but also to create a way of life despite their unfortunate and imposed circumstances.

After the coal bust came the addiction to *the draw*. The compensation given by the government and coal moguls was intended to temporarily sustain families who suffered economically and medically from the downsizing or the closing of the coal mines. A nominal payment was made to those who had engaged in the dangers of the mines for years, only later to find themselves in the sinking sand of an economic catastrophe and the lack of health care for chronic, even terminal illnesses such as black lung and tuberculosis. Local politicians made their promises toward the recovery of the region and its people.

Thus came the rotating rhetoric of the politicians. Many local pundits with name recognition were elected by their passionate hell-fire-and-brimstone demagoguery that deferred all the blame for the plight of the region on the powerful *outsiders* their elected and ineffective predecessors.Said Timberline County Mayor James T. Cunning:

"It's devastating! It's heartbreaking now to see this place. There's no better place to live than here. To see our economy ripped out of these hollers is heartbreaking. Stopping further decline will be crucial to coal's survival. What we really need is the ability to build new coal-burning plants and keep the existing coal fire burning.

My re-election will be a large factor in coal's future and in the lives of our mountain families! It's easy to point out what our problem is, but hey, who's got a solution? Who's gonna help us? Who's got an idea? That's what I'm looking for in this year's election. Who is going to put together a plan for our homeplace? By God, I WILL!"

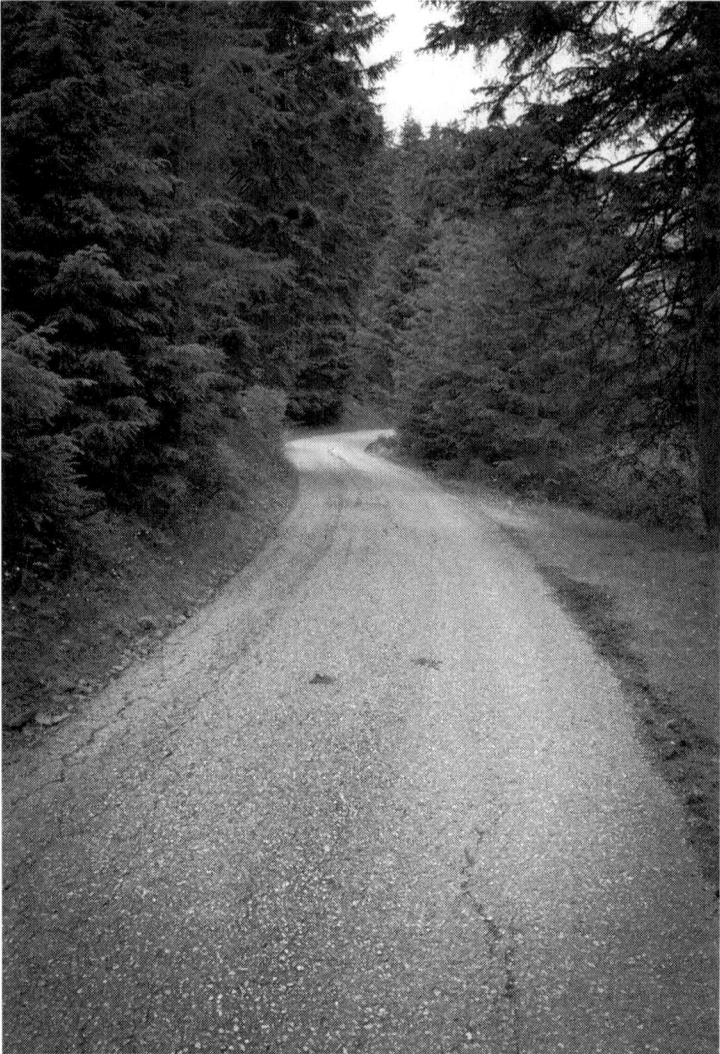

Observations of an Empathetic Bystander

There remains a hollowness in the hollers. It has been incurred through generations of inhaling the dust of things once lingering in the breeze-- the dangerous toxins from exploitive industries—what self-acclaimed Timberline "Apostle" Grace (Kilbride) Dazzlingstar prophesied as the "powers and principalities that still hover over hollers like the slithering serpent in the Garden!"

The boom and then bust in the strip-mining industry with the subsequent disruption of the Appalachian ecosystem had long-term effects on the noble legacy of how communities in the mountains had learned to adapt their lives to the hollers. Much of what transpired since the booming years of extracting coal was both a blessing and a curse. The blessing regards an appreciation for the sudden economic prosperity in a depressed community, as well as a mutual appreciation for the natural resources of the land. *The curse?* The exploitation of the community by political pundits, a depreciation for the mountain culture, as well as the plundering of terrain: runoff toxins from gouging the hilltops, waylaying the timberline, and thus, contaminating streams and the exploitation of vulnerable families. All of which contributed to challenges to a person's physical health and general peace of mind.

With the downturn of the coal industry, misbegotten promises of the coal moguls, and the subsequent displacement of jobs, Appalachian personhood-in-community was diminished by depression and despair. Their once-interdependence in the community was degraded to a dependence on the government "draw" and a desperate quest for survival and dignity.

The coming and going of the roads. And a people unprepared for the exploitation that followed. evolved into an emerging, unhealthy system: an unrelenting addiction to the government *draw*, the influx and success of the marijuana, opiate, methamphetamine, and fentanyl business, an ever-deepening social depression, and at times, the darksome behavior of Social Darwinism: "natural selection as decided by holler law."

To break free from the effects of what has been perpetrated upon them, the indignities of the past, the holler communities will have to rediscover the nobility and interdependence that is their true Appalachian heritage. The essentials for the recovery of Timberline County? An informed faith in the greater possibilities of what has been rebuffed as impossible, a renewed respect and stewardship for the natural resources and landscape, an investment in opportunities for student-specific education, a resurgence of interdependence within a healthier community and clan; and, moreover, as sub-creators with the Divine, initiate a momentum toward a restoration of "Eden:" the majestic, pristine and fragile environment of the hollers. (Author)

*

Marcus: The Parable

"I saw the poor that day in Appalachia with my own eyes…the gaunt, defeated men whom the land had abandoned; their tired, despairing wives; their pale, undernourished children…poverty summed up in fear."(President Lyndon B. Johnson, from Vantage Point, 1971, p. 79)

"In my hour of darkness

In my time of need,

O Lord, grant me vision,

O Lord, grant me speed."(Gram Parsons & Emmylou Harris, 1974)

"Being of these hills, I cannot pass beyond." (James Still, Heritage, 1935)

Miraculously, or as if by some providence, his father's pick-up truck survived the tri-fold hardships of Appalachian life: potholes, rust, and patchwork repair. Marcus himself had survived many such tormenting times, yet he was daunted by the darkness, tenuously negotiating the mountain service road during a torrential downpour such as this. The roads were slick. Slimy water flowed down the hillsides and over the road, which occasioned him to feel as though its momentum would carry him over the narrow embankment. Nothing on this run was naturally cooperative with the wing-and-a-prayer maneuvering condition of Aiden Kilbride's legacy.

Marcus sighed when he finally saw the God-rock. Illumined by his dimming headlights, he saw the familiar graffitied boulder, a signpost spray-painted in red: *"GOD VISITS FOR SIN."* Here, at this remote stretch of road, the deal would be made again. It was here he could brake in neutral and get his bearings. Take a breather. Still, the constant pounding of the storm was unnerving. The truck was wafting in the wind, and the worn old tires gave him little confidence on the slippery pavement. Even to one as youthfully fit as Marcus Kilbride, such night squalls reminded him of those frightening nights he experienced as a boy. He hated those stormy nights in the hollers!

The radio was crackling with static. The rain pummeled the roof of the truck. The intermittent screeching of the wipers was unnerving. He stomped the knob on the floor; the headlights flashed to *brighten* the message painted on the boulder. The faded red letters illumined: *"GOD VISITS FOR SIN."* Carefully, he directed the truck to the side of the road, surrendered the truck to neutral, and waited.

12:34 am. Marcus was late for the transaction. But the storm was certainly a valid excuse. It had never mattered much to his business partner in the past. But tonight was different; Marcus was intentionally hesitant—intimated by the storm, yes, but also uneasy about determining this transaction to be his last. He grew more pensive. Those invested in his part of the deal would not be at ease with his decision. The truck sputtered. Fumes of oily gas spewed from the spastic engine. Its pungent aroma drifted into the inside of the truck until the windows surrounding him became foggy with residue. He nearly choked at the smell, but he was relieved that with the shrouded windows, he could not readily be identified.

At 12:35, the passenger door flung open. Carl "Casper" Jaspers leaped in, breathless and drenched. "Shit! Marcus! Just shit!" He yelled, wiping his face with his palm. "You know how long I've been trenched? Damn, kid! Where the hell have you been? My contact ain't ...well, of a normal nature."

Although a year or two older than Marcus, Carl Jaspers was his high school chum. Now, he was more of a colleague when it came to sensitive business transactions. Timing became important as the competition between the locals and the cartels intensified in the hill country. He never knew when and where the outside players might "notice" his personal Timberline "investments." At this point, he, Marcus, and Carl's secret distributor carried on a successful clandestine operation in Timberline County with little regard from those outsiders. Jaspers could run his operation with little notice from anyone. In fact, as a child, Carl Jaspers was nicknamed "Casper" because he was always there and gone, flitting about from venture to misadventure, appearing and disappearing like the misbegotten ghost.

Marcus reached under his seat and tossed to him a bulging bag of bills. "Here! I ran the run. Ever-body paid."Casper reached into the bag and pulled out the bounty. He sorted the bills with his fingers. "Looks to be all here. You're an honest courier, Marc. Good for you…a good run!"

Marcus stared at his colleague and extended an open hand to retrieve his pay. Casper grinned, swiping his dripping sleeve over his chum's face. "Here's your cut."He folded a few bills, placed them in a hidden pocket in the glove compartment, and slammed it shut. "There you go. Done."

"I'm done, Carl. Last run. Can't use the truck for…"

"Huh?"

"I'm done. Can't do it no more."

"Huh? What the hell?"

"No more runs…I'm done."

"SHEEE-IT! You're in this." Casper scoffed.

Marcus shook his head. "No more."

"Can't give you no more right now, Marc. Shit, the other guys want'in more too! Can't do it right now!'"

Marcus bit his upper lip. "Count the change."

"Huh? The change?" he repeated.

"Yeah." Marcus exclaimed again, "Count the damn change! Every penny!

Casper shook the bag. The coins leftover in the bag sounded like jingle bells. "So, you want the change? Fine! We can settle for the change!"

"I don't want the change! Ain't it shit that we got coins, Carl? Where'd the change come from?"

"So?"

Marcus shook his head as he continued. "Them coins came from a kid! A kid 'bout seven or eight. Just a kid. My stop at the cemetery—his daddy sent him...paid with change— 'probly HIS own dimes and nickels! A little kid, never seen him before."

"It is what it is, Marc," Carl assured him. "Survival."

Marcus shook his head again. "No. I can't do this no more."

"You can't ditch me! Hell, Marcus, you need this as much as the rest of us. What the hell else you gonna do? Work at the Food Mart? Just make the damn run—get the money, drop the shit and run! You don't have to be Jesus for anybody!"

"It's not the same: shine was shine. Weed was weed. But this shit… no more."

Casper huffed, "So you gonna work *for* Rawley? Huh? He'll put you in the dirt. You won't last a day! It'll bury you. This 'shit' is what it is now, kid! This is your future." He tossed the bag onto the front seat beside Marcus. "Take the damned change!"

Marcus snapped back. "Is my full cut in that glove compartment?"

"Mostly." Casper smiled.

"Damn, Carl!"

Casper countered, "You get what I can afford. The other guy! You don't know him, but if you did, you'd know he ain't nobody to screw with. You make the delivery; I'll bicker with the loser. Hell, Marcus, be patient!"

Suddenly, a dull beam of a flashlight hit the side mirror of the truck. After a moment or two, a man exited what looked to be a dilapidated old car. Casper turned around to see a shadowy figure stepping slowly, precariously toward the truck, then stopped a few feet away. "Wait for me. I gotta negotiate." He clenched a wad of bills in his fist and, creaking open the passenger door of the truck, stepped outside.

The rain had subsided for the moment. He leaned in toward Marcus. "Don't go *nowhere!*" He whispered, "I'll up yer cut now…tonight! Don't leave me, Marc! You're my delivery boy, not a damned Food City bag boy! Keep yer truck in neutral. I'll be right back."

The flickering, dim beam from the connection behind reflected on the truck's rearview mirror again. Marcus sunk low into the seat to conceal his presence. Casper turned quickly to the approaching beam, shielding his eyes. The shadow man stopped several feet away, standing in a drizzling mist. Marcus peeked over the seat to the back window of the truck. He could only see the image of the connection, which was not targeting the beam of his flashlight directly at Casper. A clump of trash bags dangling from the man's fist was thrown over his head and into the bed of the truck.

Casper slammed the door of the truck securely behind him. He took a pensive step toward the shadow man, extending to him a fist of bills. As the two drew closer, suddenly, the transaction went array. From inside the truck, Marcus heard a muffled but angry altercation of obscenities between the two men. The broken defroster on the truck would not allow him to see any more than their images crossing back and forth around each other like two cocks gearing up for a fight, leering for the lessor's wounds.

With a torrential wind came another downpour. Casper Jaspers and the shadow man were tussling— shoving one another, swapping fists, their arms flaying about. They were screaming at each other now. As Casper stepped toward him, he lost his footing in the mud. When he did, the shadow man thrust his fist again and again into Casper's frame, falling him to the ground. Carl Jaspers didn't move.

Marcus gasped and turned away, holding firmly to his steering wheel. He prepared to put the car in "D."Haplessly, he pressed the brake pedal. The one brake light that still worked lit up the back of the truck. The two men were now illumined in a dim red glow. In the rearview mirror, Marcus saw the shadow man straighten his back and jerk his head away from his friend—his eyes aglow, reflecting the red light. Jaspers was lying still in a moist, reddish puddle. The red light awakened the shadow man to his nemesis in the truck.

Hastily, Marcus sat up, shifted the truck into "D," and stepped on the gas. But the truck merely sputtered and stalled. The light on the dash dimly flashed "E.""Oh my God." Marcus whimpered.

Quickly, he creaked open the driver's side door and slithered out, crawling on his hands and knees to the front of the truck. The shadow man was coming closer. In a panic, Marcus, slipping in the muck, leaped off the ridge and slid downward into the dark ravine, into the concealment of the darksome terrain. Down--down the mountainside, he fell, bounding lower in the mire, the thickets, and jagged rocks until he was caught suddenly, held fast by a protrusion of outstretched limbs. He was wounded but was too terrified to bother. He glanced upward toward the beams from both the shadow man's flashlight and from his daddy's truck. There, yards away, he could see the shadow man, looking down, casting the torch and scanning about for the one who "could not get away."

"God." Marcus whispered scarcely above a breath, "God."

Marcus's body was aching everywhere, but he remained motionless. The shadow man stood his ground just atop the ridge. Without seeing Marcus huddled in the camouflage, he cursed the truck and twitched away in retreat. Marcus stayed where he was, crouching like an aborted fetus in the oozing mud and mire. The ridge with the God-rock was only a hike away from his mother's home. He waited, concealed by the darkness.Despite the slimy residue of the runoff from the mountainside that bathed his limp and shivering body, Marcus was determined not to move until he was certain the shadow man was gone.

The rain subsided a bit. His hiding place now seemed to offer some shelter. Then he noticed the headlight of his truck was shifting—moving in spasms. His father's truck was curving toward the edge of the precipice. It slid in the mud, curving and leaning now until the headlight was pointing down directly toward him. Then down came the truck—over the edge of the mountainside, an avalanche of metal—crashing, squealing, booming into the trees and rock, ripping off the rusting parts from its body and tearing apart its remains all about the terrain until it finally came to lodge in the thick underbrush below him a few yards away.

Marcus was scarcely moving, nearly fainted away. He glanced subtly upward. The shadow man appeared again, pointing his flashlight downward, inspecting his directed demolition. Marcus's face was smeared with muddy, black run-off. It provided him with ready camouflage. Evidently satisfied with his work, the shadow man retreated from the ledge and disappeared.

Marcus could smell the smoldering truck, hissing and groaning.He lay still.His shoulder ached from displacement, and his mind was discombobulated with thoughts of what had just happened to him…and whatever came of Casper Jaspers?He managed to usher himself into a small cleft where he would be sheltered from the rain and, at most, be hidden from the shadow man if he were to return. He eased his breathing, inhaling a malodorous blend of fuel and sweat. He was consumed by both fright and fatigue. Adrift between the ethereal and the earthly, the aroma prompted him into a reminiscence of a moment he had once-prayed long-forgotten.

"In Timberline County, if you're living, you're still working in coal. If you ain't got the mines, you ain't got much." bellowed Aiden Kilbride to his sons. "If you're going to live in these hills, then you got to shovel whatever shit you can. I ain't afraid to shovel it back to any of 'em!"

The serpentine backroads to Timberline, even in the best of conditions, was an adventurous route. On a dark, drizzling night as this was, even the likes of Aiden Kilbride, who had driven these winding, cheap concrete roads since he was a young boy, was agitated. His hands gripped the steering wheel until his fingers were numb. 50-55-60 mph., then a sudden break for the curve…30 mph.The truck shifted from side to side with the curvature of the road. The wipers randomly swept the windshield. One headlight led the way, and the other flickered now and then.It was a horridly hypnotic ride for eight-year-old, Marcus.

"Whoa!" Aiden mumbled as his truck weaved abruptly around a narrow curve, "Now you don't get scared, boy! Stop that whimpering! I know what I'm do'in. This truck and me been run'in shine long before you was even thought of. It's our gospel ship! A vessel of salvation!"Marcus glared with large, open eyes, staring at the condensation on the windshield. His jacket was unzipped, and he was trembling with the chill. "Zip up, Marcus! Your momma will have a fit if you come home with a chill."

Every now and then, the wearied brakes on the man's truck groaned and then squealed. *"Slow down,"* Marcus thought to himself.Sparks of adrenaline ignited with each jerk of the steering wheel. But the boy remained silent, held fast by a frayed seatbelt and a strap fastened snuggly around his small torso.

"Want to hear the radio?" his daddy asked. "Maybe you won't be such a pount'in possum boy over there with the radio."

Marcus didn't care one way or the other. No tune coming over the airwaves would remedy either his nauseous belly or his trauma.He kept silent.Aidan tweaked the dial to "ON." Amidst the static, the boy heard a fiery preacher from up one of the nearby hollers. While the words were hard to discern, the holy rage in the man's voice was not. He hated sin and those who blatantly committed it: "The drunkards and the cussers, the adulterers and the haters of the church"were all the targets of his bully radio pulpit. God was positioning Himself even at that moment to pour heaven's wrath upon "blasphemers, sluggards, hell-bound politicians who took prayer out of school, and children who were disobedient to their parents!" The tirade ebbed and flowed through the vexing frequency of the car radio. Now and then, lightning would flash and prompt more static—and another jolt of fear in the young boy: "God is angry."

"It is time for repentance! Time for God's deliverance from the wiles of the devil!" preached the voice of God through the airwaves.

"This is good." Aidan began, "We'll get your holy licks on the radio tonight, so you won't have to get up and go with your momma in the morning." He adjusted the dial on the radio with one hand steered the wheel firmly with the other."Damn. This run took longer than I thought. Didn't know it would be a hard rain and…all."

The boy stared blankly out the side window. The rain pelted the glass. He shuddered again with a sudden chill and wrapped his arms around his chest. After a breath or two, his father smiled, "Nah! Don't fret about your momma…she'll be real glad we got this cash on hand. It weren't a good time for us this month. But don't fret 'bout it, Marcus. You did real good today. Don't fret about noth'in. You'll get used to it. We all get used to whatever we got to do."

The radio preacher closed his sermon. A "hymn of invitation" overtook the airwaves:

"I will arise and go to Jesus; he will embrace me in his arms,
In the arms of my dear savior, oh, there are ten thousand charms.

Come, ye sinner, poor and needy, weak and wounded, sick and sore,
Jesus ready stands to save you, full of pity, love, and power."

Suddenly, Aidan sang ill-harmoniously the last chorus, "'I will arise and go to Jesus, he will embrace me in his arms…' Come on, Marcus, sing it with me. You know this from Sunday School! It'll make you feel better."Then he whispered to himself, "Dammit, Lord, hoping one of those 'ten thousand charms' is gas in my tank.Runi'n low, Lord…run'in low. Seems like I'm always run'in low."

Then he insisted again, "Come on, sing Marcus.Sing! Get your mind off the lightn'in and all."

But Marcus stayed silent. He knew the words of the hymn.His mother had taught the hymn to him years ago. But he couldn't sing just now for the 'hard rain…and all.'"

The voice from God rose up suddenly, "The Bible says, "Fathers shall not be put to death because of their children…" Static overtook the voice over the airwaves"…(indistinct words) shall children be put to death because of their fathers…Each one… Deuteronomy 24…" Aidan abruptly turned it off.

Marcus sighed as they crossed the makeshift bridge to their holler. Now, the boy didn't care a snit about hell. He just hoped that God would *deliver* him safely across Eden Pass Bridge—home and to his bed. If nothing else, that much should be easy for a God who is "all mighty" to do.

His father slowed down and turned up the muddied lane that followed the rising creek, then with two more sharp veers, he maneuvered the old truck around the hillside to their gravel lot. Marcus raised—and loosened the shoulder strap. He could have cried, but he didn't. There before him, despite the downpour, he could see the flickering of a lantern from a window—a small flame, but an ever-present flame, his mother's keeping watch, wooing him to the front porch.

The truck sputtered a bit and rested at the edge of the house. Before his father could stop the sputtering of the engine, Marcus pushed open the car door and slammed it closed. He stood in the pouring rain, looking upward, motionless...deeply breathing. The drizzling rain fell soft upon his eyes and mingled with a residue of tears. Luckily, his father would only notice the rain on his face.

"Your momma's spying on us. See her?" Aiden chuckled and yelled to his wife, "It was a good run, Eva! We made a good run!" He climbed the step to the front porch and called back to his son, "What are you doing standing there, boy? Get yourself inside!"

Marcus wiped his face with the sleeve of his jacket and followed his father up to the porch. As he did, Aidan turned the boy's face upward to his and sternly reminded him, "Now don't tell your momma about... noth'in! She doesn't like me run'in the route as it is. Ya hear me, boy? She doesn't understand business with outsiders. But we men gotta do things to outsiders to get by! On this run, we had to do things to get by. An eye fer an eye...tooth fer tooth...snit for snit."

Aiden put a firm hand on his son's shoulder, ushered him through the threshold of the door, and securely locked it behind him. With one last sputter, the truck exhaled to an exhausted halt.

Chapter Two:
"Blest Be the Ties that Bind"

Nothing here e're dies,
N'er no thought or word or deed;
They fester like the kudzu vine
from misbegotten seed.
A moment in time yields
another moment in time--daring, dowdy, or dormant
But in all, 'n any time, our clan raises its shield
Despite the dormant-ed torment.
Memories, myths or lore,
Them unrepentant lies,
All live in the realm and lure
Of our timeless lullabies. (A poem by Marcus Kilbride, date
unknown)

Appalachian life has survived its most noble and nefarious heritage. From their earliest beginnings as immigrants to this ruggedly pristine region to more contemporary times, the clans in the hollers have endured the outside demand for natural resources (of timber and coal), the insidious exploitation and ownership of the land, and subsequent abandonment by the political and economic moguls of the outside world. The mountain clans have learned in whatever condition they might confront-- to therein either find a way out of no way or perhaps just become resigned to their despair.

Outsiders call it a "hollow." But to those who were raised in those valleys between ancient mountains, it is called a "holler." The living space winds through the valley, following the curvature of a stream *or crick* like a snake with both a head and a tail. Kith and kin live within a healthy proximity of one another, keeping a watchful eye out for predators and for knowing when someone within the holler is in need of prayer: God's provision and protection. Here, one can raise a voice to a neighbor up the holler and be heard.

Children and other wildlife run free, at times cooling off in the deeper sinkholes of the crik or scaling the top of the ridge where they might breathe a fresh breeze, bemused by the frameless landscape of God's mystic, natural cathedrals: the Appalachian mountains…home.

"O yes—these paths are haunted,

For we are each a ghost

A ghost where wraith is taunted.

By memories, it lost." (Robert Penn Warren, Nocturne, 1943)

The Kilbride clan has survived through generations of devotion to God, the land, and one another. Through fertile and sometimes barren fields, feuds and fests, moonshine and music, recipes and remedies—they have survived the challenges of their holler in cooperation with the harsh realities of an ever-encroaching outside world. After generations of clearing their own trails and rows of crops, the mountain communities not only carved out their own way of life but were mostly successful in insulating themselves from the whims of a modern way of life that was meandering its way ever-closer to them through the coming of the roads.

Many believed in a God who would protect their way of life through the presence of the Holy Spirit, who honored their unyielding devotion to the Gospel. The bulwark of churches was a haven for believers who were destined for heaven or for the unrepentant and un*saved* a constant reminder that they were headed for hell.When the church bells resonate on Sunday mornings, echoing in minor chords off from the mountainsides and deep into the valleys, the clans are reminded of their *respective* "payday someday," coming soon, when no one is immune from either the favor or the fire of God!

One of those bells awakened Marcus. It echoed through the misty hills of this arduous Sunday morning like reveille. Although his shoulder had somehow eased itself back into place through the night, it was still aching in the dampness of the woods and the hard ground on which he slept. He opened his eyes to the burgeoning specks of sunlight through the trees. As he roused himself, he saw the remains of his father's truck. "Damn," he whispered.His hair was stiffened with a coal-black residue from the run-off of the hillside the night before.His torn tee shirt was soaked, and his sturdy frame was unable to keep from shivering.He removed his shirt, rung it out as best he could, and quickly put it on again, but it gave him little warmth in the chill of the morning.

He had always been thought of as a "ragamuffin-child," noticeably handsome, strangely enthralling. Now, in his twenties, he was more a rugged misanthrope—weathered-weary and somehow as misbegotten as a wandering minstrel searching for the lyrics of a song.While the melody lingered here and about in his mind, the words became lost--amiss in the ruckus and ramblings in the holler.

Slowly, leaning on the cleft rock for leverage, he raised himself to his feet. His shoulder ached up and down his arm. From the tears in his jeans, he saw his legs were bloodied and bruised. He couldn't waste time to acknowledge his pain. It would be a mucky hike, but he knew the trail well enough through this part of the mountain to reach home and care for his wounds...perhaps even before his mother got home from church?

He carefully descended, slithering artfully down the slippery slope. He hesitated for a moment to examine the truck for anything worth saving—anything salvageable. It was torn asunder, almost without recognition, bent, twisted, smoldering, and wheezing. Debris was cast about everywhere—even bits of glass intermingled here and about, glistening in the sunlight with scattered dimes and nickels -- the coins his boy "customer" had given to him on his run the night before.

"Nothing worth saving." Marcus grimaced. "Damn."

To his mother, Eva Kilbride, her dead husband's truck was sacred; Elijah's fiery chariot offered a way out of no way…to a heavenly realm. Now Marcus had destroyed that vessel of her response. "Damn," he repeated.

He slid further down the slope. In his haste, he didn't notice the brutalized body of Carl "Casper" Jaspers, caught in a thicket of thorny vines just a few yards away.(As the shadow man had presumed, "Ole Casper won't be missed. Nobody ever really *seen* him no way anyhow.")On that foggy Sunday morning, neither did Marcus notice him. He was too gratified about his own survival and resolute about making his way homeward than to worry about his now-former business partner. Anyway, Carl was one who could always fend for himself. Whoever the shadow man was, he certainly could not contend with the business savvy of "Casper" Jaspers.

*

Sundays in the mountains were always a moment set apart from the other days of the week. Generations reserved Sundays to reconstitute God in their lives through a weekly reunion called "church."

Timberline County was a haven of churches: holy houses of worship; centers of social interaction, for the sharing of blessings and burdens. Church sanctuaries were a weekly reunion between denominational clans with their respective perceptions of God and all things designated holy. Although not everyone regularly attended Sunday services, all were in some way *churched* by indoctrinated influences and traditions, birth rites or death rituals, weddings, and wantonness. The churches in Timberline County stood like the stanchion of a mighty invisible fortress, weathering the vicissitudes of the seasons and keeping watch for any invasions by outsiders or any other demons.

Most of the established churches in Timberline County emerged from nineteenth-century camp meetings or evangelical revivals. In the early days, when a new preacher came to the hills, wagonloads of pilgrims from the hollers came to hear him, following the Spirit toward repentance and salvation. From the frenzy of the camp meetings came the fervency of devotion to the many respective meeting houses throughout Appalachia. Just as there was absolute devotion to one's clan, so was their complete loyalty to one's chosen mode of salvation—Baptists were decisively Baptist, Methodists were devotedly Methodist, Presbyterians were undeniably Presbyterian, and almost none of them could tolerate anything else. Mostly Catholics and non-believers who did not accept the proscribed "ways of salvation" were not only assumed to be treading the heathen-path-to hell; moreover, they were mostly shunned by the gospel-loyalists who knew themselves to be whisking upward on angel's wings toward the hallowed gates of Heaven.

Denominationally driven preachers promoted their clans as legitimately biblical and as originating from THE holiest icons in the history of Heaven-on-earth. The Baptist clan traced their heritage back to John the Baptist. The Methodists lifted John Wesley at Aldersgate. Presbyterians held strong to John Knox, their patriarch in the old country of Scotland. Those churches were usually and decisively led by a pastor from the holler or thereabouts, trusted by the clan. Some were formally trained, and others were merely informally ordained to oversee their congregants.

Other than through some benevolent missionary venture, rarely would anyone see a Catholic church in the holler. The communities just couldn't abide being told what to do by some outsider priest or Pope. These churches believed in their own spiritual autonomy, the priesthood of the believer. There was a resounding insistence upon the Spirit speaking to each individual for salvation without the interference of a higher authority other than God himself.

Sunday morning triggered a holy feeling –an inner aura, within the holler households. One either celebrated the new dawn or fretted over the delinquency of the night before, merriment or mourning, redemption or repentance on this set-apart day the Lord had made. In the hollers, there was an instinctive regard for Heaven and Hell and how one truly gets "saved."Feuds sometimes flared not only over how a sinner secures but also how one subsequently sustains salvation. For the *saved* were in a state of transition from Earth to Eternity. Systems toward sanctification—holy by-laws, constitutions, doctrinal statements, creeds, and guidelines toward legitimate worship had to be articulated in this transition toward future entry into the Kingdom of God. Some sanctuaries swelled for hours with music from a piano, organ, or even a banjo or guitar. Others banned such melodic frivolity as profane or as an irreverent encroachment of Satan-- the world of "outer darkness"—the outsiders who bring the tempo of the flesh into the holy sanctuary.

All the churches believed themselves to be citadels of salvation in the hollers and for a lost world. Each taunted their denominational clan as the true church preaching the *true gospel*. One mainstream denomination could not tolerate the rites or traditions of the other. The demons were crouching in such details. Offsetting the established churches were the hybrid movements. These fellowships usually emerged through disgruntled members who wanted to purge what (or who) was wrong in their church body by pulling out and planting a purified settlement elsewhere. Sometimes, the overseers of these fellowships even preached a purging fire against those misguided congregations who had gone astray. Nonetheless, each denominational clan believed they were planted by the Holy Spirit to *save the lost* in Timberline County from the influences of a sin-infested world. In the thinking of many, the first church to *save the world* would be the one most favored by God in the Kingdom to come—after the torment of sinners in the apocalypse of fire and universal bloodletting. Many spent their lifetime wondering which denomination would be God's first choice or His last choice and which of them would not be chosen at all!

Saving sinners from future torment was the common mission of the churches in the hollers. They justified tormenting others with their decries of hellfire as a warning about the eternal torment yet to come. They saw this as the mission commissioned by Jesus to his disciples in the Bible and for the ages of churches to come: *to seek and to save the lost.*

However, there did arise hybrid movements of those who sought to purify the gospel from those who had placated it. Prophetic voices echo in the hills, seeding various and sundry hollers with their sermons, restoring the pure message of the true Gospel. Of such was the *call* of Grace Kilbride. While Baptists, Methodists, and Presbyterians followed their man-made by-laws and ordinances, Gracie Kilbride, Aidan's younger sister, emerged a self-proclaimed prophetess, restoring the "pure way!" Soon, like many others, she was shunned by the loyalists.

The dowdily plump, gray, frazzled-haired frump would not be so easily desensitized or deceived. As she testified, she was so disillusioned from her efforts to reform the Timberline County churches that she just "wandered away into the hills… one day up the holler near her brother Aidan's still, I was suddenly jolted by the Holy Ghost! I fell to the ground before a Holy Presence. Then God spoke to me. He told me to start a restoration revolution by raising up a fellowship of the shunned dissenters to set right what those social club churches had compromised."

Thus, it came to pass that as Grace Kilbride's voice was heard throughout the county, many who had likewise grown dismayed with their churches gathered in a clearing in the Kilbride holler. They began to meet every Sunday morning under a large, used tent on a secluded section of her inherited property. As her congregation grew to nearly thirty, she spoke with authority and in favor of her congregants. They anointed and ordained her as their pastor, dubbing her a prophetess, like a "dazzling star in the darkness." She became known as Sister Grace Dazzlingstar! (As the name Jesus was reflective of his humanity, Grace's sir name, Kilbride, reflected hers. As the title Christ signified the divinity (or otherness) of Jesus, so too, the title, Dazzlingstar was intended to set Grace apart as a divinely prophetic utterance in the holler.)

She became so revered by her congregants that when she announced she was "with child" (at her age, with no recollection of any sexual activity or the identity of the father), it was deemed a "mystery" or a "miracle" of such magnitude that the name of her only child would be Emmanuel—or Manny for short.

Marcus traversed through the thickets, descending the spiraling, chaotic mountain terrain. In the distance, he heard the clanging of church bells echoing through the hollers. Some resonated melodically, others were noticeably malodorous, but each sounded with the hope of awakening sluggards from their beds, arousing souls toward salvation. Marcus knew the terrain well enough, but the sound of the bells helped him map his way. As the sun pierced through the heavy mist of the morning, he could see clearer his wounds, his bruises, thorn-torn shirt and jeans, and the gash in his leg. Although he had set his shoulder back into place, it stiffened and ached in the chill.

He finally reached the main road. He paused for a moment to sit on a stump. Alone. He exhaled, and in his misty breath, he envisioned the events of the night before: sitting in his father's truck with Carl. This was to be his last delivery. He told him it was getting too risky! He told him so. The stranger appeared behind them. Who the hell was that in the shadows? The fight between Casper and the shadow man! He fled down the mountain. Then he gasped…his father's truck…"Oh God," he thought, "the truck!"

He stretched his aching arms and legs, tenderly rounded his aching shoulder, and proceeded down to the main road. He wrapped his thin, water-soaked denim jacket around him. His thick, ruddy-red hair, caked with mud, looked almost as brunette as the rest of the Kilbride clan. How could he explain his outrageous appearance to his mother? He hated upsetting her with bad news—especially when it regarded his own ridiculous behavior. He has done some injurious stunts before, but now… he totaled Aidan Kilbride's truck! Eva entrusted it to him after her husband died. How could he ever be trusted again?

He continued along the main road, cautiously glancing over his injured shoulder every now and then for any passing vehicle. Every so often, he would scurry by a church. As he passed by those sacred hives in the holler, one-by-one, he heard similar arrangements of the same Sunday song:

Blessed be the tie that binds…

Timberline Baptist Church was known not only for it's annual tent meetings but mostly for giving Christmas packages to needy families in the hollers every year. They collected items every month for this event. In the springtime, the Baptists invited everyone to celebrate new life: baptisms in Timberline Creek.

Our hearts in Christian love…

First Methodist Church has a gospel quartet that actually recorded a record and sang in " community gospel sings" all over the state, even once somewhere in Nashville. They were the congregation that sponsored a pig roast every summer for everyone in the county to promote the *trading post* in the basement of their building—a center for the more destitute to find free or inexpensive essentials throughout the year.

The fellowship of kindred minds…

A mile or so down the road was the Presbyterian Church. They owned the organ that was brought from Edinburgh. It not only journeyed shipboard across the ocean but survived an arduous trek in a wagon over the Appalachian Mountains. It still played as only a staunch, vintage instrument can play. This congregation was known for its emergency handiwork. During times of flood or other *acts of God,* the members rallied resources to each occasion.

Are like to that above. Amen.

Another mile or so down the main road was a sudden and unsuspecting graveled entrance. That was the swerve off the road that Marcus reluctantly decided to take. He reluctantly conceded, he needed help. He would try to get it from his Aunt Grace, especially since she was Grace and not *always* Dazzlingstar. He couldn't let his mother see him in such a naked shamble. There would be too many questions to answer. At his Aunt Grace's, he could shower, mend his wounds, and perhaps retrieve some clean clothes; something fit-able from his cousin Emmanuel's closet.

An anthem from Dazzlingstar's humble congregation sounded. It grew louder—outrageously so.He hesitated for a moment. He heard the syncopated rudiments of a drum, the chattering of tambourines, the strumming of vintage guitars, and the shrill-but-harmonious voices unashamedly raised in unbridled praise.

Worship at the Gospel Light Church of Timberline County was ignited! Their tent of sanctuary was comprised of wooden folding chairs set up under a grove of oak trees a few yards from Grace's house. Every Sunday morning, Grace Kilbride made her sojourn across the yard to a makeshift pulpit—a large stump from a fallen tree. As Grace drew near to her pulpit, she was somehow transformed into the prophetess. As she stepped up to her hallowed platform, the stump-turned-pulpit, she *evolved* into *Sister Dazzlingstar!* (This identity she would be for the next several hours of the morning—for as long as the Holy Ghost channeled the message of God within her.)

A gash was still seeping from a splintered thorn that pierced and held fast to Marcus' thigh. His shoulder ached even more in the morning chill. Strands of his stringy reddish hair were matted with mossy mud, disguising him as more an intruder than kin. His face was unshaven with tiny red bristles appearing on his lower chin. Unlike his elder brother, Rawley, he had little body hair. Although he was also smaller of frame, not bulky like Rawley, he was tightly muscled. Marcus's physique always lent itself to more agility; running, nearly gliding through misbegotten trails, vaulting over mounds, around burrowed-in copperheads, all the while with the flow of the terrain, blending with his habitat. He knew the holler well, even the most secret places wherein a boy could hide.

He in-heaved a breath of gall and sneaked around to the back door of Aunt Grace's house. To Grace, locked doors displayed a lack of faith. Her back door was always unlocked, especially for any repentant sinner to enter. Marcus thought, "If she is truly *like Jesus*, she wouldn't mind me borrowing some stuff."

Marcus pulled back the screen door. It creaked as it always did, but the sound was muffled in the uprising from the grove. He stepped cautiously inside. He knew Sister Dazzlingstar's performance would allow him at least enough time to shower, care for his wounds, and put on some clean clothes. Perhaps he could even do all of that and make it back home before his mother returned from her church and the Kilbride's Sunday dinner. He couldn't go home in the condition he was in. Especially not on Sunday! Eva Kilbride would not stand for his mess on Lord's Day. Moreover, his older brother, Rawley, would joust the hell out of him!

"Oh, damn!" Marcus suddenly remembered Rawley. His brother was outraged when their mother gave Marcus the keys to their father's truck. Although everyone in the clan was sentimental about the vehicle, for Rawley, it was a vessel that rendered the presence of his daddy, an icon "in remembrance of him," as a perpetual reality. "'Yeah, Rawley,'" Marcus mused, "' the truck got pushed over the mountain and slammed in the trees-- 'cause I was 'shin'n a delivery to somebody who made a shitty deal with somebody else. I got away, but the truck is dead!'"

"I can hear him: 'Damn you, Marcus! You are nothing but shit in this family! Daddy did everything for you, and this is how you thank him! You are chicken shit!'" Although his older brother Rawley was his bulkier brother, Marcus's physique always lent itself to more agility; running, nearly gliding through misbegotten trails, vaulting over mounds, around burrowed-in copperheads, all the while with the flow of the terrain, blending with his habitat. He knew the holler well, even the most secret places wherein a boy could hide.

Marcus angrily whipped away the tears from his eyes with his clenched fist, then silently stepped down the narrow hallway to the bathroom. He paused to hear the music swelling from the grove:

46

"Come morning, I'll walk by the river,

I'll rest 'neath the evergreen tree;

So, I'll carry my cross through the midnight,

Come morning, there's a glory for me."

Marcus stepped out of his soggy boots, ripped off what remained of his tee shirt, and slowly removed his tattered and bloodied jeans. Carefully, he revealed a large thorn protruding from his thigh. An inch or so was still jammed under his skin.He reached over and turned on the shower.While the water was warming, he looked for tweezers in the medicine cabinet. He discovered a pair of rusty hognose pliers. They would have to do. Quickly he grabbed the edge of the thorn with the tip of the pliers and winced as he yanked the sliver from his thigh.The puncture was still moist. He stepped into the tub and cleansed the wound. Although his shoulder ached and the puncture on his thigh stung, he was warmed by the falling spray. It soothed his aching flesh and washed the muddy residue from his face.

His mind was swirling now with the beating of the water on his chest. The peace of the moment infiltrated his soul. He thought of praying; after all, it WAS Sunday morning, but he couldn't think of any to say to God. It had been a long time since the boy referenced or revered God. The last time he did, he jeered Him, scolded him for not answering his prayers—and told Him that, in Him, he no longer believed! Yet, somehow even in his unbelief, he had to believe if he was to survive.

The water was turning lukewarm. He was not sure how long he had been in the shower. He turned off the flow and listened. There it was: the 70-some-year-old, frowsy chords of Dazzlingstar echoing against the stone walls around the holler through an antiquated microphone, heralding her sermon in sanctimonious tones. He heard only moments in the message when the prophetess raised her voice to emphasize words between breaths, like "hell, wrath, judgment," along with her admonition to "raise a holy ruckus!" There were times, too when it seemed his Aunt Grace appeared, speaking more softly, uttering words like "grace, love, mercy" and... "Jesus."

He grabbed a towel and swiftly dried himself. He had to hurry to find some clothes from his cousin Emmanuel's closet if he was to make his escape before Dazzlingstar discovered a "sinner" treading her holy ground. The prophetess was uncompromisingly intolerant of any meth-running, "hell-bound" sinner interrupting the anointing of the Holy Ghost on her premises. A son of her brother notwithstanding, "a sinner is a sinner until a sinner comes to salvation!"

While his Aunt Grace would understand her nephew needing her home to mend his bloody wounds, Sister Dazzlingstar would never be so empathetic. Grace or Dazzlingstar? The distinction was at times, unsettling.Marcus never knew which one would greet him in her house.

Marcus stepped down the hallway to Emmanuel's room. Quickly, he put on some underwear and a tee shirt from a chest of drawers, then pulled on some floppy jeans from Emmanuel's closet. Emmanuel's fashion was as colorless and non-descript as was he. His cousin's tee shirts were a dingy gray, and his jeans were both large and extra-large and purchased from the local thrift store. Emmanuel was around the same age as Marcus. Perhaps a few months older.No one knew for sure. Grace had moved away several months before her son was born, and it was only sometime after, upon her return to the Kilbride holler, that anyone even knew of Emmanuel. He had been kept a secret for longer than anyone knew. Moreover, no one really knew who his father was. Dazzlingstar explained his conception was "mysterious." Emmanuel grew up in seclusion for several years. He was home-schooled, indoctrinated by the whims of Grace Kilbride and Dazzlingstar. Fearful of social interaction, Emmanuel was hidden away until Grace was finally inclined to reveal his presence at the graveside funeral of her brother, Aidan. "Manie," as he was later called by the clan, was nearing twenty years old when he emerged from his mother's holler.

The music swelled again. The service was concluding. Marcus quickly finished dressing, gathered up his own muddy clothes, and surreptitiously scampered out the back door like a mischievous waif playing hooky from school. In his haste, he forgot his soggy boots. Bare-footed, he fled through the camouflage of trees down the gravel drive to the main road. He could still hear the congregation raising a righteous ruckus behind him. He tossed his filthy clothes into the thicket and diverted his path through the wooded Kilbride holler along Timberline Creek-- a shortcut toward home. He tamed his aching shoulder and stretched the bruises on his legs and torso as he ran, dodging fallen trunks and slippery rock.

He survived the night and managed to tend to his wounds without his kin knowing anything about his situation. He would make it home before his mother returned from church, and she, too, would not be any the wiser. Despite the ache in his shoulder and the gash in his thigh, his stamina was certain. He sprinted the last swath of the way, shunning the pain.

As usual, Marcus expected Rawley's daughter, Wanda, and the brothers' older sister, Fern, to be preoccupied in Eva's kitchen, preparing the Sunday feast. He stopped for a moment to concoct his plan. He would climb through the window of his bedroom (because the lock had broken many years ago) and crawl into bed for an hour or so until Rawley and their mother returned from church. After his mother got home, he would rise as if he had been there all along.

He was truly a "cunning," he thought to himself, a "survivor." He reached the clearing. Before him was the harvested field between himself and his mother's house. His bedroom window was in view. As he stepped onto the field, his bare feet stomped on fallen stocks from the harvested corn. He suddenly realized he was not so cunning after all: he had forgotten his soggy boots. They were left in

Emmanuel's room: evidence-- left behind on Dazzlingstar's holy ground.

*

Up the holler, downstream along Fallen Timber Creek, in the bottomland, ever-stood the chink-log abode of the Kilbride clan. Built by kin themselves in the early nineteenth century, it held "staunch 'n sturdy" with a clan some dignity despite the onslaught of weather and want throughout the years. Here, decades ago, the post-adolescent coal miner, Aidan Kilbride, and his bride, the pre-adolescent Eva Fernwald, lived in holy wedlock, mostly. Not long after their vows in the First Baptist Church came their series of offspring. First came her daughter, Fern. Aidan was a bit disappointed at the time. He was "bent on hav'in a boy," but after Fern grew to be a help to his wife, he obliged that even a daughter could be "useful."

Next arrived the first-born son. Aidan named him Rawley, "like… Rawhide," his favorite television Western. Fern and Rawley were followed by Dorothy, Dolly, and finally, Marcus. Marcus was a breached birth. Eva was close to sixty at the time and had a most difficult tenure with Marcus before, during, and after his birth. Aidan was most pleased with Rawley since Marcus was an unexpected afterthought.

In this scanty shack, Aidan and Eva Kilbride provided as best they could for their offspring. From here, Aidan scratched out a living, Eva enforced home rule, and the siblings created their lives. It was a sacred space secluded in their hallowed holler. Inside their threshold was an array of artifacts and faded photographic memorabilia, arranged meticulously on the walls and tables and shelves in remembrance of Kilbride and Fernwald ancestors never-to-be-forgotten. The framed icons seemed to be not only a remembrance of kin, but also a fortress of witnesses, keeping watch over the household, like kinsmen standing guard --placed strategically on a mountain watchtower.

50

It was a decade after Aidan's untimely death, but his offspring and their children were expected by clan tradition to return to the dwelling every Sunday, preferably after church, for their weekly Kilbride dinner. Eva was insistent that everyone within the sound of her influence would follow the clan rule to be at table with one another "by the time she and Rawley got back from church!" This was a rule that, if "squandered," was punishable by an Eva Fernwald Kilbride matriarchal tirade, followed by the Sunday shunning of the more compliant offspring around the family table.

As the extended family grew, the timing for their Sunday ritual became more compromised. Those who were not in church were expected by their matriarch to perform pre-meal chores. Absence from church or working on Sunday was "forbidden by God" and by Eva Kilbride. Thus, penance was the cost of such infractions. Members of the clan absent from God's house were expected to clean the Kilbride home—in detail—and to start the Sunday meal for those who would arrive after their commitment to God and Eva had been fulfilled. (Of such was usually the plight of Eva's oldest daughter, Fern, and Wanda Kilbride Sorley, her oldest grandchild, the sparklingly moody daughter of Rawley Kilbride.)

Now in her early twenties, Wanda decisively refused to attend church, nor did she insist on such for her own children. She had grown stone-hearted by her last church experience when she was abruptly "shunned by the pastor" in the wake of her refusal to marry the birthfather of her third child, Donny.

"Why should I marry *him*? He's a bum!" she scolded the inquisitive pastor. "Hell, if *he* married every girl he'd seeded, he'd have to marry more than one wife. Now, that's a sin, ain't it? He ain't gonna quit seed'in women even if he *did* marry me, so why would I marry a flat-out, ly'in muskrat? It's God's will this way. He won't influence Donny and the other kids if he ain't in the house!" But her perspective had no reckoning with the pastor. So, she quit that church and tried another and then another.

Wanda tried to reason with two other disgruntled pastors from two other churches before she decided that "no church was for her." She grew numb to any need for it. For her, Sundays would be set aside for cleaning her Mamaw's house and preparing the Sunday meal. "I can worship God in my own way," she insisted."I don't need be'in burnt at no stake ever-time I walk in them churches." (In her absence, rumors about Wanda spread with folks in those church halls.Her erratic church behavior, reinforced by her waitress job and notable intemperance with boys at the HUB Bar 'n Grill, labeled her a "hamp" in church circles. A "hamp" is considered in Timberline County to be *both a hick and a tramp.* Wanda heard of the term and, while tending tables at the HUB, unbuttoned the top button on her blouse. She displayed her cleavage, flaunting her heirlooms like medals of honor.)

Wanda was high on romantic schemes but grounded on practical dreams. At twenty-some, she appeared more harshly middle-aged than sweetly fair. After graduating from Timberline High School, she married due to a rabid infatuation with a wild boy she aspired to *own.* They contrived a convenient romance, consummated it several times, and soon conspired to wed, making their romance more "legal."

Although her wild boy was a "roam'in rascal," Wanda was certain she could tame the beast in him and make him her gallant knight. But roughneck Bucky Sorley was not the hero she designed him to be. He was in no way pliable. After quitting school in the middle of the 10th grade, Bucky worked a brief stint in the mine, but he determined cutt'in coal was too "confin'in." So, he abruptly quit and found himself taking on some night work on the road, taking on whatever he could find to keep the home fires burning whether he was there or not.

Their first child was a girl. Bucky named her Denise after "the first girl he ever kissed." Next came their son, Dusty. A week before Dusty was born, Bucky caught on to a rumor that somewhere in the

Appalachian Mountains was a hidden treasure worth millions! The rumor was that during the Revolutionary War, when the British thought they had the Americans on the run, they sailed over an extraordinarily crafted cannon. This cannon was intended to fire the decisive blast that would end the war in favor of the King. The explosion would resound throughout the hills for centuries with the message of the superiority of the British empire. "I'm going to find that cannon." he announced to Wanda.

"The hell you will!" she shrieked. "You can get down to the coal office, and my daddy'll give you somethin' honest to do to take care of your kids!"

"When I find that cannon, I won't need to dig no shithole!"

"There ain't no damned cannon, Bucky! You're just gett'in outta here 'cause you can't take on no kids!"

Bucky grinned that grin that had so often wooed Wanda to submission. "Not a 'damned cannon,' Wanda, a *gold*en 'un. The King of England ordered a cannon made it 'o gold...to fire it when they won the war. But they didn't.When they went retreat'in, the Red Coats hid it in some cave...out in the hills. It's out there, wait'n to be found. I'm gonna find it. Nobody knows these mountains and caves better than me? Hell fire, I've run 'em all my life."

He assured Wanda what he was doing was for her, Denise, and the new "baby right there in yer belly." Before the week's end, Bucky packed his gear. He promised to return with a "family fortune." He kissed Wanda and Denise goodbye, patted her on her belly, and smirked, "See ya son. I think I'll name you Dusty after my old '68 Chevy."Then he turned his resolute head to the hills— decisively abandoning them all "for a few days...or thereabouts."

Shortly thereafter, Wanda moved herself, Denise, and her newborn son, Dusty, to her daddy's home just up the creek from Mamaw Kilbride's. Rawley Kilbride kept his daughter's room just as it was when she left it to marry Bucky Sorley. After the first month of Bucky's absence, Wanda, Denise, and Dusty moved from their scrounging lifestyle in a small apartment to Wanda's childhood home. In her old room, Rawley added a small cot for Denise and Wanda's old crib for Dusty. Wanda, *the hamp,* and her halflings could always find refuge with the clan, especially with her Daddy.

She called her misbegotten middle children, Donny and then Donna, and her last child, Dara, *"re-bound babies."* They were conceived respectively by way of other shining, amorous nights of Wanda's schemes with other *wild boys* from the HUB. They were not at all random picks; they usually reminded her of Bucky. Rawley embraced Denise and Dusty Sorely, then Donny, Donna, and Dara as Kilbride's flesh and blood, and insisted they were clan-worthy of a seat at the Kilbride Sunday table. Wanda refused to ever identify the birth fathers of her last three. Rawley stopped asking. After a while, it didn't matter to him.

Sunday morning, 11:15 am. Wanda had just over an hour to prepare the table for the clan. Mamaw would be insistent that all be ready by the time she got back from church. (Some Sundays, when Preacher Benny Peyton of Silent Spring Baptist Church had too many points to his sermon, Wanda could find time to take a breath or two. But that was unpredictable. Most Sundays, she had to stay on task, having everything warmed, arranged on the table, and ready for Mamaw Kilbride's approval by 12:15. As a hostess at the HUB, she was used to watching the clock.

The ruckus in the living room was out of control. "What the hell you kids doing?" Wanda frowned as she whipped the potatoes in the bowl, now in a frenzy. Her herd in the living room ignored their mother's bellowing. "You all have your orders! You'd better be do'in 'em 'fore your Papaw gets here with Great Mamaw! He'll have a fit if you all are just mess'in around!"

They decided not to go to church. Mamaw's prescribed penance? Denise was to clean the bathroom while Dusty swept the floors. Donny was to dust the furniture. Donna's only job was to

54

keep little Dara occupied. But while their mother was preoccupied in the kitchen, thirteen-year-old Denise was lounging on the couch, gaping at teenybopper pictures in a Tiger Beat magazine. Twelve-year-old Dusty and his ten-year-old half-brother, Donny were embroiled in a round of Memphis-style wrestling, clad in their threadbare undershorts. Donna, now eight, was keeping little Dara, now five years old, busy playing beauty parlor. Donna found the paint brushes and watercolors in their Great Mamaw's toy box and decided to tint some colorful highlights in her half-sister's long, silky-blonde hair.

"You kids better damn well be at what I told you to do!" Wanda yelled again.

Dusty was about to pin his younger brother to the floor and into submission. He yelled, "Momma, you said 'damn!'"

"You said 'damn,' Momma!" echoed Denise, looking up with a sly grin, still ogling at a centerfold of mop-headed Leif Garrett—one of her "future husbands." "You said, 'damn'… on Sunday!" she repeated.

"Great, Mamaw won't like that!" Donny managed to utter, straining to exhale from beneath the weight of Dusty's knees, compressing his chest.

"Y'all better be do'in what I told you! I ain't got time for yer shit!" Wanda snorted. "You ain't gonna tell her noth'in…ever! Yer grandpa will whip yer little asses if you ever tell her anyth'in that would make her stroke out!"

Dusty eased off Donny. They stood to their feet, staring each other down, preparing themselves for a second bout. Then Denise called her mom again, smirking as only a teenager can do. "But you said 'damn,' on Sunday, Momma! We don't have to tell Great Mamaw noth'in. God heard you, and God tells her everything!"

Wanda stomped to the living room and squinted her eyes, glaring them down. "Y'all just shut up! I'm your momma; I can say whatever I damned well, shitty-shit-shit-shit want to—especially to bratty kids! I can say whatever the hell I want to say, and you don't tell yer great Mamaw noth'in! 'Else I'll beat the shit outta yew!"She retreated toward the kitchen again, then in haste turned around to them, "And God doesn't *say* noth-in to anybody anyway! So shut up!"

Donna was carefully gliding a thin brush of green paint along a strand of little Dara's hair. Dara liked the sensation of her sister's touch in her hair. She sat very still, taking one quick breath at a time so her sister would not paint outside the lines. "How old do I have to be 'fore I can say bad words too, Momma?" Donna asked.

"Especially the BAD ONE?" yelled Dusty.

"Yeah, the BAD ONE?" echoed Donny. "Dusty says that one all the time. When can WE say it?"

Wanda paused for a moment, then bellowed again, "When I'm dead! That's when!"She gazed at the clock again, 12 noon.She made it!Her preparations were in sync with the clock. The meal was ready for Mamaw and the clan. The ham was warming in the oven, the side fair was simmering on the top of the stove, and the table was set. She sat down at the table to catch her breath and lit a cigarette.

Undaunted, Dusty leaped at Donny, locking his neck in a vice grip with his elbow, twisting his little body, and forcing him to the floor. Donny wailed from under his bulkier older brother, flailing his skinny legs from some escape. Dusty yelled in triumph, holding tightly to his grip. "I'm Country Boy Clem! You're the Sheik of Iraq-nia! The battle fight of the century!"

Donny was pinned. "I give up, Dusty! Get off a-me! I can't breathe! I can't move! Get off'a me!"

Suddenly, Denise intervened. "Get off of him, Dusty! Before you really hurt him again."

Dusty obliged. He stood and raised his arms over Donny's conquered torso. "Country Boy Clem wins again!" He yelled, pulling up his bedraggled shorts as he strutted around his victim.

Donny struggled to his feet."You always get to be Clem! Ain't fair!"

Then Denise pleaded, "Momma, make them quit fighting...PLEASE! I'm trying to read! And it stinks in here! They smell like pigs!"

Wanda called from the kitchen, "Dustin! Donald! You all quit your fight'in! And go put yer clothes on! NOW! Donna, go wash that paint out of Dara's hair! NOW!"

Dusty pushed Donny aside. "Big baby! Can't take noth'in!" He grabbed his tee shirt and jeans from the couch. "Anyways, I'm *always* Country Boy Clem 'cause I'm the oldest! I fight like MY daddy."

Donny reached for his jeans. He stood nearly naked before his siblings. The boys stared at each other in a sort of mutual submission. "That don't mean noth'in!" the younger boy whimpered. "Anyways, Dusty, your pits smell like poop!"

Dusty glared at him and smirked, "But I have a daddy! Who's YOUR daddy? See, you don't even know."

Donny was motionless now. His lower lip quivered as it always did when he was alone. Neither one of them said anything more. Keeping the battle raging from that point was more real than their wrestling match was. Dusty grabbed Donny's tee shirt and helped his half-brother dress himself.

*

All the Kilbride offspring knew the house rules. The code of their clan they usually adhered to, at least when Mamaw and Rawley were around. Either by inscription in their DNA or through environmental adaptation, they followed holler law for clan survival in an ever-intrusive world of roads and bypasses. The Kilbrides adapted holler law for their own household.

The Ten Commandments of the Kilbride Clan evolved through generations:

1. There was no greater loyalty than to your own kin.
2. Never tell family business outside the holler.
3. Only cuss when necessary. Never on Sunday.
4. Everyone is to be at the family table on the Lord's Day.
5. Always be obedient to your daddy and mama. No questions asked!
6. Work for what you get. Only give what is yours to give.
7. Control your flesh urges; it could get you into trouble.
8. Don't steal nothing that ain't yours.
9. Always tell the truth to your family. Others, if necessary.
10. God always gives you what you deserve. Don't bargain with Him.

*

There was a raw elegance to Eva Kilbride, especially when she returned home from church. She was angelic in her lace-sleeved dress, cameo broach, and finely braided gray hair. Although she had a walker to use around the house, she never used it when she entered the sanctuary; proving God's to the bystanders around her that God's grace was "all-sufficient." Even so, her eldest son, Rawley was always by her side too, there to grasp her arm and steady her steps.Her aged, petite physique moved rhythmically down the aisle to her pew with the fervor of the deep gospel tempo that accompanied her and in God's favor.

By the time Rawley and his momma arrived home, the oldest daughter, Fern, and her husband managed to make it to the dining table only minutes before they did.

"How was church this morning, Mamaw?" asked Fern, nibbling on a slice of spiced apple.

"Well, honey," Eva replied, "if was glorious. You all should have been there...could've filled the pews 'stead of fill'in yer bellies."

"There you go again, Momma, should 'in on people," Fern said."Should not lest ye be should on.'"

Rawley answered, "It was rowdy as usual. Mama got her tithes worth."

Everyone had their respective places around the table. Eva Kilbride saw to it that no one in her clan was anonymous or unaccounted for, especially on the Lord's Day.Her late husband would not be pleased with anything less than seeing his offspring *"propered—"* in his and her place at the table. Eva sat to the right of an empty high-backed chair placed at one far-end head of the table. After Aidan's untimely death, that chair remained empty, *propered-in-place* where it always had been for Aidan, now placed in remembrance of him.Rawley assumed his place at the foot of the table directly across from his daddy's empty chair. Everyone else knew their respective *proper places* as well: Dorothy Kilbride Jackson, the middle-aged daughter of Aidan and Eva, sat with her husband, Perry, on one side of the table. Parallel to them were two places, one set for the youngest daughter, Dolly—and the other was empty, awaiting the presence of their prodigal baby brother, Marcus.

A card table was pitched in the living room for Wanda and her children: Denise and Dusty, Donny, Donna, and little Dara.Dorothy's sons, Presley, a heartily rugged nineteen, and his brother Hank, a slim and agile seventeen, sat in the living room, eating their Sunday buffet on wooden trays. While the boys mostly tolerated, at times even liked, their smaller cousins, they usually avoided them at mealtime.

At the kitchen table sat Eva and Aidan's eldest daughter, Fern Kilbride Walker, and her husband, Dean. Now, in her waning years, she had the tender soul of her momma with the tenacious ire of her daddy. While she was always ready for a heated debate, she usually argued more from her heart than her head. Always a conundrum, Fern was an impetuous family-thorn to be reckoned with, yet at the same time, a fragile and tender petal to protect. Even deciding her name was a conundrum for her parents. Aidan wanted to name her after his own beloved mother, Lucille. Eva insisted, after all the labor she did with the help of her midwife and Aunt Fern, that the child be named Fern.

Aidan insisted they called their first daughter, Lucy-Fern. Eva refused, stating that she had NOT given birth to the devil—"LUCIFER." She agreed to name her Fern Lucille—especially Fern, for it described well her daughter's prominent features: she was a feathery frond emerging with a determination to grow, even in the harshest of environments. It could be trampled on, starved of care, or smothered with the driven residue in the holler, dormant in the dead of winter, yet return, resilient in Spring. Thus, she was never called Fern-Lucille. She was *just* Fern, a feathery and feisty force to be reckoned with.

Rawley Kilbride dominated the table proceedings. It was from his position as the eldest son, in sight of the empty chair at the head of the table, that Rawley voiced their Sunday prayer: "Our Father in Heaven, we thank you for your bounty here at this table. And for each one in his place around it. Or MOST of us, anyway… May we all be worthy of your provision and mercy. Amen."

"Very nice, Rawley," Eva whispered. "Could've left out that one part, but it was nice."

"Thank you, Mama." Rawley replied. As they passed the peas, Rawley spoke up with the question they all were pondering, "So, where's 'possum boy', Momma?"

"Rawley," responded his younger sister, Dolly from a couple of chairs away, "stop that. He hates that name."

"His chair is empty-- again." Rawley returned, "I was just wondering."

"He might've driven to church."Dorothy smirked.

"More likely he's hang'in 'round Leah McCreary." Dolly smiled. "Spent the night with her. He wishes. But that girl won't do noth'in without a ring on her finger."

"Lord, I hope he might've gone to church! The trucks gone."Eva suggested.

Fern could hold her peace no longer. "Marcus ain't never gonna go to church, Momma. He quit that when he was a kid. Your prayers ain't reach'in beyond the ceiling with that one."

Fern passed the pinto beans to Rawley. "He's *try'in* children. He's really try'in."

Fern grumbled, "He's *trying* alright, Momma. He's *trying* everybody!"

Always the mistress of mountain laurel, middle daughter Dorothy had to speak up. "He has always been a… vagabond, yes, that's it…a vagabond. Out and wander'in for something he just can't seem to find. A vagabond…"

Just then, her husband, Perry Jackson, spoke up, "Yep," he said, Marcus is a vagabond…" (He paused a moment to finish chewing a bit of ham, then proceeded.) "And a vagrant."

"What's a vagabond?" asked Dorothy and Perry's son, Hank from across the room.

Fern was going to answer, but Rawley halted her with a glare. "…a fugitive from justice! It's in the Bible. Cain was a fugitive -- outcast from the garden for slaying his brother. Pastor Benny preached about how Cain was a 'vagabond running from God.' Running straight to hell fire for what he had done to his brother. What's right is right, and what's wrong is wrong. Period. Marcus better starts squaring himself. There's a plumb line dangling from his daddy's hand! He should know better!"

Hank called again from the living room, "So, you all think Uncle Marcus is going to hell, Uncle Rawley? Personally, I like him. He's just figur'in things out."

Dorothy grinned and whispered to her siblings at the table. "Hank thinks he's cool. Presley thinks he's a criminal."

Dolly couldn't no longer abide the table talk. She slammed her hand on the table. "Marcus ain't going to hell! You all got no right speculat'in 'bout the eternity of Marcus Kilbride! Going to hell? Would you toss our brother in hell? For no God-almighty reason 'cept he ain't at *yer* almighty table?Send'in anybody to hell is nobody's call at this table but God's! At times I don't think Jesus blessed Christ could sit long at this table either!"

Rawley and the others were stifled for a moment, but as his youngest sister was so apt to tantrums, he just smiled. Few ever took her too seriously.

Dolly was Aidan and Eva's youngest daughter. After her second birthday, the whole family decided never to have another child. She was the cantankerous and moody Kilbride baby who refused to behave herself simply for the sake of following orders. Most things had to be proven to her if she was to follow the Kilbride rules. She spoke her own mind and was more than hesitant to give her heart to anyone she deemed unworthy of her trust.

Dolly was a voluptuous mountain girl: untidied, skinny, with adventuresome dark eyes and sleek-swirling brown hair. She was always a bit mysterious, unlabeled; somewhat darksome, yet with an unbridled, adventuresome spirit that intimidated even the most rambunctious of Timberline boys at the HUB. Even in high school, while she was approachable, Dolly Kilbride was what she called *"sleazy-easy."* While she could have been successful in most anything she set her mind to, she was content to just glide along, alone, day-by-day, with a Fresca in one hand and an unfiltered cigarette in the other, waiting to see whatever happened next. Perhaps that's why Dolly became an indispensable manager at the HUB, the epicenter of the town and clan. She was content in the holler, devotedly loved her Momma, and seemed to be the only one of her siblings who was always empathetic for her little brother, Marcus.

"Hell, damn well, ain't YOUR call, Dolly!I think Pastor Benny and his Bible know more about it than you do." Rawley scoffed.

Eva could tolerate their Sunday insolence no longer. "Children! No bicker'in at the table! Lord! Lord! Lord! Forgive me, Jesus, if'n I've raised a pack of heathen.

"Sorry, Mama." Rawley grinned and asked, "…any more red-eye gravy from breakfast?"

*

After Marcus strolled through the harvested field and to his momma's house, he jerked-open his bedroom window and vaulted himself inside. His shoulder was aching even more, the puncture from the thorn in his flesh was sore, and his belly was nagging from hunger. Yet, more so, he was exhausted and in need of an embrace— some open arms to *"welcome him home."* His momma? Dolly? Hank? Wanda's kids? They were prominent in his mind.

As always, the door to his bedroom was securely locked. But the aroma in the house was compelling. But the risk of Fern's analytical stares or a confrontation with Rawley kept him from leaving his bedroom. By the time he reached his bed, he was too exhausted to venture into the well-lit household. He surrendered to his fatigue, swept himself into a cocoon of disheveled quilts, and heaved a heavy sigh. He tried to sleep. Yet his brain was racing in circles with thoughts of his midnight run, of Casper and the shadow man, his father's demolished truck… and… the shoes he left behind in his cousin Emmanuel's room.

"Damn," he whispered. He lifted one of the quilts over his head and, for the moment, slumbered away. At least for the moment, he was safe…at least, he was home.

Chapter Three:
Table Talk and Ton'in

"Essential wisdom accumulates in a community much as fertility builds up in the soil." (Wendell Berry, The Art of Place: Interview New Prospectus Quarterly, 1992)

"...in the Eastern Kentucky coalfields...Those mountaineers are rugged people...If you got grandma out in front, Lordy mercy, anything can happen!" (Governor Albert "Happy" Chandler, from Heroes, Plain Folks and Skunks, 1989)

As the first-born son of the Kilbride clan, Rawley held a position of esteem. By holler law, privileges for the first born son were his birth rite. When Aidan died, Rawley owned the role bequeathed him, and he wore that mantle well. By that same hallowed Law, his older sister, Fern, was not and would never be considered for such a position. Although she had the Kilbride spunk, she didn't own the hardware for such a task. It was not that she was unable to handle such privileges as title to property, economic power of attorney, and expressing her opinions, but as a daughter, she was engendered to the house rules regarding her place in line. Still, she could be a force of nature to be reckoned with.

Fern Lucille Kilbride married Dean Walker after they graduated from McGuffey High School. Rather than pursue her career in nursing in a romantic swept-off-her-feet roust-about, she committed herself to the whims of Dean Walker. It was through Dean that Fern discovered a life course that would whisk her away from the hollers of Timberline County. Dean enlisted in the Army toward the end of his Senior year before he proposed to the aspiring nurse. The tension between them began when Dean waited to tell his bride of his commitment to his country until after their wedding vows to one another. On the day that were wed, he not only married Fern, but he also recruited her for his stations in the army. From that point on, she was never to be in control of her destiny. It was in keeping with Holler Law.

Only a week after their wedding, Dean drove his new bride in his, *"God, I hope we make it" Ford Fairlane* –west toward California. As they drove down the main highway and away from the Kilbride holler, Fern suffered the pangs (and guilt) of leaving her clan behind. But as they traveled further down the expressway and away from the sheltering Appalachians, across the Mississippi River, and the flatlands and deserts, with the promise of seeing the Pacific Ocean for the first time, her demeanor changed. She dreamed herself riding a mighty steed—with her arms wrapped tightly around the torso of a knight in shining armor. She embarked on an adventure she had never dreamed possible before.

For Dean, serving his country was fulfilling, and honor, if not a dangerous and advantageous deployment. There was no real action at the time. He was, for the most part, in basic training and in reserve for any possibility of war. In wartime or peacetime, Dean was committed to serving his country—and seeing what the world was like outside the holler.

For Fern Kilbride Walker, the lessons she learned through the arduous support she gave her husband in the military were enriching. She learned through navigating this time in her worldview more diplomacy than a formal diploma could have offered her. Fern not only learned with a remarkable capacity for education, but she also grew with discernment. When Dean was called away on orders, she took adult education courses (usually at the local high school) in whatever ignited her interest: literature, accounting, history, and self-preservation. All the while, she tended to the care of herself and her two young sons-- creating meals from scantily stored cupboards, disinfecting ominous new housing assignments, exterminating bugs and ridding their perimeter of other predatory creatures, packing and unpacking with little warning, and staying sane in the process of keeping a new husband and family safe, healthy and content. "A nursing *degree?*" she often thought to herself, "who needs to waste time and money on a piece of parchment? I just do what I gotta do and go on to the next thing."

After twenty-four years of various deployments from Southern California to the Philippines, to Oklahoma, and to *"God only knows where the hell we are,"* Dean and Fern decided to return to their holler. With the land Dean inherited from his mother, he built for his family of four a comfortable home in the bottom land of Fallen Timber Creek. Now in their sixties, with their two sons, Bobby and Chisholm away, living in cities, one in New York and the other in Chicago (locations they described as more "civilized"), Fern and Dean settled resolutely from their globetrotting to be near Eva Kilbride in her later years.

*

Fern cleared the table. Wanda's children helped a bit by dumping their own plates in the kitchen sink and then scurried out the screen door. "You kids watch for snakes!" their Great Mamaw reminded them sternly. "Them snakes is still mov'in this time of year!"

Dean remarked, "There were plenty of 'em in the field when I took in the beans."

"Don't know why there are so many this year," Fern added.

Dorothy slid a bowl into the sudsy water in the sink and spoke up assertively, "I know what I heard. It's 'cause some government program is trapp'in 'em from around housing projects in Louisville...rounding 'em up in crates and dumping them out of helicopters all 'round here! That's why there's so many of 'em."

Most at the table were alarmed by the news. Always the disclaimer, Fern just chuckled, "That's not true, Dorothy. Where'd you hear that?"

"It's so, Sister. I heard it on *Perry's* station!" Dorothy replied. "It was on the news."

"Perry Jackson, you ought to censor that malarky before it goes out on the radio." insisted Dean.

Perry Jackson was indigenous to Timberline County.What he lacked in physical stature, he overcompensated with ambition and attitude.He entered the clan first as the childhood chum of Rawley before and throughout their school years.It was Perry who taught Rawley how to smoke and tolerate the taste of moonshine.It was Rawley who taught Perry how to repair cars. It was also Rawley who encouraged Perry to devise a plan of how to cultivate a romantic relationship with his sister, Dorothy, more a mediocre wallflower than a mountain wildflower.

After high school, when Rawley found his way to the coal mine, Perry's plan for personal and political gain emerged in earnest. He wooed Dorothy into marriage and moved to Henry Clay College to study public administration and communications. Four years later, Perry returned to Timberline County with his degree in hand and Dorothy and their young sons, Presley and Hank, at his side. By then, he owned an unquenchable hankering for fame. Perry was determined that he would one day be catapulted to the State House of Representatives. He hoped that his boys would be the next Nashville singing sensations. He had little expectations for Dorothy beyond supporting his campaigns.

Upon his return to Timberline County, both his ambitions and his renown began to unfold. He opened a used car lot and managed the local food market. Later, he overtook the local AM radio station. He became a prominent columnist in the local paper, often editorializing the promise of bringing a post-coal vibrance back to Timberline County. He determined he was reaching out with a new hope-- his voice, self-professed as one "crying in the wilderness*"*— echoed throughout the Appalachian Mountains. Then he ascended from print to the airwaves. His radio program, *"Perry Jackson: The*

Voice of Timberline," launched him into local notoriety. On a clear night, his voice carried on the airwaves resounding beyond Timberline County.

Fern asked abruptly, "Why would anyone bother to drop snakes in the hills?"

With his on-the-air intonation, Perry asserted, "for new housing developments, gated communities. Cities expanding into county land! Wildlife has to go somewhere. City people don't want copperheads and rattlesnakes in their fancy petunia gardens. So, the government rounds 'em up and dumps 'em on us 'cause *we're* supposed to know how to live with 'em. It's always been like that." Perry continued while adding another dose of sugar to his iced tea, "I don't remember that story on my station. But if Dorothy heard in there, it must be true."

Dean replied. "I can't imagine *this* administration doing anything like that. That's a little far-fetched – don't you think, Dottie?"

"It's the government, Perry."Dorothy replied, "ain't *nothing* too far for them to fetch…"

Rawley shifted his chair forward and parted the residue of table crumbs with a swift swipe of his hand."*This* administration?"he repeated with a last gulp of his tea and a first breath of sarcasm. "The same administration that shut down the mines? You think they wouldn't dump on us for the sake of padd'in their pews?"

"They didn't shut down the mines, Rawley. The coal companies sunk bottom." Perry began suddenly. "Fossil fuel is dying like all you dinosaurs, Rawley."

Rawley was triggered all the more. "You damned liberals baled on us, Perry.My God, who's side are you on?They left this county with noth'in but empty promises. Lying about temporary layoffs, decent severance pay, and health insurance--promises of re-opening.

They saved their own assets … their own asses. This administration did nothing but shit on their people! People are addicted to the draw because they can't do anything else but hope for coal to come back. Well, hell, bring it back. Subsidize new mining technology! Make it safe. I'm more about reality than reptiles."

"Rawley, this ain't the day to get riled over this." interrupted Eva.

"I'll watch myself, Momma," Rawley assured his mother.

Dolly smirked, "Yeah, It's Sunday, Fellas! We don't want to make Jesus mad!"

Perry scooted his chair forward, poised in political protocol, with an analytical stare at Rawley. He cupped his hands together as if in prayer and began his homily in a well-rehearsed tone: "The impact of the big companies leasing our land was horrendous. Coal extraction was not only dangerous; it led to innumerable deaths and diseases, horrible accidents from unsafe working conditions, and black lung! And it takes its toll on *your mental health*!So, in their lust for coal, New York bastards and their cronies—who've never been on site here-- decided such news was bad for public relations, so they opted to strip the mountains; wash away the surface to suck out the coal and leave us with noth'in but contaminated soil and desperate kin."

Rawley turned his head away and cleared his throat. Perry raised his voice above his brother-in-law's fit of congestion. (Rawley was content for the moment to let Perry rant. He patiently waited his turn.)

"It was an ecological disaster!Look at the toxins in our creeks, our poisoned land! That's now! Who knows what that raping of the mountains will cause in the future?When the ecosystem suffers, the hollers suffer too.This administration wants to diversify, Rawley.Coal is dead! It was a frenzied, monetary orgasm—a quick cash flow, that made moguls rich, but it took its toll in the hollers!

70

But we've come to our senses. You can't exploit the ecosystem; the virgin landscape, and it does not impact the hollers for future generations! I say we should let it go! Diversify! The depleted demand for coal is a sign of the times. An Appalachian Apocalypse!" With that, Perry leaned back on his chair and wiped his spittle from his mouth with his napkin.

Rawley leaned forward, facing Perry, resting his bulging forearms on the table. "The roads came." Rawley began in a tone just above a whisper, then gradually grew louder. "There was no cash flow back then. Jobs? Not much. We could have been smarter in how we leased the land. But nobody knew much about 'industry' thinking. We should've demanded guidelines. But the hollers were sucker punched. We trusted the wrong people—the 'moguls,' like you said. We just trusted that people were good and we'd all be taken care of: JOBS! JOBS! JOBS! True, a lot of people up there got rich, but it trickled down to us too. Not all the benefits they promised ever came; they gave this county a pittance for what they promised. But that pittance was more than what we had to live on before the mining *industry*! Strip mining was a way to safeguard our people. It wasn't just an experiment to get more coal. It was an investment in our economy."

Rawley raised and leaned on his elbows and cupped his two hands in front of him into one rounded fist. "Then came your liberal mayhem! Instead of just demanding more guidelines and economic compensation, you all just want to close the industry completely. Just when we learned 'bout clean coal and safer mechanics, you just want to shut down the mines! Your rant'in has put us out of business. NO JOBS! NO JOBS! That's what has taken its toll in Timberline County, Perry! YOUR administration does do a good job at using us for their big speeches 'bout how they are gonna help us hillbillies down here! Sure, they do! The DRAW! From a penny to a PISS-ance! They buy our votes every four years with promises they make that will never change anything! All we wanted was a way to make a living! The coal industry gives us that! Now, people—REAL

PERSONS-- have to choose between doing nothing and taking the damned government draw or moving away from Timberline County! Either way, Perry, we're abandoned by the big shots to fend for ourselves. Most of them bastards at the Capital ain't ever crossed over our county line, but they sure as hell count themselves, 'for the people!'"

Perry was about to speak, but Rawley began again, overriding his kin's veto. "Hell, we can't even run moonshine anymore—the government runs their own distilleries all over the state. But we survive. That's our heritage. We're a strong county! Marijuana and meth! Whatever people must do to survive!WHY?Because *liberal-mania* took over everything with self-righteous regulations and raped ever-body down here! And YOU want to be one of *them*!"

Perry chuckled, unmoved by Rawley's dictum. "Rawley," he smiled, rather menacingly now, "We want to move forward beyond coal. Diversify: low-cost housing developments, recreation sites for tourists: fishing lakes, hiking, cycling trails, camping, and caring for the ecosystem at the same time. Maybe even a new prison! In the future, coal can be replaced by music festivals—bring in the tourists! Be creative! Sell 'em tee shirts, coffee mugs, and sourwood honey! Resurface the roads! All we need to do is cater to their hankering to see their idea of Appalachia. BE the hillbillies they come to spend their money to see! Suck the funds from those big, fat city wallets when they ain't look'in!"

Abruptly, Dorothy interrupted, "They ain't gonna come here if the government is dumping snakes on their heads."

"We don't need tourists in here *look'in at us* like we're some freak-a'nature!" Rawley insisted. "The government just needs to stay out'a our way! We can figure out a way to market what we have, like the Bible says, 'strengthen what remains,' re-open the mines, *while* keeping our people safe. We can send a damned rocket to the moon; so, we can extract clean coal and have a decent economy in the hollers again."

Perry Jackson refused to relent. "Economy, yes, but not at the expense of ecology. I have plans for water treatment installations to purify the acid water and grant money for local sanitary disposal projects. There are also ideas being discussed for rehabilitation of the air—of the noxious fumes caught in the hollers. Not to mention the closing of abandoned underground mines and the reclaiming of streams and fields damaged by surface mining and clearing of timber. All of this takes time and funding, Rawley. It takes leaders with vision to make it happen."

Rawley exhaled a long breath. He leaned back in his chair. "You never did cut coal, did you, Perry?"

Perry shook his head, "No."

"I have. You phrase words real purity, *Senator Jackson*... especially for one who left the county. You think you can replace the coal industry with tee shirts and coffee mugs! How about this, Perry? Clean up the government *ego-system* and the ecology, come up with a healthy way to cut and burn clean coal, then re-open the mines and sell it to the world as... *black diamonds—the wonder of Appalachia*! How about that, *Senator*, or whatever you're gonna be? *Create* the damned market like they do with ever-thang else! Save Timberline County! Don't use it for some goddamned campaign promise. Perry Jackson, not *Senator* Jackson, needs to get down to where he came from and SEE things: the mountains, not some marble-floored watchtower. These are real people down here, not campaign commodities."

Before Perry could answer, Eva raised the palms of her hands. She sat with her hands open in front of her, her eyes closed, speaking softly but in earnest. "It all started when that Mr. Devlin from the... what did they call it, Rawley? That man that came down here and talked at the school gym that time?"

Rawley cleared his throat, "Arte Devlin...from the LUCI Firm... the Land Underwriters Corporation International...it was a land lease thing. He slithered in here promising better 'provisions and prosperity.' I remember that. A slick offer! People believed him. The LUCI Firm took it's fill and ran. My daddy didn't fall for it. Never leased our land to him. He took me aside and looked me in the eye: 'We'll do with what we got 'fore we buy what they're a-sell'in…them…predators. We'll do what we have to do to keep from those damned letchers.' Daddy tended to ever-thing… always did what he had to do without leasing our holler."

Eva spoke again. "My Aidan cut coal, ran shine... I ne're liked it, 'specially the 'shining. But he did whatever he had to do to keep our land; 'we can eat corn cakes and cook up a sell a'jug a'vigors to feed our kids.'For your daddy, come hell or high water, he was going to make us a living--got tougher as the mines run out, but he would not sell out noth'in to that…LUCI-Firm!"

Dolly had enough of what she called "…qubbl'in." She gathered her lighter and a pack of Marlboros and strolled toward the door to the back porch. "God, I've heard all this before and before and before."

At that moment, she crossed the path of Hank Jackson, Perry's adolescent son, retrieving another plate of beans and cornbread in the kitchen. "Aunt Dolly," he said, "Tak'in a smoke on the porch?"She nodded with a frown. "Oh." Hank smiled and turned toward the table to talk, "Coal again? …blah di blah di blah."

"…and blasé. Come on, Henry," Dolly said, "Get yer beans and sit with me on the porch 'til this blows over."He happily obliged her.

Dorothy tried to negotiate the debate. "You both need to hear one another. But neither one of you listen to the other one."

Eva continued her story. "He'd get up at four in the morn'in. You had to get up at four in the morn'in to do what's fitt'in! He put on his long cottons—it was cold in those days… that blue jacket and overalls and heavy boots. Many-a- morn'in, I saw him tromp in the mud in those boots. Weighted him down, but he did it anyway 'cause it had to be done.He headed off with that old torch on his helmet—trust'in that light. That's all the light he had.I packed him a pail of whatever I could find. Every morn'in, I prayed for him!He got in that coal car, water dripp'in down everywhere… sometimes he crawled 'round down there like one of them blind-eyeds sallie-manders.*Safety timbers*? There weren't no safety noth'in down that shaft. All day, he'd crouch and stoop and kneel and peck at the cut line.Sometimes, it was my Aidan who had to drill, powder, and light the fuse to the cylinder to crack the rock.Safety? How far back away can you go from an explosion down there to not kill you?I hated those days! But he had to do it to keep ever-body fed.

You *both* talk fine up here atop the ground-- Perry Jackson, with yer government-mental fixes, and Rawley, with all yer whin'in and wishful think'in!But this is our *holler*; it ain't politics! We ain't talk'in 'bout politics or profits; it 'bout people whose really liv'in here -ever-day!Real people, try'in to just make good, car'in for one another."

"What does that mean, Momma?" asked Fern.

"Well, missy, all I know is when Gladys Norris up the holler is ail'in with her arthur-i-tis, I don't wait for some policy to tell me what to do or wait til she pays me someth'in. I take her the poultice myself! When Floyd Sease down the way is hungered, I take him what I canned! That's the way I know of. Don't take any political noth'in to take care of people. It just takes people who care." She finished her sermon and began to clear the table.

Fern snickered, "I guess she burnt your toast… boys!" Dean sat nearby, sipping his tea, rather unimpressed by the chatter. Fern invited him into the fray. "Dean," she began, "you haven't said anything."

"Nope…" He muttered. "Sometimes it's better not to."

"Come on, Dean." Rawley insisted. "Off the record."

Dean took another sip and sat his cup in front of him. "I think you're both obsolete."

"Huh?" they asked.

"COAL!" Dean continued, "My God, you'd think we had nothing before or since coal! Y'all need to quit living your life by coal!"

Fern began again, "If the truth be told…"

Then Dean interrupted her ever-so-softly, "Truth emerges from the ashes. All will be well…eventually. But you gotta sift through the ashes. Your talk is obsolete, fellas. Sift through the ashes…find an ember."

Hastily, Dorothy asserted, "Tell them about your new commercial on the radio, Perry! Momma, Perry has a tv commercial for his campaign coming on today!"

"I don't want to hear no more fuss'in 'bout Perry Jackson politics!" Eva commanded, "I would rather do these dishes…"

"Or hear the boys sing?" Dorothy suggested, "The boys have songs for the Festival."

For Presley and Hank Jackson, the music of the mountains was a welcome inheritance. For as long as they could remember, they heard Appalachian melodies echoing from their grandfather's radio. Bluegrass and Rockabilly, Bill Monroe, Ralph Stanley, and the Stonemans. Then came Elvis, Cash, Hank Williams—Senior and Junior, and other latter-day song-saints. Their ancient, lyrical psalms filled their imaginations, entering their souls with melodies echoing the pristine modulations of life-- the vicissitudes of the seasons of life in the mountains. Once smitten by the wonder of the songs, they pleaded with their Uncle Marcus to teach them how to play his guitar. Presley was content imitating the records he played repeatedly. Once Marcus taught Hank the basic G, D, and C chords, the youngster took it up a fret or two from there, composing his music--what he felt deep inside.

Nineteen-year-old Presley Jackson was more interested in the piety of his performance than he was in the presence of his soul. He spent hour upon hour devising ways not only to imitate the *king of rock 'n roll* but to channel his crowd-pleasing appeal as well. When he performed (especially for a predominantly female audience), he would sneer at them with an upturned lip, rotate his knee, and gyrate his sturdy, hairy chest—revealed shamelessly yet intentionally-- through an unbuttoned shirt. He threw himself heart, mind, soul, and torso at them!(As his back up band, in the shadows behind him, Hank just saw his older brother, "Pres," in action as a "boney and bow-legged, butt-flitt-in wanna-be.")

Hank's real name was Henry. He preferred that name. Hank became a stage nickname imposed on him "for publicity" by his dad to imply some recollection of the country icon. He disliked the nickname. But after a while, no one called him by his given name anymore. Henry was more kindred with the mountains than his older brother.He found romance there. He was devoted to composing lyrics that reflected the lure of the landscape. To him, this was the real world.

He played backup for Pres's performances, in the shadows. He used *his own music* as a safe space—a place to sense a deeper presence within himself. For Henry Jackson, music was more a sacred experience with something…supra-rational than a performance for his renown. At seventeen, Henry was contemplative and thoughtful. He was slightly in stature, not as muscular as Pres. Pres was a competitive lineman on the football team. Henry was content to be a distance runner, and a rock climber, content with being non-competitive.

Pres and Hank both had deep black hair; the older brother styled his, slicking it back tightly over his forehead, the younger leaving his hairstyle to the whims of the breeze. Perry bought them a secondhand guitar in a flea market to practice with. Although the bridge was slightly warped, Hank creatively compensated for its imperfection with gentle adjustments on the frets. It was always a challenge to keep the instrument tuned well in the changing environment, but somehow Hank managed to keep it somewhat in tune. Still, at times, the flea market bargain was difficult to play.

On Sundays at Mamaw's, Marcus was given carte-blanche permission to practice with his Uncle Marcus's Gibson guitar. (The one granted to a youthful Marcus by Aidan as a reward for "jobs well done.") It was kept given to Hank after Sunday supper, leaning at Marcus's bedside.

"I wanna hear my grandson's song!"demanded Eva.

The boys overheard Mamaw's command. They needed little prodding. Rarely did either grandson linger when Eva Kilbride requested anything of them. They were swift to please and/or appease her. Pres gobbled his second slice of apple pie and combed back his greasy black pompadour. Hank returned from the porch with Dolly. He grabbed a bottle of Mountain Dew from the fridge and guzzled it down. He and Dolly walked down the narrow hallway to Marcus' bedroom door. "Is Uncle Marcus in there?" He asked.

"Don't know." She rattled the doorknob. "It's locked. But it's always locked. I'll get the key in my dresser drawer." She retrieved the key, stuck it into the lock, and slowly nudged the door open. "Shhh! Can't never tell who might be in here."

"Is Uncle Marcus in there?" Hank whispered again.

"…don't think so." Dolly answered, "The truck ain't outside."

The room was dark. The weathered hunter-green curtains were pulled shut, waving randomly with an incoming breeze. Hank had enough light to lead him to the guitar, leaning against the wall near the headboard. Marcus was hidden in his cocoon; his body wrapped in a shroud of quilts; his head covered with pillows. Hank reached for the neck of the guitar, and as he did, Marcus...*moved*! Hank panicked, pulling back the strings with his fingers. A sudden strum of a dour chord on the instrument roused his uncle.

"Oh my God!" Dolly uttered. "It lives!"

Startled by the discordant alarm from the shroud, Marcus peered at them with one open eye from under his pillow. Dolly and Hank stood motionless, silhouetted in the doorway. "What... are you... doing?" he groaned.

Hank whispered, "Sorry, Uncle Marcus. I'm getting your guitar for Mamaw."

"Just...get...it, Hank." He moaned. Hank gingerly grasped the vintage heirloom.

"Thanks, Uncle Marcus," Hank nodded, "I'll be careful."

Marcus closed his eyes. "Uh huh...You will."

I hope you feel better." his nephew whispered quickly, then escaped from the room.

Dolly closed the door to the edge of the frame and sat on the edge of her brother's bed. He remained still. "Marc?" she began. "Marcus?"

He didn't budge.

"MARC-US?" she said more assertively. Then, after a pause, asked, "So...what happened to Daddy's truck?"

Marcus widened both eyes. "God, if you're there, help me." He thought to himself.

*

"Turn it up!" demanded Dorothy. Perry's first public service announcement was scheduled to be broadcast from his local radio station precisely at 2 pm. This was strategic: the waves would be clear and give enough time to allow everyone to have finished Sunday dinner to turn up their radios.

"What are you running for, Dad?" asked Presley.

"His life," Fern remarked. "It's out there somewhere."

"Your daddy is up for State Representative for this entire district!" retorted Dorothy. "That makes him a high ranking in the state."

"Yes." Fern replied again, "He *ranks*. This'll make him *rank* all the more!"

2:00pm. Perry Jackson's announcement took to the airwaves. The narration was set to Bill Monroe's "Muleskinner Blues" in the background: *"Good morning, Captain...do you need another muleskinner...etc."*

"WHO IS PERRY JACKSON?

A man of Christian compassion—visiting local hospitals, praying with victims of black lung and tuberculosis.

WHO IS PERRY JACKSON?

A man of organization—helping local churches distribute food and clothes to the hungry and cold. Like Santa Claus' helper, he delivers toys to those children who otherwise would never know what Christmas was all about.

WHO IS PERRY JACKSON?

An achiever—one of us who worked from meager means to college graduate to a media manager for our mountain community.

WHO IS PERRY JACKSON?

A leader for out times! No empty promises. He knows what Timberline County needs to move forward.

So, WHO IS PERRY JACKSON?

With your help, our next State Senator.

Vote Perry Jackson...He's one of us."

(Fade out the music: "Mule Skinner Blues.")

Fern switched off the radio. There was a pensive pause around the family circle in the room. Eva broke the silence, "Well, honey, that was really nice. Should get you some votes."

Rawley added, "Sounded like a man who needs a job. Come by the mine, we can talk..."

Perry was not amused. "Coal is obsolete, Rawley. When you get that, even *you* can move forward, maybe even vote for me."

"Dammit, Perry, this is a coal county! The world'll always need what we've got stockpiled! Market it, Perry! If yer damned regulators would get the hell out of the way...There's a thousand years of coal in Timberline County. Coal is our birth right*!"*

Perry fumed, "It's our birth defect! That coal can just lie there! We need better education, new technology, and connecting to the world! Nobody wants coal anymore! *Coal is dead!* That's my platform!"

"You keep talk'in, Perry Jackson," Rawley warned, "And some folks 'round here will see you lying with the coal. You get rid of coal, what do YOU plan to replace it with?"

"Timberline Marijuana!" sang Fern, "It's hillbilly sown and mountain grown!" She laughed to herself, then grew sullen. "Noth'in will ever do what coal did for this county, boys. But Perry's right, it's gone."

Dorothy inserted thoughtfully, "What to replace it with? There's college, starting new stores, learning a trade...something new. You don't have to be a victim if you don't want to be."

Perry continued, "Yeah, Rawley...wipe the soot from your eyes...and BREATHE fresh air!"

Hank returned to the living room, tuning the frets on his uncle's guitar. "You all still harping 'bout coal?" asked.

"No, they ain't." asserted Eva, "What are you going to play, honey?"

"Play that one you wrote about your girlfriend," Dorothy said. "She'll love that one."

"You got a girlfriend, Hank?" Rawley asked.

"Not really." contended Presley with a sly grin. "He wrote a song for Sandy Alcorn... *my ex.* He wanted her...bad! Not a chance. She needed someone...bigger. He's a little dreamer...*very little.*"

"Shut up, Pres." Hank replied. "I wrote it for Mamaw and Papaw, not for Sandy Alcorn. And I'd rather be a little dreamer than a big dork. That's pro'bly why she quit you."

Perry clapped his hands. "Come on, boys, you can't act that way at the Festival. You get along-- brotherly love and all. Tourists like that kind of thing."

"Play your song for me, Henry." His grandmother whispered.

Hank arranged himself on a footstool near his Mamaw's easy chair. She gave him a nod and patted him on his shoulder. He looked into her eyes, "It's kind of a love song 'bout you and Papaw. Maybe how Papaw saw you back then? It's called 'Lady of All Seasons.'" Hank took a breath, then gently began stroking the strings with his fingertips, singing softly:

Lady Fair, you linger easy on my mind,
A feather bed in winter,
A warming taste of vintage wine.
If I didn't know you better,
I would swear you've seen my soul.

Rest your head here beside me,
Keep my mind from growing old.
Lady Fair, you whisper rainbows with your sighs,
Like the breezes in Springtime,
Breeze of honeysuckle vines.
Let the rain fall on my shoulders,
Or the thunder moan,
Your embrace is my shelter,
In this lonely world, I'm not alone.
Lady Fairr, wildflower meadows in your eyes,
Summer o'er the hillside,
New morning lullabies.
In the rush of the morning,
In the heat of my every day,
You entice me with your radiance,
I'm just a puppy dog at play.
Lady Fair, each sigh you breathe is life to me,
Inhaling memories of our autumns:
Moonbeams through falling leaves.
In the firelight, I see us aging,
Together—tenderly.
We share a love for every season,
For our time...and eternity."

Hank moved his fingers poetically through the last strum of the melody, keeping his eyes low, demurring in awareness of the clan. He sighed and lowered the guitar against the footstool. The response around the circle from "very nice" to "has potential." But Eva Kilbride gazed lovingly at Henry, putting her palm on his cheek, "it was perfect." She said.

"Very nice, Hank." affirmed Dorothy.

"*Nice* is a tickle," began Perry, "but it won't 'rouse those girls at the Festival. Now, Presley's stuff...that's potent! When he wins the talent contest, he'll kick it up on Saturday night! Hank, sing

"Country Boys Can Survive…" Then his father himself proceeded to sing the lyrics to his son:

"We grow good-ole tomatoes and homemade wine

And a country boy can survive

Country folks can survive

Country boys can survive…" *(Written and recorded by American musician Hank Williams Jr. The song was released as a single in January 1982)*

"You keep those boys out late on Saturday night, and they won't be up for church come Sunday morning." stated Eva. "Keep 'em outta church, and they won't survive noth'in!"

"Oh, Momma," responded Dorothy, "you don't turn down a deal. They need exposure if they're gonna get somewhere."

"I don't want them boys to end up 'somewhere.' I want 'em in church!"

Perry chuckled. "Nashville is better! All they need is the right exposure to a producer."

"Or some criminal stalker!" Eva continued. "They're some strange wheeler-dealers out there."

"Oh, Momma. We're careful with our boys." Dorothy scoffed.

Eva grew stern. "Don't farce with me, Dottie Kilbride! I know what's out there! Stalkers who pick up children on the highway…Podiatrists they're called on the news. They do horrible things to children.

"Pedophiles, Momma?" Fern answered.

Eva paid her no mind. "If ya'll got back in church, you'd know 'bout the world of sin out there! That's where you want to send your boys into! You all need to read your Bibles. The world ain't what it's supposed to be. You go along think'in the world is fine. That's when you get bit by the devil! NO! You keep close to them… You make 'em play music… in church!"

"Where do all of them '*podiatrists*' hide…in church!" laughed Perry.

Dorothy insisted, "Momma, our boys are safe."

Eva calmed herself and glanced at her grandsons. "You two be here for Sunday dinners, you hear me?" Keep yerselves justified in Jesus."

"To God's 'plumb line.'" Rawley added.

Presley rolled his eyes, then turned away with a sheepish grin at his daddy. Hank strummed a string or two on the guitar and whispered to his Mamaw, "I promise."

Chapter Four:
Aidan Kilbride

"We must be responsive to siltation control...Reports I hear from the effects of strip mining are the most appalling revelations...'the rape of our mountains' isn't strong enough to describe what we have found."

(Governor Wendell Ford, Public Papers, 1972)

"For us, it was hard to believe there was any 'rest of the world,' and if there should be such a thing, why, we trusted in the mountains to protect us from it." (Jean Ritchie, Singing Family of the Cumberlands, 1980)

Dusk was veiling the holler. The air was brisk, scented with vintage honeysuckle. The last of the season's wisteria was drooping from the trees around and about Eva's homeplace. There was a soft wisp of falling leaves—everywhere, everywhere trickling, drifting lazily, willy-nilly about the yard. The peepers were chirping in endless chatter. Echoing somewhere in the woods was a whooping 'yoo-hoo' of an owl. In the autumn sky, a canvas of the gloaming was emerging as if a consummate artist was playing with fanciful watercolors. The fiery timbre of the day was surrendering to the deeper blue diamonds of solitude-- the inevitable eventide was drawing near.

At first glance, it was merely a small, open-air deck, an extension of the house. But it was more. From Eva Kilbride's back porch, one could enter another dimension where past and present were one-in-the-same. Mamaw's back porch wooed the weary into solitude—a sheltering wing from the woes of the world. There was a raw wooden swing secured on the ceiling of the porch by a rusty chain. It gently swung back and forth in a soothing syncopation; it's wafting sound heard like a lullaby to those who reclined in its arms. A high-backed wicker chair was set near the swing. It was padded with a holey quilt, Eva's favorite patchwork. There were wooden trays to rest glasses of sweet tea, copies of the newspaper, or pouches of Sir Walter Raleigh pipe tobacco.

Dorothy and Perry and their boys, Fern and Dean, Rawley and Wanda, and her kids left for their own homes. Only Dolly and Marcus remained at home with Eva.Every Sunday evening, after everyone departed for their respective homes, it was on her back porch that Eva could find refuge; solitude... time alone with Aidan. For a lifetime, this was their meeting place. No matter how far away from each other they might have been on their back porch, they could always find their way back to one another.

Marcus emerged from his exile (after everyone had gone) and was at the table nibbling on the last slice of apple pie. Dolly finished drying the last plate from dinner and stepped onto the porch. "Mama, you, okay?" Dolly asked. "Need anything?"

"...a little air..."she answered. "...a little quiet." Dolly understood her meaning and retreated into the kitchen.Her mother wanted her time alone, in a sacred space.

Eva was fragile but not frail.She could still find her place on the porch. She eased herself into the wicker chair; it creaked beneath her. The October breeze was brisk, and it chilled her. She wrapped the quilt around her shoulders and sat back with a Sunday evening sigh, closed her eyes, and waited.

"Eva?"She heard him; Aidan?

She kept her eyes closed and smiled. "I'm fine tonight, Aidan." she purred. After a moment, she uttered, "Coal's burning tonight. Smells sooty. But you always liked it that way."

"That's 'old-de-colon' to me, Eva."

"How're the boys do'in?"

"They're young, but they'll do what they gotta do. *You showed 'em*...always did." Eva opened her eyes and inhaled the breeze. "We can't keep 'em in the mines, Aidan. They need school'in."

"They'll leave... never come back. The roads'll take 'em away. I can't let 'em run off. "

(Eva remembered a Sunday evening like this many years before as their sons were reaching their respective "ages of clan accountability.")

"BOYS! Rawley! Marcus! Come out here! Your momma and me are spat'in over your duties! She don't want you cutt'in coal. You gonna snap shucky-beans or cut coal? I know Rawley ain't feared of do 'in *his* duty. Marcus? You gonna do what's rightful? God gave this land to us; it's our duty, by dog, to keep anybody from steal'n it! Gotta keep a paycheck com'in."

He winked with a nod to Rawley. At twelve, he had already committed to doing his duty in the mine alongside his daddy. But Marcus was not as bold as his older brother. Although he wanted to please Aidan, at only eight years old, such exploits underground was a terror.

Aidan addressed both sons again but stared sternly at little Marcus. "Boys, it's a dark time. You can almost breeeeeathe the dark. But we got the light in our gut. You don't have to be a-feared of the dark. We do what we gotta do. Ever-one of us has to do what he can do to keep that light shin'in in our holler. If that ceiling in the hole should fall, we'll be buried with a smile 'cause we weren't a-feared to do what we had to do."He glared now at Marcus. "Right, boy?" Marcus looked downward, away from Aidan. He crossed his arms in front of his chest and held firmly to his cupped his hands on his little boy's biceps.

Aidan turned away from Marcus and toward Rawley. "But your momma wants you a top 'a the ground, plow'in a poisoned field. Since the flood, that plot we got ain't much fertile no more. We all got to do what we gotta do cause it's gett'in dark! It's our…duty! Gotta protect your momma and Fern, and Dorothy, and Dolly.Hell, Jesus said, we gotta do what we can do… *'while it is day..'.* or else the night's gonna come and take it all away.*"*

Aidan twitched his face away from Rawley and took a menacing step toward Marcus. The halfling looked up at Aidan's face and flinched, instinctively taking a step away from him. "Boys," the man began again, "You'll do your duty, or by God or the devil, it might be a day, but I'll make it *your last one!*"

Eva opened her eyes. The mirage dissipated into the primitive cacophony of night sounds in the holler. She held to the affirming arms of her chair and leaned her fragile torso forward, bowing her head for a breath of fresh prayer. Then she sang softly to herself a hymn her mother always sang to her as a child, A. P. Carter's *"Pale Wildwood Flower:"*

"O you taught me to love you and promised to love

And to think of me always all others above;

But you've loved, and you've left me in one fleeing hour,

Gone and forgotten your pale wildwood flower."

"Momma, I put that load of laundry back in the washer," said Dolly, stepping onto the porch. "Wanda forgot to dry them, and they soured." She exhaled her cigarette and batted the smoke away from Eva. "You think'in 'bout Daddy?"

"Everything's odd when you get older, Dolly. Why is it we remember some things and forget other things, like things we thought we'd never forget? We forget 'em. And other things we want to forget and can't never forget?"

"Guess God made it that a'way."

"Sometimes God makes sense, and sometimes He don't. Beautiful flowers in Spring …only wilt away. He makes the trees full of leaves, but they just fall. Don't make no sense sometimes. God gives but eventually takes it all away."

Dolly exhaled a billow of smoke. "Hell, Momma, if you're gonna talk like this, I'm going back in the house and finish the damned laundry." But instead, she sat in the swing, listening to Eva's wicker chair.

Eva smiled. "Sometimes God don't seem...justified in things. I don't mean to blas-a-pheem, but... He's too much to understand sometimes." She paused and raised her eyes to the distant backwoods beyond the porch. "Ever see the wild dogs foller after yer daddy? They did. They weren't a-feared a-him, and he weren't of them. Yer daddy weren't never a-feared a-noth'in! When Aidan was a boy, he was a handsome feller with a wind-blown face, boldly shoulders, darksome eyes, and a nose that flared when anyone crossed him. He had a mean streak; and he could be spiteful. But he always akindly way for those wild dogs. He used to talk to them dogs—and they'd do whatever he said.

And those clumpy boots he wore all the time? Went up the ridge in 'em even after a slide in the mud. He loved those boots; he said they made him taller. But no. They just made 'em feel that way. Clomp, clomp, clomp! Dolly, I swear sometimes I still hear those boots on the porch and ... listen to those dogs out there...like they're look'in for him."

"Or maybe its squirrels clomp'in on the roof?" Dolly said. "And dogs barking at coons and such?"

Eva sighed, "Maybe so."

Dolly tossed her cigarette off the porch. "I remember Daddy carry'in me on his back up the ridge to plant someth'in or other. I was on one shoulder and he flung a hoe on the other. He could always find a patch of grow 'in sod up there—even in the rocky places. He could plant in the dry season, stormy or cold, and someth'in would grow. Daddy taught me to grow. First season, I planted too shallow; the next season, I planted too deep—but things still grew…when the critters didn't get at 'em. I reckon our time here is to teach us how to grow."

There was silence between them for a moment. Dolly lit a fresh cigarette and balanced it on the edge of an old ashtray. The white smoke ascended around her, and she inhaled it. Through the smoke, she recalled a path that led from Fallen Timbre Creek and up the mountainside. (The path Dolly remembered was misbegotten now. The clan was content to commute on paved roads rather than commune with the trails of their childhood.)

Dolly's thoughts led her to a time before she graduated from Squire Boone High School when she and her daddy followed the path through the backwoods and along the creek. Every now and then, Aidan would stop to remove debris from damming the flow— fallen branches or things unnatural, like beer cans and trash bags. Aidan tried to remove as best he could anything that obstructed the stream.

Along their way, her daddy took notice of everything around him. The fauna he knew by nature and by name. He pointed out to Dolly the wildflowers: alum, wild strawberry, sassafras, percoon root, raw iris, and whippoorwill blossoms. He was obliged to direct her sight to a hawk's nest, secluded dens where foxes or other predators could hide, and the scratching of bear claws on tree trunks that marked territory as its own. He paused to distinguish how the trunk of one tree, "if you listen close, tonated differently from the 'tother, when they come a-humm'in with the wind." Along the way, he pocketed chestnuts on the ground -- always careful first to look for snakes. Copperheads and outsiders were the only creatures that Aidan ever feared.

They scaled a steeper path to the top of a plateau overlooking the holler bottomland. After a breath or two, Aidan and Dolly climbed to a ridge, a natural ledge that allowed them to see a more far-reaching purview of Appalachia. From here, Dolly grasped how their holler was a small but essential link in the fullness of everything in the mountains. From that height, the world was indeed more wonderful than she could imagine. Mystical waves of autumn woodlands were ebbing and flowing as they had since "nobody really knows but God." At dusk, the deep emerald of the pines mellowed the ruddy amber of the leaves. Standing at top of this small ridge, *their ridge,* Dolly inhaled the awe and the aura of absolute solitude. They stood together for a moment. Aidan took his teenage daughter's hand and said, "When you get a hanker'in for what you ain't got, daughter, climb up this ridge. Look at what you got. But remember, Dolly, we tend to things here, but we don't *own* it. Nobody really *owns* what they don't create out-a-noth'in. We *tend to* things… and things *tend to* us."

Dolly flicked the remnant of her cigarette into the yard and wafted away the smoke. She smiled as she reminisced out loud. "On our way back down the mountain, he took me to another path...used, but hidden. It was like he took me explor'in. But he knew where he was going. I smelt it 'fore we got there. There were some embers still red: daddy's still! Sitting there as big as you please. Right there, Momma, out in front of my eyes: the legend come true! 'Course we all knew it was up there," She smiled again, "but that was the first time I actually seen it."

Eva responded with half a smile and half-a-frown. "I hated those *runs!*"

"No! Momma! I was honored." Dolly returned. "Hell, Rawley didn't even know where it was. He just knew it go'in on… somewhere. Daddy was good at hid'in it. We just hiked back and never talked 'bout it again. Daddy said he would be there if I ever needed it. 'Outsiders,' he said, 'will buy it no matter how new or how old the batch. They like to own what they ain't supposed to have.' 'Thou shalt not covet"—tak'in control over someth'in that ain't yours to control.He told me, 'When you can make people think they can own something they ain't supposed to have, you can sell 'em...anything...good batch or bad.'"

Eva got up from her chair and strolled to the back door. "I hated those runs, Dolly. At least, I hope when he sold a batch, it was a good batch!"

"I'm sure it was, Momma. Daddy always sold his best." Dolly assured her and followed Eva into the house.

*

Dean Walker's bottom land was in view from the upper hillside of the Kilbride property. Years ago, a land settlement was negotiated between the Walkers and the Kilbrides to decide how the connection between the two homesteads could be negotiated to defuse a possible feud over rightful access to the bridge. Although Dean had a legitimate claim to the fertile bottom land, they did not have a claim to the bridge, the entrance to his rightful property. In years long past, there was tension between the two clans over which clan owned the bridge.After Dean married Fern, the tension eased. A settlement was agreed to when it was fortified with both a nod and the wedlock of Dean Walker and Fern Kilbride. The vows were made. But now and then, Aiden reminded his son-in-law that "by rights," the Kilbrides still owned the bridge between their properties. With the untimely death of Aidan Kilbride, the bridge became the inheritance, not of Fern, but her brother, Rawley: for his discretion alone.

Sunday evening. Dean drove across the narrow bridge over Fallen Timber Creek and down his gravel drive toward their home. "We gonna miss 60 Minutes."Fern grumbled.

As they got closer to their house, the headlights on Dean's car caught the fluorescent eyes of a rotund black bear rummaging through their trash cans. "Didn't you tie down the lids?" Fern yelled.

"I thought I did." Dean answered in a sweat. (At times, he was more intimidated by his wife than he was by the bears.)

"Well, you didn't!" she snorted. "Shine your brights! Drive up there and scare the damn thing away!" Dean followed her orders and accelerated toward the intruder. The bear was startled, but merely snarled, turned its back to the approaching vehicle, and kept chewing some choice piece of rubbish. Dean slowed down, cautious so as not to agitate the wild in the animal.

"What are you slowing down for?" Fern exclaimed. She stretched her hand to the steering wheel and sounded the horn. The bear merely turned his head around, still chewing voraciously, but gave them a leisurely glance; annoyed but undaunted. Not to be outdone, Fern stretched her foot over the console of the front seat and slammed down the gas pedal, overriding her husband's foot. The car fishtailed in the gravel and accelerated down the lane. "Damned bear!" she yelled. Dean held the wheel but in the panic of the moment, steered the car into the drainage ditch.

"My God, Dean, get it out of the ditch." she demanded.But before he could maneuver anything, Fern was out of the car, tromping in attack mode up the driveway. Dean pulled out of the ditch and slowly followed her. The car lights on "bright." There was the bulky black bear, mouthing chomping, eyes alert. It turned now, looking at the approaching woman, the firstborn of Aidan Kilbride. Her hands were flying in the air, and her voice resonated through the holler, "GET OUTTA THERE! GO ON! LOOK AT THIS MESS!" The bear bolted into the woods. She stopped. Dean did as well. Then she turned around, glaring at her husband. "Look at that mess, Dean!" she scolded. "I told you to always tie down the lids!"

She turned sharply around to Dean, who was still easing the car toward her. "You get out here and help me clean this up."

Dean parked the car, and marched resolutely toward his wife. "What are you doing, honey?" he exclaimed, "That bear could've charged you!"

"Help me clean this up." she returned. "Ain't no damn bear going to tromp in my trash or anything else on this property!" With that, she scurried about picking up the scattered refuse and stuffing it back into the cans. In the back of her mind, she pictured her daddy smoking his pipe and watching her on the hillside nearby. "He would be pleased." Fern thought to herself. "No cussed bear is going to make me miss 60 Minutes." she exclaimed.

*

A poem written by a young Marcus Kilbride one evening while sitting on his momma's back porch:

"My Holler Home"
Wak'in to the whistl'in rumble of the L&N train,
And the smell of bak'in biscuits, gravy, and grits with a spoonful a' sorghum cane;
Ris'in in the sun,
Free from fear or feign.
Roam'in 'round our holler,
Barefooted on my course;
Wading chest high in Fallen Timbre
Baptizing my soul with no remorse.
Smok'in home-grown, raw tobacco
Guzzl'in RCs—the empties I could sell
Trad'in stories and holler secrets
Only the stories God allowed to tell.
Learn'in letters from schoolbooks and grow'in grace in Sunday School
Sunday hymns Momma sang by heart, memory, and the golden rule
Her prayers ascended into Heaven to keep us from temptation and to Jesus-purity

That one day, we might be together in Heaven's security.
The smells of Momma's kitchen—fix'ins of holler-fared cuisine:
Home-growed maters, red or fried- breaded olive-green
Rhubarb pie, thick baloney and sassafras tea
Cane pressed to black molasses, purified to an amber gleam.
Boiling collards, shuck'in beans and husk'in corn
No need for shirts, just summer britches—bare-thin and worn
Catching fireflies in the even'in —then sitt'in on the porch,
Til the nighttime stops me roam'in and my dream'in to be re-born.

*

Marcus sat in his usual place at the table, clad in nothing but his own boxer shorts. He poured himself another glass of sweet tea stirred with half a lemon and another spoonful of sugar. Dolly sat at the table across from him and observed him sipping his Sunday evening concoction. "I never understood drink'in iced tea." she observed, "It's bitter, so you make it sweet. Then you sour-it-up. Then you add more sugar? Is it 'cause you like it bitter-sweet or sweetlie-bitter? Don't really make sense, Marc. When is it good enough?"

Marcus raised his glass to his sister, "Cheers," he said, smiling, as he guzzled a gulp of bittersweet tea.

Eva sat in her rightful place at the table and watched them both. She was silent long enough for Marcus to sense an awkwardness in the room.

Marcus turned to his mother, "Did Hank play his song for you, Momma?"

"Yes, he did. It was nice." Eva remarked sternly. "You should have been 'round to hear it." She shifted her chair a bit and folded her hands in front of her as if preparing to pray. "Where've you been, Marcus?"

"Here-- eat'in apple pie." he grinned. "Nobody does apples like Eva Kilbride."

"No, where've you *been*?" she insisted again. "With your daddy's truck?"

"I had a *run*," he replied.

"All night?"

"Mostly."

"Doing *what*?"

"Mak'in a liv'in!" Marcus growled.

"Where's your daddy's truck?" she asked again.

He gulped the tea to empty. "I...wrecked it."

Eva's eyes sank. "Lord, Lord, Lord..." she gasped.

Dolly lit a cigarette and sat very still.

"Momma. I was com'in over the ridge. The road was slick. I guess I was driv'in too fast. It slid over the side. I was lucky. I jumped out. The truck crashed somewhere in the trees...the rocks...I don't know...just stuck there."

"Well, are *you* hurt?"

"Noth'in to worry about. You know I always reckon with ever-thang, Momma."

"I've told you not to take that ridge road at night—especially when it's rain'in. How many times has your daddy told you not to take that road? He's told you! I've told you! Rawley's told you not to make that run—at all! You don't listen to anybody..."

Marcus slapped his empty glass on the table. "I listen to *ever-body*, Momma! EVER—BODY!"

"Well, you listen, but you don't HEAR anyth'in!"

98

Marcus leaned on his elbows and rubbed his fingers over his bloodshot eyes. "I hear everything! Everything! Until I just can't hear no more! My heads explod'in with everything I hear!"

Eva's voice became shallow and strained. "Why don't you just do what's right? ...run'in 'round at night! I have no idea what you're do'in."

"It doesn't matter." Marcus replied under his breath. Then he replied fervently, "I'm just mak'in a living... work'in, Momma."

"It can't be no *good* work--- at night! You wrecked your daddy's truck! Lord, Lord, Lord! What would your daddy say?"

"He'd say, 'Hey, possum boy! Don't bother your momma for noth'in'! You make that run a good'in!' That's what I do for your momma: make my run a 'good'in.'"

"Talk with Rawley." Eva suggested. "He can find you some REAL work."

"Momma, I don't need no help from Rawley!" Marcus shrugged.

"He don't need to go back to the mine, Momma." Dolly interrupted. "Marcus is not like Rawley or Daddy."

"Your daddy was a brave man!" Eva continued, "...he was chivalry*!* Did what he had to do for all of us."

Marcus's mind was triggered, set adrift to old dreams and visions. He remembered the soliloquy his father gave to him while the boy was riding shotgun in his truck many years before. *Your clan braved this holler. They defended this land from foes, the Feds, and every wild thing that comes down outta those hills. That's chivalry, possum boy! Chivalry!"*

Eva stood from her chair. "You just think about that, Marcus. Think good and long about how you're going to make good on that truck. Call that Carl Jaspers tomorrow and get that truck home." She insisted as she stepped away.

Marcus raised his empty glass. "Cheers!" he grimaced, "Cheers all around!"

"You gotta the truck back." Dolly insisted. "She ain't gonna let that go."

"I'll get it down. I'll call Casper. We'll get it down. But it ain't worth it no more. It's wrecked for good, Dolly. It's damn wrecked for good!"

Marcus stood and headed toward his bedroom. He had only taken one step when Dolly called him again. "Outta ever-thang you ever done…now daddy's truck?"

Her brother stopped and turned to her, "Stop 'grandiz'in that damned truck, Dolly! You always 'grandize every…thing!"

At night, the mountains seem to rise to become a bulwark against the outside world. The burdens of the day fade in the solace of home, wherein one can rest. Nighttime in the hollers reverberates with a consistency of sounds, unhindered by time or human machination: the trickling of Fallen Timber Creek over branches, logs, and stone, the woodwinds whistling gently through haggard hillsides, the deep moaning chant of vintage oaks in harmony with the tender strings of the willows. As evening falls, a chorus of peepers and raspy crickets scat their jazziest licks, while field larks and owls add a lofty improvisation to the respite fare.

A train was coming. It was rumbling in the distance down a misbegotten rail echoing through the Timberlines. Marcus shuddered with a sudden chill down his back. He left the table and scurried to the porch-- to listen. From his youth, he was intoxicated by the sound of a train screeching its wheels on the metal track, rumbling along with the momentum of its engine. For him, the sound was an invitation, a beckoning, to enter the threshold of some unknown world. He sat in his mama's wicker chair and listened and listened. He closed his eyes, transfixed on the rhythm on the rails and every *screech* on the track, louder and louder until it began to fade away. It never lasted long enough. It always faded away. Out of reach.

A poem written by a young Marcus Kilbride:
The restless train sighs shrill
In the evening autumn chill
In the throes of a coming wintry nil
The helmsman with a thorny thistle
Modulates a syncopated tune
To a darksome, lonely whistle
The steady track of that locomotion
Treks roundabout in sad commotion
Hurried, 'fore its final rust and motion
In the evening autumn chill
'tween summer bliss and winter nil.

The sound of the train faded. Marcus awakened from the lull of the train's lullaby by a sudden remembrance of Aidan's haunting voice. "You're a damned possum boy! A-feared of ever'thang! A pussy willer in the wind! Pout'in 'bout getting 'board some train? What's all this pout'in gonna get you or anybody in this clan? You ain't got no business board'in no train outta here! You got chores in this holler! Rid'in a train won't pay for noth'in'! Get that idea outta your head now, possum boy! If you're MY son, you're gonna give what what you got, possum boy! Are you listen'in, Marcus? Are you listen'in?"

Marcus stood suddenly. His fists were clenched, and his teeth were grinding. The wound in his thigh from the thorn he pulled from his flesh was nagging. His shoulder was aching in the chill of nightfall. He walked back into the house to his room. He laid back down in his bed for the night, heaving a heavy sigh, exhaling the voice of Aidan Kilbride as he did. As he reached to turn off the bedside lamp, he noticed his window was wide open. He got up to close it. He pulled back the curtains. There balanced on the windowsill were the sneakers he had left behind at his Aunt Grace's home. Inserted in the soul of one of the shoes was a crumbled gospel tract titled "Where Will You Spend Eternity?" The little pamphlet was roughly inscribed, "From Emmanuel, and you can keep my clothes!"

Marcus grabbed his sneakers and read the note on the tract. He leaned his head out the window and scanned the field. An autumn moon was shrouded behind ill-routed clouds. His cousin was nowhere in view. He shut his window, latched it as tightly as it could be latched, and closed the curtains.

From the other side of the harvested field, hidden in the high brush, crouched his cousin, Emmanuel Kilbride. He watched from a distance as Marcus closed the curtains. As he scampered down the road toward home, he snickered, gratified in doing his alms…*in secret.*

Emmanuel's benevolence had not gone unobserved. Across the field, behind a clump of fodder shocks, Emmanuel had also been observed. Another pair of eyes was scanning the window of Marcus's bedroom. Once wide open, it was shuttered now. Frustrated, the shadow man retreated into the woods. For him, it was all in the timing.

Chapter Five:
The First Day After Sunday

Codas, Caves and Copperheads

"What about the disease of a mediocre education…that keeps a child from reaching his or her potential?" (Governor Louie B. Nunn, Public Papers, 1985)

"The surface of Kentucky is dissected by an almost endless pattern of ridges and valleys…Stream courses formed inlets, coves, and valleys that can become entrapments." (Thomas D. Clark, A History of Kentucky)

"No longer can the plow and the pickax sustain a thriving economy. Education fuels growth." (Governor Martha Layne Collins, Public Papers, 1983)

William Holmes McGuffey High School benefited significantly by many of the reforms in education during the era of the late 1970s and 1980s. The goal of such reforms was envisioned as ways toward offering equity to all schools across the region, both urban and rural, and enabling students *to "grow through a better understanding of themselves and the world in which they live, to a productive and rewarding future as adults."(Governor Wendell Ford, Public Papers, 1974)*

Enlisted in the effort focused on the education of children in McGuffey High School were not only school administrators and teachers but also counselors and politicians. Their intention was not to usurp the role of parental authority but to create an atmosphere and supply the *machinery* through which students might succeed personally and professionally in their respective communities. During a special summit on education in the early 1980's, then-governor Martha Layne Collins pronounced, "The quality of education offered in public schools will determine the quality of life available in Kentucky." (Governor Martha Layne Collins, Public Papers, 1983)

In the 1980s, under the mandate of Section 183 of the Kentucky constitution, the Legislative body in Frankfort was required to provide equal support to conduct educational opportunities in all schools, including those in Appalachia that may have been less equipped in implementing such progressive reforms. As those reforms took root throughout the state, so were the seeds of possibility sewn in the lives of students in the hollers. The more inquisitive students began to see beyond the demise of the mining industry to consider making a living independent of the government *draw*. The 1980s were a time of transition from hopelessness due to the exploitation of the land to a resurgence of hope—new possibilities for life in Appalachia without a dependence on coal.

While education was key to the notion of economic progress in Appalachia, employment was still hard to come by. There remained in the hollers tension between the obligation of students to settle in their birthplace with little opportunity for life-sustaining jobs or leave their clan and holler to discover more lucrative employment elsewhere.

*

William Holmes McGuffey was a professor at Miami University in Oxford, Ohio. He taught classes in Latin, Hebrew, Greek, and moral philosophy. He also became a sympathizer with the unschooled, the illiterate; people in Appalachia without a value-centered or formal education. While in his career, he was also an ordained minister in the Presbyterian church and later became president, respectively, of Cincinnati College (1836) and Ohio University (1843); his major accomplishment was his role as president of Woodward Free Grammar School in Cincinnati, where he was determined to offer a quality education for all persons, especially children.

He is best known for *Readers,* the first widely used series of elementary level education textbooks. *McGuffey Readers* were sold in the multi-millions between 1836 and into the 1960s. The accumulated sales of the *McGuffey Reader* placed it in a category rivaling both the Holy Bible and Webster's Dictionary.His focus on value-centered education included literary passages from the Bible; as well as selections from Shakespeare, poets John Milton and Lord Byron, novelists Washington Irving and Walter Scott, Thomas Jefferson, and the Noah Webster Dictionary. In addition to spelling and grammar, the Readers had parables on the importance of honesty, courage, loyalty, family, compassion, patriotism, thrift, duty, kindness, temperance, and faith.

William H. McGuffey High School emerged from the consolidation of three facilities in the region: Timberline County School, Fallen Timbre Academy, and Daniel Boone Junior High School. As the population in the county decreased, there was less need for three schools in the same district. As the trio of facilities became more difficult to manage, and in the reality of a dwindling student population, consolidation seemed to be the answer both economically and politically. Mayor James T. Cunning, the County School Board, and the City Council agreed unanimously to the project.

As the State Legislature appropriated funding for the consolidation of schools, the population in the area became more intrigued with the possibilities of a new facility—bringing together what the state provided along with a collection of what was salvageable and of sentimental value from the three dilapidated and outdated facilities. The students themselves had high hopes for the merging of the schools: stronger athletic teams—basketball in a regulation gym and football under a lighted field-- and a better lunch menu in the new cafeteria. Extra funding from the city brought improvements in the curriculum and the athletic program. Even some wealthy business owners from surrounding counties and local bankers contributed to the Astro-turf campaign and posted a new, lighted scoreboard for the new football field. Soon, the district offered better sports equipment, uniforms, pom-poms, and school spirit in the county.

The expectations for the new educational facility ran high. Mayor Cunning assured his constituents, "A new educational facility was the answer to the challenges in Timberline County." (The community agreed that their children needed both an education and the salvation of Jesus to live successfully.)The appropriation of the State Capitol ignited a renewed excitement: William H. McGuffey was born.The Grand Opening was complete with much pomp and circumstance. Tours were offered through the decorated hallways. Teachers were present to explain their respective curricula in science, math, history, and English. Still, while those doors were open, most visitors lingered merrily in the state-of-the-art gymnasium or on the newly turfed football field.

(It was assumed by many that William Holmes McGuffey himself would be pleased with his namesake. Still others simply didn't know (or care) who William H. McGuffey, "a city boy," was at all. So, it was determined at a community forum that the school mascot would not be the McGuffey "Readers" as was first suggested, but the Timberline County "Raiders." Certainly, it would be the "Raiders" not the "Readers" who would win for games!)

Monday.

The dismissal bell rang. Hank had just enough time to gather his end-of-the-school-day wits about him and meet Presley in the parking lot. Their father, Perry Jackson had a full post-school chore for his sons. Although there were for Hank other alternatives offered Hank after the bell: cross country conditioning, class in Appalachian Storytelling, and the possibility of a quality conversation at his locker with Sandy Alcorn, all else had to be suspended for this season of his father's political fervor. Duty called. Perry Jackson was running for state office. Presley and Hank were enlisted to post their daddy's campaign posters on prominent landmarks around town and throughout Timberline County. Hank stuffed his backpack with essentials and scurried through a maze of his peers in the hallways to the exit.

Hank met Presley at the wheel of their daddy's van.By the lowered brow of his older brother's face, Hank knew he was not in sync with his older brother's schedule. Hank loaded his backpack in the back seat and took his rightful place as co-pilot.

"We've got a hundred of these posters. Gotta get 'em up 'fore daddy signs off the air." Presley insisted snidely. He slammed the gas pedal to the floor. "Then we got rehearsal. I can't wait for you all day, Hank!" Presley turned sharply."And...you know you ain't gonna play your *stuff* at the Fest. You know that, right?" The van raced past a startled Letitia Rawlings, the vintage school-crossing guard, screeching its tires onto the main thoroughfare toward town.

"My '*stuff*'?" asked Hank.

"That sloppy crap you played at Mamaw's last night. It was just for her, right?"

Hank was silent for a moment. "Oh, you mean my *songs?*"

Presley nodded with a sly grin, "Yeah. Your *stuff!* Your shitty-witty. You ain't gonna play that shit at my show. Nobody wants to smell that stuff. They like 'Country Boys Can Survive.'"

"It ain't shit, Pres*!*"

Presley whipped back, "It ain't go'in nowhere."

Hank shook his head, looking out the window and away from his brother. Presley continued: "We play what people want to hear. We ain't going nowhere with what you've been blow'in out your ass!"

"It's new. People will catch on to it."

"Ain't gonna get us nowhere." Presley turned sharply again into the lot of the Commonwealth Bank and parked the van. "You can practice it all you want. Ain't nobody at the Festival gonna like it. It ain't got market potential. Nobody'll get it."

"Come on, Pres!" Hank began, "Nobody got Dylan either. Now he's a genius. He was shit to people when he was just *Bob Dylan*, but now he's, well...*DYLAN*! He kept playing his stuff and people learned to like it. It's like...*acquired*."

Presley leaned over his seat and thrust a stack of posters at his younger brother. "First, you ain't Dylan. Second..." he grinned again, "I ain't gonna play your whinny-sloppy stuff at the Festival. Third, take these and post 'em, or I'll tell Daddy that you're being a little whinny bastard!" He thought for a moment then grinned that grin that so triggered his little brother. "Or better—I'll tell Sandy Alcorn yer real name.

"Shut up, Pres!" Hank grimaced.

"Bocephus! HANK *'Bo-Oh-Oh Ceee-fuss'* Jackson!"

"Shut up!"

Hank snatched the posters from Presley. Then he sang to his brother a re-arrangement of a famous Dylan song via a Dylan brogue: "How does if feel? Hold hands with girls like an eel? Without me, you'll never get a record deal. 'cause from Elvis' pelvis you steal!"

Presley got out of the van. "I gotta lyric for you, Hank. Let's see what rhymes with *steal?*'" He snapped at his brother, "I got it, Hank: go eat shit for a meal*!"*

The boys grabbed their share of posters and took to opposite sides of Main Street. Being the only thoroughfare through town, the light posts, telephone poles, and street signs were the most productive sites on which to display their daddy's picture—his eyes airbrushed with empathy, his thinning hair tinted Lincoln black, and a smile that would undoubtedly win the votes of all the widows and wallflowers in Timberline County. The only words on the poster reflected the candidate's formula for success in the upcoming election--name recognition and a memorable slogan:

PERRY JACKSON. "HE'S ONE OF US!"

Hank and Presley were determined to finish their assignment before nightfall. They wanted to display as many posters as necessary in town, then move out into the county, putting them on fences and trees and wherever else they could flaunt their daddy's image.

Hank was just about to duct-tape a poster on a STOP sign when a sharp-toned, well-honed baritone voice halted him, "Hey!" sounded a Deputy Sheriff from his patrol car across the street. His unfamiliar voice was as jolting to the boy as if the officer had suddenly ignited his siren. "Kid! Stop what you're do'in! You can't do that!" Hank turned around to see Deputy Sheriff Travis Hudson crossing to him in a double-time-strut. His fisted hands held firmly on his hips, he said, "You know you're creating a menace?"

Hank demurred, trembling a bit in the sight of the man's badge. "Sir?"

"...those posters..." continued the Deputy. "I'm the Sheriff's new deputy in town. Deputy Sheriff Travis Hudson. Who are you, kid?"

He knew Sheriff Keith Boswell, but he had never met his new deputy. Travis Hudson was a towering man—not so much in altitude as in attitude. The new county deputy was slick--from his starched shirt and the shiny inscribed badge that draped his chest like military metal to his razor-creased britches and protruding pistol. Travis Hudson was ready and more than willing to serve and preserve the law in Timberline County and anywhere else he could make his presence known. He truly believed he represented not only the Sheriff's office but the overarching rule of law on the earth.

Deputy Hudson scanned the poster. "What's your name?"

"Hank Jackson."

"A relative of this guy on the poster?"

"He's my daddy...run'in for..."

"Yeah...run'in for something. Think he'll get elected?"

"Don't know..."

"Well, Hank Jackson, he ain't gonna get elected if his kid is arrested defacing a STOP sign. Funny! See, the irony: it says STOP! Stop means STOP! It's meant to be followed. Defacing public property is a menace! What if a car drives by and only sees your daddy's face? Doesn't see the sign? Could be a tragedy! Do know what a tragedy looks like?"

Hank perused the beefy public servant. Then, he studdered under his breath, "Um, yessir. I think I understand what a tragedy looks like."

Travis Hudson removed the duct tape from the poster and handed it back to Hank. "You take your posters and hang them where they won't be a menace to traffic."

"Yes, sir," Hank said, retrieving the poster.

Deputy Hudson crossed the street to his patrol car. He climbed into the open door, then called back to Hank. "You got your warning, Frank!" He slid into the front seat of his chariot of the law and slammed the door. As he drove away down Main Street he smiled and gazed back at Hank one more time in his authorized rear-view mirror.

*

Presley ran down Main Street, catching up to his brother. He had only a few posters left. It would be dark soon, and if they wanted to please their daddy, they had to come home empty-handed. "I know the perfect place for the rest of 'em!" Pres said, "Come on!" They climbed into the van, and drove down Main Street to the county service road. They parked off the road every now and then at a fence post or two, but Presley was insistent they get to his perfect place for posting their propaganda.

"Where are we going, Pres?" asked Hank. drove

Presley smiled. "The *GOD ROCK*. Daddy's face on the GOD rock! People will think God is calling Daddy to save Timberline County... or something like that! He'll love it! It's perfect!"

Hank sighed with a subtle sarcasm, "Yeah. Perry Jackson: Senator and Savior."

They continued hastily along the winding, narrow service road, up its steep, unrestricted incline to the graveled edge of the sharp precipice from where lodged the God *rock*. There was the renowned boulder. On its side was the sanctimonious graffiti: "GOD VISITS FOR SIN." It had been painted on the boulder a generation or so before by a radical band of Pentecostal deacons. It was almost as hallowed by many in Timberline as the tablets of Moses. It served as a reminder of the grace of God for the repentant and a warning of impending doom for those who continued along a path of rebellion against God and Hollow Law. Now somewhat faded by the whims of weather, the words were still recognizable.

Presley parked the van carefully near the safest edge of the road, enough to keep it from being sideswiped by any oncoming vehicle, far enough from tilting over the edge. They climbed out of the van and took to their daddy's business duct-taping the posters around the God-rock.

They taped the last poster as securely as they could with duct tape to the smoother edges of the rock. Then they spied an indentation in the stone and gleefully mounted the God rock. They climbed to the flat surface of the boulder as if they were performing on stage at the Ryman. Presley imitated Willie and Waylon's, "On the Road Again," while Hank was content with Haggard's "Sing Me Back Home."Their voices echoed about the ridge and into the woodlands.With his boots, Presley clogged atop the God rock, singing into the hills, echoing his voice into the wilderness.

They had frolicked on the stone for only a short while when a strobing red light flashed around them. From up and around the bend of the service road came the Deputy Sheriff's patrol car. Deputy Travis Hudson was at the wheel. He accelerated "justifiably" toward the boys. His tires ignited a mound of dust off the side of the road as he parked strategically behind their van, blocking any escape they might try. He paused for a moment and glared at them through his windshield. He let the blaze of red continue for a while, then switched his siren on and off—to get their attention. He turned off the strobes, slowly got out of the patrol car with a noticeable scowl, then meandered toward them—his lips were tight and rolling around like he was sucking on raw horehound root.

"Boys? What are you all doing now? Defacing that rock?" he called. He didn't wait for a response. "You boys better get down from there…NOW!"

Hank dutifully slid down the rock. But Presley intentionally took his time. He looked for a way to descend the boulder that was not so demeaning. *"Who IS this guy anyway?"* he thought. "He ain't Sheriff Boswell." As he was looking for a way to climb down the rock, he noticed the disheveled trail of the fallen truck.Saplings and dense thickets were displaced in a disturbing pattern down the mountainside.Then nearly hidden in the shade of the last bastion of sunlight, he saw the wreckage.He leaped from the rock into the dust and hurried to the edge of the ridge. "God! Is that…Papaw's truck?" he yelled. In an instant, he was sliding down the slope!

Deputy Hudson endeavored to stop him. "Whoa, kid!" he ordered. "You can't do that—it might be a crime scene! Don't touch anything!" But it was to no avail. Presley was skidding and tripping and sliding without restraint toward the wreckage. Hank watched his brother, but his arm was suddenly held firmly by the lawman."You all can't go down there either, *Frank*. That's gotta be reported. I have to call this into the Sheriff." He ushered Hank to the patrol car and leaned in the window for his pen and pad. "Jackson, right? Frank Jackson?"

Hank ignored the question. He tried to pull away from the Deputy. "Can I get my brother? That might be our papaw's truck."

"Kid, you're staying put!Your brother's name?" he asked, scribbling quickly on his official pad.

Hank turned pale. He kept looking toward the cliff as he answered the man's questions. "Presley."

"Presley. Like Elvis?"

"Yeah. Sort of."

"And that truck down there? You think that's your papaw's truck? Your 'papaw'? What's your papaw's name?" Hank was too stunned to respond. He could not let his eyes wander from his brother's descent. "Listen, you can't go down there 'til the Sheriff gets here. Now I need the name of the owner of the truck. What's your papaw's name?"

"*Aidan Kilbride*...But he died. It's not HIS anymore... Listen, Sir, I gotta get down there with Pres!"

Hudson wrote down the name. "Kilbride...with one L, right?" Hank nodded nervously. "How do you spell the first name?"

"A – I – D - A -N!" Hank snapped, "But he's dead. A copperhead bit him...he was hoeing up the field, and ...he died...It's not *his* anymore...Can I go down there now?"

Hudson paused for a moment and glared at Hank, "Then who owns the truck?" Hank said nothing. He inquired again, drawing out each syllable of each word. "Does Elvis drive the truck?"

Hank thought for a moment, then glared back at the officer. "We don't drive the truck." He paused for a moment not wanting to divulge any more information to the lawman. " I don't know who drove the truck down there." he quipped.

"I have to call this in." Hudson insisted. "Don't you move?" He reached inside the patrol car to radio the Sheriff.

Suddenly Presley shrieked from the down the hillside, a shrill howl that reached to the top of the ridge. Hank pulled away from Deputy Hudson and ran to the edge. Presley was clumsy, in a frenzy, scurrying up the slope, groping for traction with his haunches and grabbing for anything he could to pull himself upward. Pres was yelling something at Hank, but it was too frenzied for his brother to comprehend. As Presley drew nearer the top of the ridge, Hank inched his way cautiously down the slope, reaching out his hand to his brother.

"Hank! Hank!" Presley yelled breathlessly. "A body! There's a dead body down there!" He grabbed his brother's hand. Hank pulled him up. "It's Papaw's truck," he whimpered. "…and a body…it's all bloody…"

While Deputy Hudson ranted on his radio with his dispatcher what he could distinguish of the scene, Presley grasped his brother's shoulders. "Hank," Presley whispered, "It's Papaw's truck and a dead body… It's Carl Jaspers…I think."

The Deputy finished his call and rejoined the boys. "You Hank's brother?" asked Hudson.

Presley nodded.

"Your name Elvis?"

"No! Presley… Jackson."

"That's definitely your Papaw's vehicle?"

"Yes, sir." Pres stammered.

114

"And...a body?" Hudson inquired, "You found a *human* body? Not a deer?"

Presley swallowed hard and grimaced in a frenzied sputter, "Yeah...a ways from the truck. It's bloody and messed up... broken...twisted... I thought it was a deer... It ain't no deer!"

The Deputy was looking at his watch to make sure he could document Sheriff Boswell's arrival on the scene. "Do you know the identity of the dead man? Think it's the driver?"

Presley answered, "No. I dunno. Maybe. Never knew this guy to ever drive it...'less he stole it or someth'in."

Deputy Hudson inhaled a long drawl of ego and shifted his feet impatiently. "Boys, if this is your papaw's truck and he is dead, *who* owns it now? Could be the murderer. This is evidence."

Presley was about to answer, but Hank silenced him with a nudge. "Clan!" Hank answered abruptly. "Just...clan."

Hudson nodded condescendingly, "Uh huh." The deputy pulled at his chin with his thumb and forefinger and impatiently glared solely at Presley. "Can *you* identify the body...Presley Jackson?"

"Looks like *Casper* Jaspers." Presley confessed. "He runs the Emporium in town."

Hudson wrote down the name on his pad. "C-A-S-P-E-R? Like *the' friendly ghost' cartoon?* Last name: J-A-S-P-E-R-S?"

"Yeah," Presley added impulsively, "he's a friend of our Uncle Marcus...They do some business thing together."

Hank tightened his lip and gritted his teeth. He looked away from his brother and kicked up some dust into the breeze.

The deputy scribbled more firmly on his pad, "Uncle... Marcus? Do you spell Marcus with a *K* or with a *C*?"

"A *C!*" Presley offered hastily, much to his brother Hank's chagrin.

Still, even as devoted a nephew as he was to Marcus, Hank himself wondered why his uncle not only hadn't notified anyone about the wreckage of the truck but, more importantly, *why* he hadn't reported the death of his...friend.

*

It was with the first hint of sunlight when Marcus dressed in his hiking gear and routed a trek back to the truck.Although the ridge was not a major road, a rather desolate place, he knew it wouldn't be long before some passerby would notice the truck. They would no doubt conclude that something erroneous happened there—and "God forbid," find the roll of cash he had left in the glove compartment. To belay any further investigation, he would get to the truck first. In doing so, he decided to take an alternative, lesser-known path through the woods, a more strenuous ascent further down the old service road. Once reaching the road he would cross along the ridge, to the God rock, and to the wreckage below.He was invigorated with the thought of fixing the situation. He envisioned somehow restoring the wreckage, but only after he retrieved his cash and covered the tracks of his late-night *run.* As always, he wanted as few people as possible to be aware of what he had done or what he had to do. He deemed this morning's subterfuge as simply another adventure.

From his early childhood, Marcus cherished the notion of adventure. His favorite books were thematically Twain. He was enthralled with the stories of David in the Old Testament—not of David, *the king*, but of David, the *shepherd* boy after "God's own heart." Marcus disliked David as a *king*. He was more drawn to David, the simple shepherd boy who rose above the shortsighted expectations of his older brothers and eventually even defeated the Philistine giant, Goliath, with one stone aimed well from one definitive snap of his leather sling. He thought the decapitation of

Goliath's head was too gruesome to include in the Bible, but he was always comfortable with stories about defeating giants.

The morning was brisk and clear. The aroma of pine mingled with the scent of Autumn leaves saturated by the first frost of October. He blazed his trail upward, following a stream of run-off water that flowed downward from the road higher up the hillside. The path led him to the top of a ridge where the nobler trees—the oaks, chestnut, and hickory stood strong. From there, he mounted a rocky bluff. He reached a primitive overlook to gain his direction, then made a sharp westward turn onto a path quite indistinguishable from any more casual hiker. Although this path was more arduous, Marcus knew it would lead him to the truck unnoticed and without fanfare.

Along this path were caves, some open, others camouflaged by dangling vines and dense thickets. A few of the openings were thresholds to hidden caverns. Along the way, Marcus imagined what it would be like to explore those caverns, underground cathedrals, a mystical nether world wherein would be the answers to fascinating questions. What could be discovered in such a subterranean wonderland? Ancient drawings, maps to misbegotten treasure, letters, forbidden diaries, skeletal remains of secret lovers, or the brocade jewelry of some lost tribe?

It was rumored that somewhere in that vast labyrinth of caverns was hidden a cannon forged of gold during the Revolutionary War. It was sailed to the mainland by the British army in their war against the colonies. They prepared to fire it at the last decisive battle. According to legend, a rogue militia of mountaineers seized the cannon, and then, when the war was won, hid it somewhere in the mountains—requiring a ransom from the King of England for its return. The ransom was never paid, and the cannon was never found. "What a find that would be!" Marcus thought. Anyone who grew up in Appalachia had at least heard of the golden cannon. Many sought to own it. Few had the gumption to pursue it.

Some caverns nearby were used as church sanctuaries for circuit-riding preachers. The covering wing of the underground provided for them a natural shelter from the heathen world above. No outside noise could distract anyone from hearing the homilies. The walls were so acoustically pure-- no one could turn a deaf ear to the Lord's voice amidst the darkness. For the messengers of God, the cavern sanctuaries were a perfect venue to hear the Gospel: "The God of nature speaks too loud here for man not to hear."

These remote dens were used during post-Civil War days as stations for the Underground Railroad. They provided temporary refuge for slaves on the run. Later, cavern chambers became experimental therapeutic *avenues* for TB patients put in quarantine. The science of the day thought the consistently cool temperature, damp air, and solitude of the chambers served as a cure for "*consumption*." Unfortunately, that science was only proven wrong. The atmosphere exacerbated the tuberculosis and eventual death of those patients.

Caves in the more remote locations were havens for bears, wild cats, copperheads, and other slithery creatures that coiled in the dark. While some caverns were used as holy sanctuaries and therapeutic domains, others harbored covens—steaming cauldrons swirled by witches musing in depravity. What looked to be an inviting port could have been a clandestine entry to a maze of passages and pits—more a precarious underworld than a pristine wonderland. Nevertheless, each cave Marcus noticed both intrigued and ignited his imagination.

He quickened his climb, diverting to a rocky embankment along the eastern side of the service road. From here, he improvised a plan. He would hike along the road until he reached the God-rock. He would immediately retrieve the cash from the glove compartment. Later, he would call Fred Bentley's Wrecker Service to raise its remains, tow it off the mountain, and stow it in the junkyard behind Carl Jasper's emporium—for good. If the rest of the clan wanted to grieve the loss, they could visit it there. Marcus was done with it!

He was determined to rid himself of his daddy's rusty pick-up and repent of his mistakes at the same time. He would start over, maybe move westward down that service road-- to the Mississippi River to the Rockies or to the Pacific North—maybe he would bunk in the wilderness with Sasquatch without anyone ever knowing his whereabouts.

"Maybe this wreck ain't all bad," he assured himself. "Ain't all things possible with God? The truth sets you free, right?"

At the top of the ridge, he reached a smooth, sun-lit plateau. The fullness of the warmth of midday refreshed his face. The rain from the days before left the air crisp. The sky was a brilliant blue. Only a few yards away was the final leg of the service road.It stretched from the God-rock in the East westward to the county line, connecting thoroughfares beyond Timberline County. But to get to the service road, he had to traverse a flat, desolated terrain of mudholes, windblown leaves, and rotted thorns and thickets. Once a meadow, it was now a wasteland of weeds and sour mud, a meadow decimated by the sooty runoff from the strip-mining operation further up the mountain.

With the sun in his eyes, he jaunted across the open field. Marcus was suddenly invigorated by the thought of impulsively turning West, away from the holler. That was his dream as a young boy of eight or nine: to take the "road less traveled."Routing westward would follow the call of the night trains he heard as a boy when his dreams led him to nobler pursuits. Routing westward would follow the paths of his heroes: pathfinders like James Fennimore Cooper's Natty Bumppo, explorers like Lewis and Clark, or Twain's Tom Sawyer. He often pondered what it would be like to soar into space like John Glenn or Neil Armstrong. These men weren't just stories; they were mentors.

But then he heard his father's voice bellowing, "Never leave the holler" and "Don't betray the clan. Follow holler law!"Yet he dreamed of flight, abounding above the hollers. "What the hell is so wrong with that?" he thought to himself, "Even Jesus flew to heaven. He left everybody in his clan!"

What or *who* might he explore along a path veering West? Leah McCreary? He suddenly remembered a song he composed for Leah McCreary when he pleaded with her to run away with him down a westbound road years before. She refused. She couldn't leave her father. Her brother had just died in a mining accident. Her mother was in a deep depression. Her father, the town physician, "needed her." She wouldn't leave her clan. Impulsively, he stormed away from her that night. Swore he would forget about her! She stood on the threshold of her home and watched him walk away.

Through the years thereafter, Marcus suppressed his regret of that night. He could not attempt to escape without her alongside him. Although he would not openly acknowledge his feelings for her again, he kept the memory of their youthful escapades in his mind. As he made his way toward the service road, he was startled by how fluently he recalled the words of her song:

"Oh, sweet lady of springtime,
More lovely than prisms of dew
Awakened my soul to her mourni'n
And my heart aches with long'in' for you.
If only this wanderer could find her
Adrift in her field of forlorn
I surely would weep at the want'in
Of the lady the wildflowers adorned.
So, I wandered alone to the meadow,
With rise of the full autumn moon
And I found the lady of springtime
Whisper'in a soft autumn tune.
Oh, sweet lady of springtime,
More lovely than prisms of dew
Awakened my soul to her morning
And my heart sings with the hold'in of you."

The nearer he got to the road, the more his romantic ruminations rekindled. His attention was so lofty he didn't notice a copperhead loitering on his path. Masquerading as a clump of autumn leaves, its darksome, chestnut-hourglass pattern against its dorsal tan was barely recognizable, particularly with Marcus's state of mind. The snake didn't budge. All but it's tongue remained ever-so-still. Marcus's advancing footfall did not intimidate the cunning, surreptitious serpent. It held its ground, coiling slightly…silently. With a flickering tongue, it detected the approach of the hapless, boney-legged intruder. It schemed for a moment of ambush—for an accurate and venomous strike.

The snake relaxed its form for a moment, then twitched its quivering head, fangs protruding a bit like an arrow in the bow. The sudden sound of the slithering in the dry leaves awakened Marcus from his stupor.He stopped short. He stared down at the copperhead. It stared back. Its tongue moved slower, elongated, mesmerizingly wooing Marcus to come closer.Marcus retreated with cautious steps backward.He looked around him. They were there, perhaps a dozen or so more snakes lying about—in the heat of the afternoon. Some were blatantly daring him to disturb them; others were less obvious and thus, more ominous, hidden in the fallen foliage.

Marcus negotiated his steps cautiously.He was determined to reach the service road, the slithering creatures notwithstanding. He swerved his way in a precarious semi-circle around whatever snakes he saw. The snakes were perturbed, poised, and ever vigilant, waiting for Marcus to trespass within their perimeter. With a skip-in-his-step and a few irreverent words of prayer, he managed to circumvent the serpents. Perhaps it was the heat of the day that anesthetized the vipers (maybe Marcus wasn't worth their effort), or Marcus's agility in dodging the predators, God's answer to his blasphemous prayer? Whatever it was, Marcus negotiated his path safely to the other side of the venomous plateau. Somewhat miraculously, he reached the median of the service road.

*

Sheriff Keith Boswell was more a statesman in Timberline County than a politician, more an empathetic overseer than an elected automaton. The Sheriff was respected in the hollers for his official title as high sheriff but affectionately more articulated by Keith. He was a man in his seventies, still sturdy and driven, with solemn facial features. His once-flaming red hair was now growing more silver-gold—more by burden than by age. As a young man, he retreated from the mines with an understanding of those who were bound or buried there and owned great empathy for the miner's kin, who were often overcome with fear or grief for their loved ones underground.

Sheriff Keith Boswell was a name that resonated throughout the district with affection and immediate respect. It held with it an assurance that not only were persons in the community accounted for, but they were also held accountable for their personal behavior and interaction with one another. It was common knowledge: Keith Boswell loved the people, had Heaven in view, and served the law as best he could in Timberline County. Even his aged eyes were enlivened with both the tenderness of a shepherd for his sheep with the intensity of a prophet for the wayward or misbegotten predator in the hollers.

The Kilbride clan revered the Sheriff of Timberline County as an elder. While long ago, Keith Boswell was once a beau of Eva Fernwald (Kilbride), now Sheriff Boswell was the clan's cherished confidante. But he was considered as such by most of the clans in the hollers. He had been elected without opposition for nearly three decades. He kept order in the county by being firmly rooted in the *intention* of the law rather than in its *letter*. At times, this meant compromising jail time as he recognized respectively the idiosyncrasies of the lawbreaker. At the same time, he was never swayed by popular opinion or political intrigue. His profession of faith (in a church whose denomination he forgot) informed him on how to best perform his profession as the high Sheriff. He balanced justice with grace and grace with justice.

Eva Kilbride once remarked about her trusted confidante: "Keith Boswell is more interested in creat'in a life-lived-well rather than to make a liv'in- for-wealth." He proved this time after time through an unyielding devotion to his constituency. That burden helped tint his amber hair with noticeable strands of silver. While the Sheriff's sparkling eyes were prophetically bold and stern, they often glistened with glimpses of mercy.

At times, he hinted at naivete, especially in the early years of his tenure as a Deputy. Through his decades of service, he learned to pursue the redemption of a person more than the retaliation of holler law. He believed he was not *guided* toward climbing to a notable career but toward an ascent to a higher calling. He was Sheriff of Timberline County.

He was never hesitant in articulating his opinions and was even known to publicly scrutinize a lawbreaker's rights in front of a crowd on Main Street. Carl Jaspers was one he always said, "knew better" than to do the "damnable" things he did. Although Sheriff Boswell never humiliated Casper he did humble him when necessary. (When it came time to arrest and jail Casper for public drunkenness at the HUB, as he slammed the cell door in the young Casper's face, Boswell simply asked, "How's this lifestyle work'in for ya, Carl? Can't keep it up forever."

Sheriff Boswell knew Carl "Casper" Jackson. He knew of the boy's traumatic upbringing. How he wasn't raised but was more *routed* as a child. He had known Carl and his brothers from their infancy and had observed their *exploits* both in school and during the Autumn Echoes Festival every year. He watched Carl ("Casper") grow up and by fourteen, usually spoke a word of warning to him whenever he crossed his path, which was quite often.

*

The sheriff arrived at the scene of the wreckage and immediately made his way to Presley and Hank, tempering the scene with his crime-side manner. "Travis." He began with a low, lion-like growl. He rubbed his stubbly-red chin as he was briefed by Deputy Hudson. Then he turned to Hank and Presley.

Still in a frenzy, Presley blurted out, "Sheriff, that's my Papaw's truck down there! And there's a dead body! Carl Jaspers, I think!"

"A body?" asked the Sheriff, "*in* the truck?"

"No sir," Pres gulped, "it's a few feet away, I guess, maybe a yard, I'm not sure. I don't know… It's all…mangled…torn up…but I saw his face. It's Carl Jaspers, the guy at the Emporium."

"You two okay?" Boswell asked.

Hank nodded, trying to keep himself from trembling.

Presley cried out, "Hell, no, I'm not ok! That's my uncle's truck down there—with a dead body all cut up!"

Boswell tightened his lips into a grin. "You both stay here with Deputy Hudson." He walked to the edge of the ridge and started his descent to the site.It was not as easy to negotiate the slope as it had been in his younger days. Nevertheless, he would never let on how this kind of thing ached in his knees and prompted duress in his chest.Strategically, he jaunted jaggedly downward from right to left, back and forth so as not to lose his footing. Down, down he went as steady and surefooted as he could be at his age.

The boys watched from the ridge as he reached their Papaw's truck. Boswell looked up at them and waved.He inspected the wreckage briefly, then crossed to the brutalized body.It was indeed Carl Jaspers, his body brutalized, arms and legs sculpted by the jetted rocks from what looked to be an unfortunate tumble down the slope. The Sheriff sighed heavily and rubbed his chin with a handkerchief from his pocket. He sighed, and his eyes went dim in the shadows of the late afternoon. Casper's demise was not merely an unfortunate tumble. He had been flayed with lacerations in his stomach and chest.

He left the body and walked back to the truck. There, he examined the empty cab.Without proper protocol (for this was *his* county), he pulled aside what remained of the door of the passenger side and looked fervently inside. Then he opened the glove compartment, retrieved the registration card and gathered a loose bundle of cash.He put them both in his pants pocket. He climbed around to the bed of the truck. In the bed were three large black bags tied firmly. One was torn open with items emerging from the plastic: stripped energizer batteries, a few empty pop bottles, some moldy coffee filters, empty packages of a generic decongestant, and rusty cans of Coleman camping fuel. "A damned lab on wheels." concluded Sheriff Boswell. "Casper's deal...gone to hell!"

He took a step back and examined the panorama before him: the truck, the trash, and the torso. He knew the truck. It belonged to Aidan Kilbride. There was no mistaking that one-of-a-kind jalopy and the hundreds of late-night deliveries of moonshine Aidan had made in it.But the registration was no longer in Aidan's name.It belonged to Marcus Kilbride. Aidan gave it to his son just before he passed a year or so before. There had been no criminal reports involving the truck since it had been in Marcus's possession. (Once Sheriff Boswell caught Marcus smoking a joint in the back seat during the Festival a while back, but after a stern warning, there was never another incident with Marcus or the truck to speak of.) But now, *this* was perilously serious.

Sheriff Boswell thought, "Aidan did run 'shine after the closing of the mine. Once or twice, there was the aroma of marijuana seep'in through the cracks in the doors, but…*this*?"He glanced up at Presley and Hank, giving them another reassuring wave as he began his ascent. His knees and lower back ached as he climbed back up the slope. Breathlessly, he whispered to himself, "Dammit, Marcus. What the hell did you do now?"

*

The early morning mist was still rising from the hillside when Marcus arrived at the site. He was alone. In the shadows, he saw the truck, decimated like the remains of some unfortunate insect in a spider's web. Aidan Kilbride's legacy of *"runn'in"* sputtered its last gasp. Now, all that was left to do was to retrieve the cash from the glove compartment and call a wrecker to haul the icon away. He would be free from *runn'in:* no more moonshine, no more weed, no more meth, *no more dreams*—those nightmares that always featured his daddy's truck.

He arduously hiked through the thickets, around rootage and rock, to the passenger door of the truck. It was bent and half-torn from its hinges. Marcus had just enough space to reach forward his arm. He reached his hand into the compartment to fish for the cash, but it had been gutted. Nothing was there, nothing at all. The cash was gone. The compartment was empty. He spent the next hour or so digging through every possible venue in and out of the wreckage.

Maybe the cash had been flung into the back seat, or under the seat, or scattered about the terrain? But there was nothing but twisted metal—and in the bed of the truck, large trash bags of bric-a-brac and wet stuff strewn about everywhere!

He stepped backward to gaze upon the horrific panorama. That's when he tripped over the body of Carl Jaspers. "Casper?"The body was so mauled. While it was not an immediate ID, it was undoubtedly Carl Jaspers, as torn asunder as the truck he commissioned to make his runs: mishappen, disfigured, and gutted. Marcus stepped away, and fell on his knees, camouflaged in the morning haze. A groundswell of grief erupted from the core of his belly. Then he fell limp to the ground, scratching into the soil with his fingernails as if digging some makeshift grave, not for Casper, but for him.

When he finally came to himself, he perched a few feet away from Casper's body and stared blankly at the *wreckage*. He knew he would be the "person of interest" in this--no longer a deal gone wrong or an unfortunate accident—but a "crime scene." For Marcus, it seemed at that moment that now, at twenty-something, his whole life had been nothing but an unfortunate accident, wreckage, or crime scene. He descended the hillside and headed back to the service road, uncertain of where to go from there. Where could he go?Casper was not only dead, he was brutally dehumanized. Casper Jaspers had always been good to him. So, why do good people suffer? Marcus had no answer. But in the silence of the woodlands he had the wherewithal to ask the question, "why?"

*

Carl "Casper" Jasper's Infamous Emporium

The Emporium was once an abandoned church located off a branch of Main Street. After the legendary sanctuary feud, the building became a bus station. Because it had restrooms, it became merely a urinal stop for weary travelers. But even the bus station became obsolete when few travelers took advantage of the facility. Later, it became a Florist and Greenery Center. Since the owner, Willard Roth, was also a licensed mortician, he included engraved headstones in his inventory of floral arrangements. His business not only thrived through being the only florist in Timberline County, but also a mortician who could offer a full package of services for the bereaved. So many appreciated his cut-rate services, he was often affectionately called "the Roth of God."(In fact, more estranged members of the former church united together in mutual grief during funerals than they ever did worship together "in one accord" during worship services. Seems mutual grief tended to unite people when mutual gratitude did not.)

When Willie Roth passed, so did his business. The building remained empty until the local churches formed an informal association to offer clothes closets for the more destitute families in the mountains. As the mines shut down, so did the donations. Those who donated items found themselves in need of the items they would have donated. Eventually, the churches set aside space for collecting whatever they could for clans within their respective churches.At different times and seasons, the storefront was used as a library, a guns and munitions shop, the headquarters for various political campaigns, and a school for martial arts.After years of neglect and disrepair, the building was left to dilapidation.

Then came Carl Jaspers! As an older child, he was bused to school from the upper holler. Until then, his clan rarely came to town, but for essentials, they couldn't grow on their own. The Jasper clan made do with the land they had and with whatever or whomever they could use to survive. In his pre-teens, Carl was not only skinny but scanty—hardly dressed at all. Faultness clothes cost money.He was so thin that, throughout the day, he had to keep pulling his oversized tee shirt up and around his shoulders and chest to cover himself. His hand-me-down britches were wrapped twice around his waist with burlap twine.

The Jaspers lived as best as they could without complaint or comment. Carl himself grew to believe that collecting things just "weighed a man down." Carl Jaspers decided at an early age, he would not be weighed down by anyone or anything.

At seventeen, a high school dropout and mining derelict, Carl Jaspers had found his business in town. From his entrepreneurial imagination arose the Emporium—a warehouse of merchandise out-of-time and customers out-of-warranty.His clientele grew with the downturn of the mining industry. His "Emporium" was a haven for those who huddled together in a momentary respite from the misery of their economic affliction. For them, it became an avenue in purgatory—neither hell nor heaven, but a respite in-between. They gathered in Jasper's sanctuary to bolster themselves through cursive conversation with doses of Casper's finest brew while swooning to Skynyrd's "Sweet Home" or Steve Miller's "Fly Like an Eagle." The customers were in the wonder and aura of Casper's vaporous incense.

All were welcome, especially those who understood the lamentations of Monroe and his bluegrass boys, the Carter Family, and Ralph Stanley's rendition:

"Come on, you young fellers, so young and so fine...seek not your fortune way down in the mine, for its dark as the dungeon...way down in the mine."

The legitimate inventory included stacks and cardboard bins of memorabilia.Used LPs, some in better condition than others, sparked a reminiscence of better days in Timberline County. In this tawdry collection of musical memorabilia, one could mine for both nuggets and pyrite (fool's gold), but for the grieving, it was all golden just the same. The décor fit Carl's scanty taste. He covered the ashen, mildewed walls with a collage of artwork. Posters were strewn about—of Jefferson Airplane, the Moody Blues, Janis Joplin, and Iron Butterfly's "IN A GODDA DA VIDA." He even covered a prominent hole in one of the walls with a poster of "Up, Up, and Away"—an invitation to a hot air balloon ride recorded by the Fifth Dimension.

He built shelves from the floor to the ceiling to cover the sagging walls and secure the thin linoleum to the floor. The black flooring had been laid years before to cover the cracks in the slab-foundation. The floor was indented now in waves due to both the cracking foundation and the weight of its use. On those shelves, Jaspers arranged the remains of things left behind in the back room: vases and vintage knick-knacks, jeweled bobbles, spoons and spools of thread, boxes of bullets, rusty pocketknives, shovels and spades, cauldrons for spells and pots for stew, evangelistic tracts and boxes of communion cups. There were leftover shirts, pants, shoes, and caps. In the main showcase were shelves displaying old tobacco pipes, rusty campaign buttons, and what looked to be tie clips.

In a separate section of the Emporium, Jaspers built a small stage with makeshift spotlights and a sound system. In front of the stage, he assembled a circle of chairs-in-the-round. Upstage, he planted a few select instruments (homemade and discount store-bought) donated by various clans. These included guitars, banjos, mandolins, fiddles, and dulcimers—some warped, others vintage, perfected through the years. All were available to anyone who entered the Emporium on Saturday nights.

Around the proscenium of the stage, Jaspers posted pictures of mountain icons in their hollers. He even lit lanterns around the stage in honor of their memory. Prominent upstage was a velvet paint-by-number depiction of Jesus in the Garden of Gethsemane and framed photographs, respectively of Carl's grandaddy Jubal holding the carcass of a large buck and its hapless fawn, Sergeant Alvin C. York in full military regalia, daredevil Evel Knievel, and President Lyndon Baines Johnson.

*

Marcus was twelve when he met Carl Jaspers for the first time. It was during summer vacation from school. Marcus had completed three *emergency runs* with his daddy, the last one being the night before the annual Vacation Bible School at the Baptist Church. Eva Kilbride insisted her children, including Marcus, were going to VBS the next morning regardless that Aidan hadn't gotten Marcus home until after 2 am. The child would promptly board the Church Bus every summer when it came 'round.

Marcus attended VBS and joined in the usual fare. First, the liturgy: "I got the joy, joy, joy, joy down in my heart...WHERE?...down in my heart...WHERE?...down in my heart to stay." (Marcus's cousin, Emmanuel, particularly liked the second verse: "And if the devil doesn't like it, he can sit on a tack...etc.... OUCH!...to stay.")Then came the arts and crafts station, where the children designed their own crosses made from popsicle sticks with glue and glitter. Afterward, the children played kickball or hide 'n seek in the churchyard. Then came lessons from *Daniel in the Lion's Den, Elijah raising a boy from the dead,* or some other story from the Bible—as told by Pastor Benny Peyton. Finally, refreshments were served: homemade cookies and Kool-Aid (i.e., "Baptist booze.") Afterward, the church bus ran on its route to deliver the children back home.

Leah McCreary (daughter of Lorna and Dr. Leland McCreary) was three years older than Marcus Kilbride. It was the first day of Vacation Bible School at the Baptist Church. During recess on the playground, Marcus noticed Leah. She was wearing a fancy pinkish blouse with pearl buttons, a plaid skirt that didn't cover her knees, ankle socks that matched her blouse, and Keds sneakers. Her wispy, long blonde hair seemed to wave at him, inviting him to come closer.

Leah noticed Marcus when he decided to interrupt her hopscotching with the other girls by chasing her around the playground with a daddy long-leg spider between his fingers. He chased her around and about until she had enough of his impishness. She stopped short, turned around, slapped the spider out of his hand, and ordered him to "grow up!" Marcus stood mesmerized by her touch, even if it was a slap on his hand.

"You need to get saved!" Leah demanded. "Play'in with spiders can kill you, Marcus!I know. My daddy is a doctor!"

After playtime, the children were ushered into the sanctuary of the church for a lesson given by the new pastor, Benny Peyton. He was jovial, even playful with the children at first. But when it came time for the gospel lesson, he mounted his pulpit as if he were Moses climbing atop Mt. Sinai. "You can't fool 'round with the devil. He'll kill you and take you to hell. You need to get saved! And NOW is the day of salvation!"

At that moment, Marcus reviewed his young life. There were things he had done he knew would not pass by the "eyes of God." Preacher Benny reminded him of things he tried to forget. Terrible things! When the altar call came, most of the children migrated to the altar to "get saved." Leah led the way.Marcus followed her. They were side-by-side when Preacher Benny guided them into the "the sinner's prayer." As he recited the prayer, line-by-line, they followed along in unison and in short, pithy phrases that assured them of a heavenly home:

"Dear God. I am a sinner. Please forgive me. I accept Jesus as my Savior, and now I know I will go to Heaven when I die. Amen."

A few weeks later came the observance of baptism! It was a community event on the bank of a channel of Fallen Timber Creek. Preacher Benny stood in his ordination robe next to his new converts. He lined them up in a single file. The children were clad in thread-bare, white gowns, beneath which were appropriate undergarments. Because the gowns were so thin, the children were instructed to wear something underneath in case the gowns would float up from the water or cling to their flesh as they climbed back onto shore.

Leah dressed appropriately with long johns and her daddy's tee shirt under her gown. Marcus was not so discerning. His gown only covered his naked body underneath. In his mind, baptism was a kind of sacred skinny dip for Jesus. Surely, God wasn't interested in what he wore anyway.

Preacher Benny stood in the middle of the creek and gestured for Marcus. The boy stepped off the bank and glided in the current of the creek toward him. As he did, his gown arose above his lower torso, revealing the boy's lack of preparation. The Preacher quickly pulled the gown down around him as best he could. But the other children on shore pointed and laughed at the sight.

Peyton ignored them and continued: "I baptize you, Marcus Kilbride. In the name of the Father, the Son, and the Holy Spirit. Buried is the old life, risen to new life. Amen."

Marcus was lowered back into the water. As much as Peyton tried to cover him, the gown was not cooperative. Marcus came up out of the water and, like the others before him, lifted his hands to the sky! Preacher Benny then guided him back toward the shore. Marcus waded in retreat to shore. He noticed spectators pointing and laughing at him.As he stepped up onto shore, his baptism gown arose above his lower body. He tried to pull it down to cover himself, but even so, the gown clung tightly to his naked body. Aidan and Eva were glaring at him. Rawley, Fern, and Dorothy were either looking at him in dismay or shaking their heads in disgust.Dolly hid her eyes. Beside Dolly stood Leah; she was not laughing. Instead, the girl ran to her father's car. In the back seat was a large woolen blanket.In one full sweep, she pulled the soft, woolen blanket from the back seat, ran to Marcus, and draped it around the boy. The spectators laughed and cheered. Marcus believed that the blanket was like a robe from God.

*

The morning after his midnight run, Marcus was sluggish and withdrawn. Nothing in the VBS itinerary could break him out of his stupor.He turned away from a smile or two from Leah McCreary. Even when his cousin, Emmanuel put a tack on the high backed chair of Pastor Benny, Marcus wasn't even roused. At twelve, Marcus came to realize "some things just ain't funny." He thought the prank was "childish." So did Pastor Benny. That day, when he sat on his high-backed chair, he was roused too. He arose quickly, but not with a shout of "glory," but a tirade on the consequences of such behavior in the "eyes of God."

134

At the end of the session, Marcus refused to board the bus back home. He lingered behind. Pastor Benny noticed Marcus standing alone with his hands in his pockets, watching the bus pull away onto Main Street. He approached the boy, but as he did, Marcus jerked away quickly and headed down the sidewalk into town. He had no more inclination to talk to Pastor Peyton, God, or anyone else that day. That was when he discovered the Emporium and Carl "Casper" Jaspers.

Marcus wandered away from the church down Main Street. For the moment, although he knew where he was, he was not concerned about where he was going. He was agitated by all things familiar. What was once glistening in store windows was now gratuitous and gray. Everything looked…spoiled. He turned a corner to a road he had never traveled when his eye caught the entrance of the Emporium. Rope lighting was busy, bulbs-chasing-bulbs, in the display window. Over the entrance was a brilliantly glittering sign, big red letters painted onto a glowing yellow background: "THE EMPORIUM: Everything you want…and more!"

Marcus entered the front door to the tinkling of an alarm bell. The door to the Emporium was a threshold into a multi-sensory mirage. Heavy incense stung his eyes and captured the boy's breath. It was a blend of sandalwood ash with a hint of mildew. Blasting in monotone through the dual speakers: *IN-A-GADDA-DA-VIDA, Baby…don't you know that I'll always be true…"* About Marcus was a paradise of props, endless bins and shelves of paraphernalia ready to explore. At the center of it all was a glass showcase. On top of the showcase was a large plate of store-bought snickerdoodles frosted with powdered sugar. The proprietor, Carl Jaspers, was hidden just to the other side of the showcase, crouched on the floor, stocking a bottom shelf with random footwear. At the sound of the bell above the entrance, he leaped up to greet his hapless patron.

Whatcha need, kid?" Jaspers grinned. He used his stinky fingers to heartily wave forward to his new customer. "Look 'round. I got it

135

all. What I ain't got, I can get. Price is no object."Still in his haze, Marcus just smiled back. "So what do you want?" Jaspers asked again. Then he spied the boy's VBS name tag "...um...Marcus...What do need...Marcus?" The man's low guttural voice somehow didn't fit his stature. He was a skinny man who looked about nineteen or twenty, with a fuzzy mustache and hypnotically azure-tinted eyes. Marcus was surprised the man called him by name until he realized he was still wearing the name tag Pastor Benny insisted he wear to "remember his name."

"Whatcha need, Marc?" Jaspers asked again. His hand was firmly leading the boy by the shoulder forward into the swap shop.Marcus said nothing, he just followed along.

Carl "Casper" Jaspers knew well his clientele. He owned wide eyes and learned to use them when observing them. From the purview of the upper holler, Carl learned to survive, not by plowing, but by pandering and at times, when it was required, pilfering whatever his customers *needed.* If what they needed was not in his inventory, he would either find it somewhere outside Timberline County or substitute it for something else. He had a talent for transforming surreal delusions of materialistic splendor, their addictions to perishable things, into euphoric gratification, all for the sake of turning a profit for himself. For the owner of the Emporium, turning someone's make-believe into the all-that-mattered was more than a career; it was a calling.

"Let's see, Marc..." Jaspers said as he perused the twelve-year-old's winsome frame. "A football? NO! You're not football. You...are...a...runner," he resolved. "Runn'in shoes! Sneakers! I've got some in the back room. Haven't put 'em out yet." He stepped up his pace away from Marcus toward the storeroom. "Hey!" he called back to the boy, "Have a snickerdoodle! They're dandy—like candy!" He disappeared behind a curtain.

Marcus removed his name tag and put it in his jeans pocket. He meandered toward the open plate about to accept the skinny man's invitation, when he noticed a black polka-dotted, green-striped gecko scampered across the counter. "Should I take the cookie or not?" he thought. He decided to ignore the plate of cookies to take in the inventory of the shop. And there it was! In the shadows—in the corner of the stage: a well-worn acoustic guitar, a rustic treasure. He could almost hear the chords vibrating—ebbing and flowing, wooing his steps forward.

Jaspers appeared suddenly from behind the curtain with a pair of sneakers. "It's a vintage Gibson." He remarked, tossing the sneakers behind the counter. "...or something like one. You play?" he asked.

Marcus shook his head.

"Pick it up."

Marcus hesitated, not feeling worthy of touching it. Jaspers grabbed the neck of the guitar and handed it to Marcus. "Here," he insisted, grinning again, "take it, kid."

Marcus took hold of the neck of the instrument, tenuously, as if it were somehow sacred, and embraced it to his chest. It seemed to whimper in his arms. "Looks like a fit." Jaspers affirmed. "Try a strum."

He did. It needed tuning, and it was a bit warped, but to Marcus, it was exquisitely vintaged.

"It's good stuff, Marc. A raw and golden nugget."

Marcus adjusted the frets. He embraced the body and strummed the strings more decisively.

Jaspers continued his sales pitch. "I think you're made for each other. Tell ya what, kid, if you'll let me teach you a few things 'bout selling, I'll sell it to you cheap. In fact, if you run some errands for me ever-now 'n then, I'll give it to ya! Whatcha think, Marc?"

"How much, mister?" the boy muttered.

"Well, you CAN talk!" Jaspers laughed. "I ain't *mister*, I'm just Carl…Jaspers. *Casper* to my friends…and my business associates. You can call me Casper."

Marcus asked again, fondling the guitar in his hands. "How much?"

"How much you got?"

"I made a *run* with my daddy last night." Marcus began.

"YOU?" Jaspers asked, "Made a *run?*"

Marcus nodded. Then he retrieved a roll of dollars from his pocket. "It's my offering money for the church. He gives it to me for my portion. But I forgot to put it in the dish."

"How much you got?" Casper smiled again.

Marcus carefully placed the guitar on the stage and carefully counted his cash. Slowly, he counted out the sum: "ten dollars."

Jaspers opened his palm. "Marc, that's a good down payment. The rest you can owe me, right?"

Marcus looked again at the cash, then at the guitar, nodded, and placed the cash in the man's hand. POOF! The instrument belonged to the boy.

Although it had been a business transaction with the Emporium, from then on, he told everyone the guitar was a gift from his daddy for a successful midnight run. Aidan never questioned Marcus about it. It was as if there was a silent business agreement between the two of them as well.

"Come on, Marc," Casper insisted. He stepped to the showcase again and picked up the plate of cookies, beckoning Marcus. "Here…have a snickerdoodle!" This time, without hesitation, Marcus obliged him. The cookie was a bit stale, but its sweetness only enhanced his delight with now owning the guitar.

For Carl "Casper" Jaspers, that guitar was a short down payment on a long-term investment with Marcus Kilbride. The kid seemed so lost; surely Casper Jaspers could at least help him find his way into the real world.

"Welcome to the Emporium!" Casper smiled. Marcus returned the man's smile with a sheepish grin. In his mind, he had made a new friend.

Chapter Six:
The Second Day After Sunday

Morning Perspectives

"The problems of Appalachia, like so many of Kentucky's other problems, point to the fact that our state's resources, financial and otherwise, are limited resources." (Kentucky Governor Edward T. Breathitt, Public Papers, 1963)

"We mountain people are a product of our history…a traditional people…we avoided mainstream life becoming self-reliant…seeking freedom from entanglements and cherishing our solitude—both our strength and our undoing." (Loyal Jones, Appalachian Values, 1994)

"…in the hollers, a man's got three choices: coal mine, moonshine, or moving on down the line." (Loretta Lynn, Still Woman Enough, 2002)

Tuesday.

Eva always awakened early for her morning ritual: shuffle in her well-worn slippers to the dining table and read a few Psalms while sipping a cup of sassafras tea. Sometimes, she would turn on the radio and listen to her son's-in-law exclusive commentary on world affairs --via the station *he owned*. But not this morning. She cherished the silence, alone with the Lord. Dolly remained in her bedroom, fanning the smoke from her first cigarette out an open window.

The knock on the back porch screen door came early. Eva wrapped her bathrobe around her. "C'mon in!" she called.

A familiar voice returned, "Eva? It's Keith." Sheriff Boswell stepped into the kitchen, much to Eva's dismay and delight.

"Well, come in!" she replied, "How are you, honey? Let me fix you some eggs and grits…Sit down here! I'll have some eggs for you in a minute!"

He smiled, "No, thank you, Eva. Sadie made me breakfast this morning. I'll just grab me a little coffee."

Dolly heard the commotion, extinguished her cigarette, and stepped into the kitchen. She knew that low, baritone voice but wondered if it was Keith or Sheriff Boswell who was visiting them. "Who's in trouble this time?" she asked, taking a bottle of Ale 8 from the fridge. Then she took her place at the table. "We never see you 'round lest we're in trouble."

Boswell carefully took a sip from his cup."That's not so, Dolly. I see you and Wanda at the Hub now and then."

"Uh huh." Dolly answered. "Usually when you're a-look'in for trouble."

Eva interrupted, "How is Sadie and ever-body?"

"They're do'in…" Boswell replied. "Sadie's busy with the Quilt'in Crew at church and keep'in up with me. How are you… all?"

"We're do'in alright, I reckon. Still miss'in Aidan…Had a good dinner with ever-body on Sunday, 'cept'in Marcus… Lord's good to us most of the time." Eva grinned.

"Whether we deserve it or not?" Boswell asserted.

Eva chuckled, "Reckon…"

"So, are we in trouble?" Dolly repeated. "It's ain't even eight o'clock yet."

The sheriff was silent for a moment. Then he inquired, "Is Marcus here?"

Eva answered, "That boy is in and outta this house. I ain't seen him since yesterday morn'in. He wrecked his daddy's truck up on that service road. Went to get it down. But I ain't seen noth'in of him since he walked off yesterday."

"Marcus in trouble?" Dolly asked soberly.

Boswell took another sip, placed the cup on the table, and sat down. He grew stern. "The ridge, at the God-rock—I got a call yesterday…Aidan's truck was found wrecked…off the edge. Not sure what happened. I know Marcus makes *runs* with his daddy's truck. I need to talk to him 'bout what happened up there."

"He doesn't make runs anymore," Dolly said. "He makes… deliveries. He told me 'the storm…the road was slick.'"

"His daddy 'bout wore out that truck, Keith. Had bad tires and all." Eva agreed. "Aidan used that old thing on more *runs* than I know of. Marcus uses it for odd jobs here and 'bouts. Mak'in a delivery and driv'in home, he just got flushed off that ridge. That's what he told me on Sunday."

Sheriff Boswell interrupted, "He on a *run now*?"

Dolly grew agitated. "He told me 'bout the accident with the truck. It was rain'in—mudslid'in across the road…baldy tires…just slid over the side. Luckily, he wasn't killed. Better the damned truck than Marcus."

"Sure," the Sheriff nodded, "I just want to get his view of it."

Eva suggested, "People've been slid'in off that ridge for years. You need a fence or someth'in up there. Since the big by-pass, nobody cares 'bout that old service road, but it's dangerous."

"Like I said," the Sheriff repeated, "I want to talk to Marcus."

"He told me about it…said he'd clean it up." Dolly insisted, "He said he was gonna—get Fred Bentley's wrecker to haul it off."

"Dolly, darl'in, there ain't noth'in left to haul off! And nobody is gonna touch that truck 'fore we know for sure what happened.Marcus's name is on the registration—he's accountable for whatever went on that ridge."He began rubbing his chin, then continued. "You haven't heard, have you?" They stared in confusion at one another. "Presley and Hank were up there hanging Perry's posters on the rock. They found the truck. Presley saw the wreck, climbed down to check it out…"

"My Lord, them boys all right?" Eva asked.

"Yeah, they're all right." He assured her. "But there *was* a body nearby. Looked like it was thrown from the truck. But it was something else."

Eva gasped, "Lord, God! It weren't our Marcus?"

"No," he replied, "not Marcus."

Eva held one hand over her mouth and the other over her breast, "Dolly," she gasped, "did Marcus tell you 'bout this?"

Dolly shook her head. "He didn't tell noth'in 'bout no dead body."

"Lord, God…" Eva whimpered a prayer. "Who was it?"

"Carl Jaspers." Boswell was sternly matter-of- fact. "Looks like he was stabbed. Not just stabbed… more *gutted*. Something went wrong up there."

Dolly stood up suddenly and stepped into the kitchen. She dropped her cup in the sink, "You think Marcus did that? Ain't no way! You know Marcus! He's an asshole, but he ain't capable of doing someth'in like that!"

Boswell continued in a more official tone. "Right now, Dolly, I don't know what he's capable of. That's why I have to talk to him. 'cause I'm telling you-- this is gonna be out my hands real soon. The truck was a mobile meth lab. This ain'tmoonshin'in! This is Federal, and they ain't gonna play no favorites! It ain't about moonshine truck sliding over the damned ridge!"

"Lord, God!" Eva prayed again.

He turned to her and looked intently into her eyes. "Was he *runn'in* meth, Eva?"

"Keith, honey, I don't know."

"Dolly?"

"All he told me was the truck slid off the ridge, and he was going to take care of it. He didn't want me talk'in 'bout it to Momma."

"Dammit, both of you! Was he making meth?" Sheriff Boswell demanded.

Eva's eyes grew wide, her face an ashen pale. "I don't know. No man in this house ever told me noth'in—especially what they were *run'in!* Aidan always did what he 'had to do,' and Marcus Follered after 'im. They just did the *run.*"

"I know 'bout moonshine runs," Keith began, "but there are *runs,* and there's *run'in.* Some things ain't never justified, even in these hollers!" He sucked the last drop from the cup, and stepped slowly toward the front door, noticeably scanning the room. He looked over his shoulder, "You tell 'im when you see him, Dolly." He pushed open the front door and then looked back at Eva. "You know I love… your clan, Eva. But this thing ain't gonna just go away. Marcus can't run from this. Thanks for the coffee. I'll tell Sadie you asked, 'bout her."

He stepped down the front steps to his patrol car. He stopped and took a glancing survey of the area, raising his ruddy eyebrows high and low, nostrils flaring, seemingly smelling the breeze for some guiding scent, intently listening for some subtle sound. That's what Sheriffs do when they are on the prowl. But this was Boswell, so perhaps he prayed as well? He climbed into his patrol car and drove

144

down the Kilbride gravel drive—periodically keeping watch in his rearview mirror as he swerved onto the main road toward town.

*

Maintaining residence in the rugged environment of the hollers was never easy. Legends, myths, and folklore about intrepid pioneers who scaled the primitive surroundings of the mountains perhaps foreshadowed how clans survived in the post-coal years of Timberline County. During their years of courting, Dean Walker and Fern Kilbride decided they would one day flee the hollers for the outside world, searching for some respite from the harsh realities of economic woes in the hollers. Dean's military appointment took them away—far away from the roads of Timberline County. Their adventure of Army life (in the in-between years of Korea and Vietnam) was both arduous and invigorating. The couple had never lived outside Timberline County, distant from their hollers, intermingling with others not of their kin.

Twelve years of service to their country offered them a panoramic view of the outside world. From Spam in San Diego to sushi in Japan to the monstrous spiders and typhoons in the Philippines, they held each other fast and survived it all—together. Their marriage triumphed over the outside world via the laws they learned in the hollers. Their wedlock was their constant. It was held sacred for over thirty years through bliss and blitz.

After their military appointment concluded, Dean and Fern returned to their roots with their young sons, Bobby (named after Robert Kennedy) and Chisholm (named precariously after a John Wayne movie, "The Chisholm Trail.") The family lived in the bottomland called "Walker Holler," in a house the couple designed together. Here, they found refuge. Here, they could observe the rest of the world from a cozy distance by reading the Timberline Times-Tribune: "All That is Printable!" and viewing "60 Minutes" every Sunday evening. Here, they could raise their sons in a healthier ecosystem and connect them to their kin before they charted their respective roads into the world.

It was immediately after Presley and Hank discovered the wreckage that Fern's flightier younger sister, Dorothy phoned to inform her sister about their daddy's truck, the discovery of Casper Jaspers, and their brother's strange disappearance. She called Rawley for the same reason. She called her Aunt Grace as well. She decided not to call Dolly, thinking she would tell their momma prematurely.

The phone call ignited Fern into a tirade about her missing and misbegotten brother Marcus. She had a fit that, while focused on Marcus, was vented on Dean. It became an endless catharsis that began in the early evening and continued sporadically without pause until the next morning. Dean poured himself a cup of coffee. It was a brisk morning, but he decided he needed fresh air. He wrapped himself in his bathrobe, donned his slippers, and stepped to his padded chair on the patio. The leaves were falling in the hills around him. There was a brilliant green in the pines in the glow of the morning sun. He was hiding behind his newspaper and sheltered in the arms of his landscape. This was his solitude. He sipped his coffee and scanned the front page of the "Timberline Times-Tribune." Suddenly Fern opened the patio door with his second cup of coffee in one hand, a broom in the other, and a dust pan under her armpit. "Here," she said, placing the cup on a tray in front of him. "So you won't have to get up and get it." Fern was noticeably agitated. She had not been able to finish her catharsis the night before when her husband fell asleep in his lounge chair. "It's one thing that you didn't talk to me 'bout this last night," she began, "It's another that you snored while I was talk'in."

Dean sipped his coffee again. "I heard you, Honey."

"You did?" She smirked, "Then what did I say last?"

"About Marcus." He answered.

"No, that wasn't it at all!"

"Then what did you say last?"

"I don't remember *now*...'probly about my mother." She scurried the patio around him—sweeping away leaves and twigs and roguish ants off her patio.Dean kept to the Timberline Times-Tribune. "There's noth'in about it in the paper yet," she observed, "especially *that* paper." Then she noticed, "Darl'in, that's last week's edition! The new one comes out tomorrow. Don't know why you read it anyway. The news is obsolete before they print it. You ain't listen'in!"

"I'm listening, Honey."

She continued her task, then stopped suddenly. "This has got to stop!"

"What, Honey? I'll put the paper down."

"NO! I mean Marcus! Our mother doesn't deserve this. He's been the runt of the litter ever since he was born."

"Now, we don't know anything but what Dottie told us yet," Dean suggested.

"I know my brother! Everything he's ever done comes to this."She said, sweeping more decisively the more petulant ants from between the cracks in the concrete.

"He's not done anything like this before. I don't think he'd hurt anybody, Honey. We don't know the whole story."

"Take his side!" she shrugged. "You are so contrary."

"I'm not taking his side, Honey. I'm just say'in you don't know it all."

"I know what he's done before. Everything changed when Marcus was born. He's been in trouble ever since he appeared in this world. Momma never should have had him at her age. I warned her

147

about complications, but no, "God would send her to hell…if…she went through with the surgery." Nobody balked at the surgery, 'cept self-righteous Rawley. I think he regrets it now. Then Aunt Grace stepped in and clinched it for Daddy. No surgery! "Abortion is an abomination!" He could never tell her 'No.' Momma's suffered with this child ever since. She was never the same after he was born. Neither was Daddy. Are you listening to me?"

"Yes, Honey…" he replied.

"What did I say?"

"Marcus is go'in to hell." He sighed.

"Daddy did everything for that boy! Rawley never did those runs with Daddy, but sure enough, Marcus did! Daddy was with Marcus like Jacob was with Joseph, the *favored child*. Even left the truck to Marcus! Are you listening to me, Dean?"

"Clear and loud." He responded with a subtle military salute.

"God only knows what all he's done run'in with that damned Carl Jaspers. What were they doing up there? Nobody in his right mind drives that old road at night unless they were up to—God knows! They were doing no good! He's been that way all his life—runn'in 'round like some rabid coon! Then, when he gets in trouble, he runs to Momma! That mess has got to stop!"

"Yes." Dean agreed, trying to calm her. "He's been crazy, but he's never killed anybody. Marcus was never a kid to march-in-line."

"He's gonna march straight to prison." Fern insisted, "And I'm sure my mother will blame herself."

Fern swept bits of gravel, the remnants of fallen leaves, and the corpses of a few remaining ants into a pile. Then she swept them up into her dustpan, poured the remains into a plastic, tied it, and tossed it into the trash can.

Dean continued, "We don't know what all he's done, but I can't see him killing Carl Jaspers, at least on purpose. He's an accident waiting to happen, I reckon, Honey. It's worrisome." Dean sighed, looking into his newspaper again. "But it'll resolve. All things work together for good…eventually."

"I ain't worried about Marcus! It's Momma. Marcus and Daddy always gave her fits. Those *runs!* She's too old to deal with Marcus." She finished sweeping and leaned her broom against the door frame. Then, she abruptly grabbed his coffee cup from Dean's hand.

"Honey," he gulped, "there's still coffee in there."

"It's cold. I just put another mug right in front of you. I'm gonna wash this one."

As she reached the patio door, she turned as she stepped into the house. "And why in hell are you reading that paper? They don't *print* the news; they *market* it! I hate when they take a little bit of news and make it into a story." she snapped.

Dean sipped from the second cup and grimaced. "Fern!" he called, "This coffee is weak!"

Fern bellowed through open the other side of the patio door. "My God, Dean! It ain't coffee. It's herbal tea…supposed to help your prostrate."

"Hell, I'm glad you diagnosed me," Dean whispered, "I didn't know I needed help with my prostrate."

*

Rawley Kilbride continued to work with the J. T. Cunning Coal Mine Corporation in the declining years of the industry. He invested most of his life in the mines, beginning as an apprentice in cutting coal, promoted to a foreman, and finally a district manager. When the industry was waning in the awakening of the world to the ecological dangers of fossil fuels, he remained steadfast as a proponent for the value of coal—*clean* coal, the grade of coal only extracted from prime Appalachian mines. He became a lobbyist for the corporations at the State House. Soon, he was promoted to serve as a District Manager in research and development. Rawley was a devoted proponent of coal and an empathetic advocate for unemployed miners.

He was a slightly plump man, middle-aged and weather worn.His thinning gray hair made him look like an Appalachian Mountain guru: church-wise, temperately sober, and attitudinally somber. He was distinctly short-sighted; whenever he read, he had to read with prescription trifocals.

The eldest Kilbride son was not a man of pretense. He viewed all things through the lens of selective scholarly resources. He responded to challenges around him with as much empirical data as possible. When his wife, Alma was killed in a collision with a late passing coal train, it was Rawley who solemnly surmised, "No one is exempt from following the rules of the rails. If you cross the tracks when the gates are lower'in, you're bound to lose your life."

When Wanda became pregnant with Denise, it was her father, Rawley Kilbride, who demanded she and Bucky Sorley (the baby's father) do the right thing and marry, *"before the child is born a bastard."* When Bucky abandoned Wanda and his children, Denise and Dusty, it was Rawley who went searching for the *"bum."* Furiously, he took to the back roads to find him. When he failed to find Bucky, it was Rawley who provided sanctuary for his daughter and grandchildren. Rawley made a covenant with Wanda: as long as she kept her job at the Hub she, Denise, and Dusty would have a safe sanctuary…at a nominal monthly rent. For Rawley Kilbride, it was the right thing to do.

Wanda Kilbride Sorley rebounded from Bucky's desertion by dating three other prospective suitors. These opportunists only added to her misery. Those trysts only resulted in the respective births of Donny, Donna, and Dara. After little Dara was born,

Rawley laid down the law: no more "hamp'in at the HUB," lest Wanda and her offspring find refuge in the trailer park! He scolded Wanda that in his house, he would not tolerate any more bums like Bucky, "whose compass in his crotch points to you!" He even removed a picture of Bucky from his daughter's bedside table. The framed photograph disappeared. He wanted no residue of Bucky Sorley in his house.

As the elder son, Rawley was always in charge of clan welfare. When Aidan died, he became the executor of his daddy's inheritance. Rawley stepped up to be sure his momma was provided for and protected. He sheltered her from the impulsive whims of kith, kin, funeral directors, and other profiteers who might exploit his momma's state of mind in the moment. Even Pastor Benny Peyton, who officiated at Aidan's funeral, was *only* given a handshake for his services along with a token donation—a designated offering *to the church*. While he appreciated the pastor's efforts, Rawley deemed it the Pastor's duty to do nothing less than officiate a funeral for a founding member of his congregation.

When Eva impulsively gave Aidan's truck to Marcus, Rawley knew it was a risky transaction. He reluctantly honored her wish to supply his younger brother with a means of transportation to and from a viable workplace. He always admired his momma's Christian charity, if not her naivete, in how she tried to "save him." But he believed his younger brother exploited her generosity. Marcus was remarkably handsome, noticeably attractive in a crowd. So much so he could often get away with mischievous, and sometimes irresponsible behavior. He would smile with dimpled cheeks and those around him (especially his momma) would just forgive whatever he had done. But to Rawley, Marcus was just foolish, a hapless runt, restless, reckless, and roaming his way through life with no ambition toward making a decent living for himself. From his point of view, Marcus didn't care to fulfill the expectations of their daddy nor cater to the needs of their momma. To his older brother, Marcus survived to manipulate everything for his own gratification or for reasons unknown.

Aidan and Rawley began calling Marcus *"possum boy"* when, as a young boy, Marcus was so terrified of going into the mine with them that he feigned being sick and wouldn't get out of bed. Then there were the days when the mine was closing, income was thin, and everyone in the family was expected to help with whatever they could do to keep food on the table. At that time, Aidan took pity on *"possum boy."* He took him to ride shotgun on extended moonshine *runs* outside the hollers. Those were tough and uncertain days for the Kilbride. Rawley remembered Aidan took Marcus on *runs* he refused to take with him. While Rawley was always willing to take those runs with his daddy, Marcus often balked at the opportunity. He was too often forced to do what Aidan insisted to be the *only* thing he could do for the clan.

After the news of the wreckage reached him, Rawley devised a plan of intervention. To protect the clan, Kilbride, Rawley predetermined to always do what was right: *"Let the truth be told and justice served, whatever the case may be."*

At first light, he dressed in his usual pressed britches, polished shoes, white shirt, and a tie, held firmly in place with the tie tack initialed *"A K."* He made sure his watch was finely tuned to the right time, then headed to the office of Sheriff Keith Boswell.

*

The town square was in preparation for the upcoming *Autumn Echoes: A Festival of Appalachia.* Beginning with the parade down Main Street, it was an annual weekend gala that attracted clans from Timberline County for yearly reunions, as well as outsiders seeking the romanticism of the mountains. Hosted by the merchants on Main Street, the Festival offered folks a celebration of their Appalachian heritage: to re-unite with kin, set up booths for respective *causes*, sell arts and crafts, gorge themselves with corn dogs or funnel cakes, and clog to the battle of the bluegrass bands. On the last night of the Festival, during the yearly inter-denominational tent meeting, folks could even come and repent of their respective sins. It was an annual celebration of traditions, community pride, passion, and garden produce.

With only two days before the weekend, Rawley had to re-route his usual course around barriers set up for crowd control. Red, white, and blue streamers were draped along from the Israel Boone Memorial Library at the head of the block to the Hub café in the middle and up to the County Courthouse at the end of Main Street. On the other side of the street, the People's Credit Union Building was ornate with bunting. The Sears catalog store, the Coffee Corner Café, Ken Fitzner's Fix-All, and Mary Turley's Flower Boutique hung American flags, adorning their entrances with patriotism. The office of Dr. Vernon Weppler not only displayed American flags but also several pennants celebrating McGuffey High School.

Adding to the faire, seemingly on every post and pole, were campaign posters: *Perry Jackson for State Senator: He's one of us!*

The colorful decorations helped to disguise the empty shops abandoned by the downturn in their economy. Then there were the less decorated businesses creeping their way into the struggling marketplace, off-shooting Main Street: Tattoos INK-Corporated, Arcade Adventure Land, and Casper Jasper's Emporium. These shops would be visited more by teens and tweens who were more interested in histrionics than history.

The Sheriff's office was adjacent to the courthouse. Rawley parked in a hard-to-find but legal space nearby. He didn't have an appointment, but he was sure Keith Boswell would see him. As he walked down Main Street, he couldn't help but notice that even the churches that lined the avenue were in preparation for the Festival. Although there were doctrinal distinctions, Rawley fit churches into behavioral categories rather than denominations. For him, there were five categories of church polity: the hokum pulpit of superstitious nonsense, the pulpit of hocus-pocus, magical spells and formulas that manipulate God's will, the pulpit of hoo-hah that threatens all with the fires of hell—the "my way or the bye-bye-way," the Hollywood pulpit with a rehearsed and spectator-pleasing performance every Sunday; or the hollow-luiah pulpit with nothing relevant to say and too much time to say it.

He passed by church row on Main Street and whispered to himself, "Where the hell is the Holy?"

He stepped into the foyer of the Sheriff's office and was officially greeted by the well-polished badge of Travis Hudson. "Can I help you, sir?" asked the Deputy. "I'm the Deputy Hudson."

"The Sheriff, please." Rawley insisted.

"He's on a case right now. I'm Deputy-on-duty." He said, straightening his belt.

"I'm Rawley Kilbride…KILBRIDE."

"Oh, yes sir. You must be related to…"

"Aidan Kilbride? My daddy owned that truck."

"Related to the person of interest? Mark Kilbride? All this about your brother didn't come at a good time, did it-- the Festival and all? Keeping us on our toes. Going to be a lot of traffic." He smirked. "But we're on your case too, Mr. Kilbride."

"What about the truck? I want to see the truck. Have you salvaged it? I want to see the truck."

"No, sir…can't do that. It's a crime scene. We've secured the whole area. No one is allowed up there. So, I can't help you there."

"Deputy, is *the* Sheriff nearby?"

"He should be back anytime. Meanwhile, I could get a statement from you, you know… about your brother…where he might be hiding through all of this investigation?"

154

Rawley stared condescendingly at the fledgling officer. "You presume a lot of shit, don't you? I have no idea where Marcus is."

Deputy Travis Hudson retrieved a small notebook and jotted down a few lines. "It's an active case, Mr. Kilbride. The investigation IS ongoing. We found a body up there. Now, it might be a murder investigation...SIR!"

He spoke snidely now. "We called the State Police for reinforcement...every precaution, especially during the Festival. We need your brother to answer some questions...routine? Maybe, maybe not. You don't know where your brother is. Don't worry, we'll find him."

Rawley half-grinned (for he knew no other way to grin). "I understand," he exclaimed, sitting decisively in a nearby chair, "and I'll wait for Sheriff Keith."

*

"The sassafras stands winter barren now.

Its leaves were torn away in autumn strife

By elements that conquered growth and plow.

Deep rooted in the earth, it dreams of life." (Jesse Stuart, Sassafras, 1949)

Presley and Hank Jackson didn't attend classes the day after the wreckage. The news about the incident was resonating throughout the county—swelling to rumors and innuendos not palpable for anyone connected to the Kilbride clan. Dorothy Kilbride Jackson was very protective of her sons. She would not allow them to be taunted or exposed to embarrassing questions about *Uncle* Marcus. Perry was likewise concerned about damage control. He could not risk Pres or Hank making impulsive remarks that could damage his campaign for State Senator. Perry himself decided he would respond *officially* to whatever questions might come their way.

Presley took the situation in stride. He wasn't deterred by his father's insistence he remain in seclusion. Instead, openly bragged about his "discovery...*repelling down the jagged mountainside to face not only his papaw's truck but also the hacked 'n slashed remains of Carl Jaspers."* It was his story of legendary proportions, especially to the teen girls who already regarded him with some giddiness. His storytelling would not be stifled! He decided to transcribe copies of his story, then autograph and sell them at his father's booth during the Festival. Moreover, he decided to share his story with literary professionals who were eager to print it at the Times-Tribune.

Hank was silent, stunned by what he saw. He slept little that night, and he was not at ease ever after. Whenever he closed his eyes, images of the ridge appeared in his mind: the wreckage, the body, and the impuse of the Deputy to *"track down"* -- M-A-R-C-U-S."Uncle Marcus wouldn't do this," he told his mother at breakfast that morning.

Dorothy answered, "Where is he *if* he didn't do it? Hid'in somewhere? You don't know, darl'in. I lived with Marcus all my life.Nobody knew what he was go'in to do next. I don't want to think he did someth'in this bad. Nobody thinks it could happen in their own family. He's always been a loner—and they say things like this happen by loners. You never know what's go'in on in their heads 'til it happens!Marcus used to hide so much—up in those mountains. Said he was hunt'in, but he never had a gun or brought back any game...just went *hunt'in.* Anyway, I don't want you 'round him."

Hank stared out the window, shaking his head. "Uncle Marcus ain't evil, Mom." he whispered, "he may be lost, but he ain't evil. Just 'cause someone is lost doesn't mean he's evil."

"Hank!" his mother scolded him, "You saw that dead body...all that meth stuff in the truck! Your Papaw's truck is gone! Marcus ain't nowhere 'round to explain none of it! He ain't *lost!* He's hid'in somewhere! That looks *evil* to me!"   *

The consummate showman, Perry Jackson believed that any news was better than no publicity at all. Although he was not happy with his wife's clan connection to the rumors around town, he was optimistic he could maneuver the details of the story toward a positive outcome for his campaign; perhaps, at the same time, devise a platform to include eradicating meth labs in the region. *"Now more than ever, he knew the challenge. This scourge affected his own clan—a threat to his own sons."* He could engage the challenge with empathy, not just political empiricism. In short, now more than ever:

"Perry Jackson for State Senate:He's one of us!"

On a clear morning, AM station KYTC resonated throughout the hills, echoing through the hollers with hours of the most heartwarming music of the mountains: Stanley, Monroe, the Osbornes, Jimmy Martin, and Del McCoury; blended with other locally known virtuoso wannabes. The daily programming was followed immediately by station owner Perry Jackson's autonomous commentary. Although only God owned the airwaves, it was Perry Jackson who managed them in Timberline County.His live, on-the-air radio call-in show was a fascination for those who listened every day from noon 'til three.He viewed his political homilies as the "Let there be Light" that echoed throughout the hills, both provoking and pleasing his listeners. But he wanted to become more to them than just a commentator. He was intent on being a significant vote in the State Legislature.He was confident he could create practical initiatives for the health and welfare of the hollers if he had the power to do it. He knew he could get the votes in his district with name recognition alone:

"Perry Jackson...He's one of us."

This day, he expected incoming calls to his show to challenge him on the heinous event at the God-rock. With his statements in hand, the prelude to his broadcast began:

(Musical introduction: *"I saw the light…I saw the light. No more in darkness, no more in night. Now I'm so happy, no sorrow in sight. Praise the Lord, I saw the light. " (Hank Williams, 1948)*

Announcer (Perry Jackson): "It's your time to speak your mind! A daily conversation round 'n about Timberline County! with your host, Perry Jackson. Now, here's Perry Jackson… *(Music fades/cue Perry)*

Perry spoke his usual platitudes—the niceties to his audience that always preceded his real agenda for the day. After articulating the conundrums of Timberline County, the phone lines were opened. It was time for anyone to offer their thoughts about things, vent their feelings, or even sell their wares on the air. Perry would conclude each call with his uniquely unequivocal solutions to the maladies of humanity, at least in Timberline County.

On that day, respective callers spoke their minds declaring:

"We need better law enforcement!"

"We just need to support our Sheriff."

Perry Jackson responded: "Sheriff Boswell has been reliable for a long time. He needs to do more than what he is doing right now. We need to protect our kids and old folks. There are a lot of predators out there. We need tough, no-nonsense leadership."

"Satan is running this county. If we all just trusted in Jesus, none of this would happen."

"If there is a God, how this kind of thing happen?"

Perry Jackson responded: "I agree, when this kind of thing happens, we all need to seek inner wisdom—deeper answers to our most serious questions. We need inspirational leadership. Bring God back into our justice system."

"I think whoever did this terrible thing needs help. Something terrible must have happened in his past."

"Seems to me it was a crime of instinct—you know, like animal passions. Like a rabid dog, he needs to be put to death...an 'eye for an eye.'"

Jackson responded: "Good mental health care is essential. Things like can be caused by psychological, social, emotional, and even economic reasons. Yes. Justice must be served at all costs. Strong leadership is the key.

"That old county road is a mess. It needs to be closed off for good... 'specially to people who don't belong up there. Drug dealers use those old roads to get the drugs in and out. Hell, close 'em off for good."

"We don't need to close our old roads, just patrol them properly. Put lights up there and maybe a patrol car. It's the new roads that bring in the drugs."

Jackson responded: "We need better infrastructure and interdiction. Roads can be a blessing or a curse. We must protect our community from illegal transactions. That happens with common sense and progressive leadership."

Then came the calls he dreaded:

"Aren't you kin to (the name the caller mentioned was bleeped)—the one on the loose?"

"The suspect is your brother-in-law, right?"

Perry Jackson was definitely non-committal in his response. "Yes. The suspect, and I repeat, the *suspect* is my wife's kin. But you all know *me* and what I stand for. I ask for your prayers and good thoughts as this investigation continues. In the meantime, we're all look'in forward to *the Autumn Echoes Festival* this weekend.Remember to stop by my campaign booth for free refreshments and maybe pick up a poster or button or two to help us out. Come hear my boy, Presley, sing at *the Local-Yocal-Vocal Show*.In the meantime, have a beautiful and safe day, everybody!"

(MUSIC BEGINS: "I Saw the Light…no more in darkness, not more in night…" (Hank Williams)

Cue the closing by Narrator Presley Jackson: "Thanks, Dad! This has been 'It's Your Time to Speak Your Mind" with Perry Jackson, host and General Manager of KYTC—listening to your voice in Timberline County.")

*

Evenings in October. The aroma of autumn-at-evening lulls folks into a momentum of calm. The radiance of the day fades with the turning of the earth, especially at autumn, when one notices the inevitable detachment from the rambunctiousness of summer. Changes come, noticeable in autumn. Seeds that have been sewn come to fruition, are harvested, and ultimately are imbibed in celebration of how life works. In the afterglow of the harvest, the precious soil, the womb wherein the seeds were sewn, is allowed to rest from the strain of the plow. It turns over under a quilt of its own bounty and rests in slumber—in winter. It rests until the coming of spring when once again, the hollers will be awakened to the sowing of new seed and hope for an even finer harvest-- in autumn.

*

Eva Kilbride believed *"all will be well—eventually,"* even with Marcus. She was certain he would return home that night. He didn't. But, as always, her faith met her fear. She was certain he had found refuge somewhere. He had always been able to run to some hidden hideaway in the hills to sulk, decompress, or at one point in his childhood, he believed he could *find a "Garden of Eden."* Those were the days of his childhood when pristine innocence was not subjected to primitive instincts. Marcus truly believed there to be such a place.

Dolly leaned back on the living room couch as she took a last sip of her Diet Pepsi. She stared over at her momma reclining in her easy chair. "Momma. Marcus didn't kill Jaspers. You know that. " she said.

"Why is he hid'in?" Eva asked. "Why ain't he here?"

"He's look'in for the damned Garden of Eden. That was gone a long time ago."

Eva thought for a moment, then continued, "Eden is home! Right here." She said as she arose from her chair and strolled to her bedroom for the night.

Chapter Seven:
The 3rd Day After Sunday:

All That's Printable and Profitable

"An Appalachian person's first obligation to himself was to reject everything about himself that betrayed his identity." (Cratis Williams, I Became a Teacher, 1995)

"It will take a little while to find him

For hunger drives no wild man home.

Dark days no hasting to a will like his,

He may dine on berries, abide where he is.

He is somewhere around. Go and look." (James Still, Of the Wild Man, 1991)

Wednesday.

TIMBERLINE TIMES-TRIBUNE:

"All That's Printable!"

Autumn Echoes Celebration of Appalachia Edition

October, 1983 (Center Insert)

Schedule of Events:

Thursday: FESTIVAL SQUARE: Pioneer Park to Main Street 6-10:00 pm

Games, Inflatables & Puppet Shows for Children

Booths featuring: Church Bake Sales & Such, Arts & Crafts,

Health Screening for Seniors, Mountain Food & Concessions

Local Business, Club & Media Booths

"Meet and Greet" Your City, District and State Representatives from

7-9 pm (Tentative, based on availability and time constraints)

Annual 'Local-Yocal Vocal Contest' 8:00 pm (Center Stage)

Friday: FESTIVAL SQUARE: Pioneer Park to Main Street 4 pm-11 pm

Craft Demonstrations:

Hand Baskets, Wood Carving, Sorghum Stir-off, Pottery Wheel,

Quilting & Weaving, Dulcimer-making, Sassafras Brew, and more!

Community Harvest Market – open all day!

Festival Rides & Tethered Hot Air Balloon, Petting & Reptile Zoo for Children

"Old Tyme Clan Dinner" @ the Baptist Church Fellowship Hall-6-7:30pm

Featuring: Soup Beans & Cornbread, Burgoo & Biscuits or

Homemade Kraut & Wieners ($5 per person / $12 per family)

Center Stage Show - 8:00 pm

Featuring: Special Guests: Grand Ladies of the Grand Ole Opry

Saturday: FESTIVAL SQUARE: Pioneer Park to Main Street 10 am-12midnight

Morning Parade w/Grand Marshalls 1983: Mayor James T. Cunning &

Ohio Valley Wrestling Star, Country Boy Clem 10 am

Center Stage Competition: *Little Miss Teenie-Weenie 1983*

Annual Inter-denominational Community Service 7 pm Pioneer Park

Featuring the Timberline County Shape-note Singers

Center State Show -10pm

The Winner of the 'Local-Yocal Vocal' Contest!

Featuring: *Legendary Ladies of the Grand Ole Opry*

Welcome all clan-folk and tourist guests! Enjoy the Celebration and keep our county safe and clean!

All events are sponsored by local businesses, churches, and civic organizations in Timberline County. For more information, contact your county officials or representatives. This page was donated by the Timberline Times-Tribune in celebration of our history and heritage.

The headline on the front page read:

Long-time Local EMPORIUM Mogul Dies from Stabbing:

Deputy Warns "Suspect Still At-Large!"

The mutilated body of Timberline resident and record store owner, Carl Jaspers of Jasper Hollow Road, was discovered Monday by two local brothers, Presley (19) and Henry (17), as they were hanging campaign posters for their father, Perry Jackson. Jackson is currently on the ballot in the upcoming election for State Senator.

According to newly sworn Deputy Travis Hudson, the boys were dancing on top of the "God-rock" when they noticed a pick-up truck that had driven off the narrow county road and crashed down the slope. As one of the brothers viewed the wrecked vehicle, he came upon the dead body of Jaspers. According to Hudson, "the body had been stabbed multiple times." Later, an official investigation reported that the bed of the pick-up was filled with trash bags full of paraphernalia used in making methamphetamine. "To me," the

164

Deputy continued, "the truck was a mobile meth lab. It all looked like a drug deal gone bad."

The truck is registered to Marcus Kilbride, the youngest son of Aidan (deceased) and Eva Kilbride of Fallen Timbre Creek and the brother-in-law to candidate for State Senate, Perry Jackson. Other residents in Timberline have said that they have known Marcus Kilbride and the deceased to have been friends and business partners in the past. Jaspers has been known to have a significant arrest record. There have been no official charges against Marcus. To date, the Sheriff's office has not been able to locate his whereabouts. "Not yet," Deputy Hudson remarked, "The main suspect is still at large."

Sheriff Keith Boswell remarked that "the investigation is ongoing" and it was "too early to know anything definitively about the case. State investigators have been alerted." Candidate Perry Jackson could not be reached for comment.

Chapter Eight:
The 4th Day After Sunday

The Gathering Grows

"The ability to remain close to the people you represent and have a sense for how your decisions affect them in their daily lives is one of the most appealing aspects of being governor…being a friend when they needed someone to lean on." (Governor Wallace G. Wilkinson, Public Papers, 1995)

"I've seen the moon ride high over the corn

When it was green, when is was autumn brown

High above old pastures fields forlorn

When golden autumn leaves came trickling down." (Jesse Stuart, Song of Approaching Autumn)

Thursday.

It was a day of preparation. Thursday trail blazed the weekend events. By midday, Pioneer Park in Timberline County was amassed with passionate zealots, preparing for the weekend celebration. By Friday afternoon, tourists and local residents alike would be clamoring for parking spaces along the main thoroughfares in and out of the county seat. It was indeed a multi-sensory gala of booths and banners. The designated area for displays was ready for those who clamored about in the annual celebration of Appalachian history every Autumn. Along the paths of Pioneer Park were tents, tables, stages, and stalls arranged appropriately for the celebration. Outsiders from everywhere would begin arriving on Friday and usually peaked in attendance by Saturday night.

(Thursday night was usually highlighted by two major events. The central entertainment venue every year was on the main stage where was held the "Local Yocal Vocal" competition. This annual competition was always the popular attraction to the weekend. But this year, at the Hub (where the beer would flow and the rock 'n roll was always raw 'n raucous), the band *RoadKill* was booked as the major spectacle in town. This year, there was a sort of rivalry for patronize between the climactic events.

By 12:00 pm, the migration from the hollers would begin. Although the opening ceremony for the Festival had not yet taken place, locals made their way into town anyway. People were mingling and laughing, hugging and harvesting stories—a reunion, catching up with one another. After a season of separation in the hollers, the Festival took on a sacred quality, an interconnection to a beloved community, wherein everyone was accounted for, and no one was anonymous. On Festival Eve, the Festival was more about mingling with persons rather than making a profit.

By 2:00 pm, the traditional music of Timberline County could be heard in rehearsal. Folks from all over the county assembled in respective, even random alcoves about town, forming impromptu mountain musicales. For mountain musicians, sitting in on a session, picking a guitar or a homemade fiddle, was better than shaking a hand; it was sharing your soul! The music exhaled through their fingertips as easily as breathing. Platitudes were unnecessary. One could just rosin up the bow and let the fiddle speak for itself. The jamboree became not only an impromptu concert, but it was also an annual community catharsis.

By 3:00 pm, the Park became like Christmas-in-Autumn. Fanciful colored lights illuminated the pathways and booths. The smells of Autumn Fest mingled with the distinctive evening aroma of the pines. On preparation day, all the fare was free. Local grills and wagons rolled in with their venison barbeque, fried frog legs, and roasted corn-on-the-cob. There were pre-festival tables for connoisseurs of caramel apples or plastic cups full of homemade banana pudding with crisp vanilla wafers. Thursday was an extended family reunion wherein the thoroughfare was ignited with a blend of scents, psalms, mountain serenades, and social rambling about with kith and kin.

Other activities were in flux in preparation for opening day. Produce and propaganda were posted throughout Pioneer Park. Various clubs and civic organizations, both for-profit and for naught, made themselves known through their banners and billboards. The Lions Club was auctioning off a large stuffed mascot to the highest bidder at the end of the weekend. The Optimists had a wheel of fortune one could spin for a nominal donation. The slots on the wheel denoted various prizes, from yardsticks to area-store gift certificates. The VFW distributed small American flags with "no donation necessary," but a dollar or two were "always appreciated."

The Baptists were hosting puppet shows at designated times throughout the evening. A large pickle jar was on their table in the hope that those who viewed the show would drop off a donation for a youth mission project in Honduras. Next to the Baptists were the Methodists, who were not to be outdone.Every hour at their booth, they sponsored a gospel quartet show to draw folks to their booth. Likewise, in between sets, the quartet was sent out into the crowd— roving about the Park, mustering up a hymn that would hopefully draw more attention to their booth. The quarter even held up an offering plate. Donations were "urgently needed" for upgrading their sanctuary.The Presbyterian booth offered pamphlets and cookbooks for a minimal fee. They even used video presentations on a large TV screen to promote their mission to the world. Further down the lane was the Catholic booth. They gave away plastic rosaries and prayer cards and hosted daily rounds of Bingo. Proceeds from their efforts were to go to their Appalachian Recovery Program and Community Thrift Shop across from the Emporium.

Government organizations were always represented as well.The Timberline County Fire Department gave tours of their Emergency

Search and Rescue Vehicle. The Water and Sanitation Department gave away free plastic drinking cups.Radio KYTC sold ball caps imprinted with its logo. The station also distributed tiny frisbees to everyone, promoting *"It's Your Time to Speak Your Mind"* with a caricature of *Perry Jackson* on the inside.

Mayor James T. Cunning and his office staff handed out lapel pins with the words *"Coal Lives!"* embossed on them. Although they did not have a booth this year, Deputy Travis Hudson and Sheriff Keith Boswell walked among the crowd and gave out facsimile sheriff badges to the children they greeted along the way.

By 5:15, Wanda's children were set free in the Park. They scattered. Denise sprinted to Mary Turley's Flower Shoppe and Boutique to peruse the latest Fall fashions. Donna's priority was a ride on the donkey used for the sorghum stalk-press wheel-- to help stir the molasses. But the cane would not be shucked until early Friday morning. Instead, she stood in the tent with the woodcarvers and weavers. Little Dara insisted Wanda take her immediately to the inflatables and then buy her a caramel apple to chew on while her mother went to work at the Hub.

Dusty and Donny searched for the Celebrity Booth. Their hero from the Cumberland Valley Wrestling Association, *Country Boy Clem*, was scheduled to appear there-- *"for real."* There he was, Country Boy Clem, the man himself, standing behind a table in his bib-overalls and tattered hat, his burly chest bulging under his overgrown beard. He waved at the crowd of "young'ins" and then sat down on a stool to greet his fans. There was a stack of ready-made photographs on the table in front of him. Dusty and Donny each wanted one, but to their surprise, Clem was selling them-- twenty dollars for and black and white 8X10 or ten dollars just to get his signature on a piece of paper, and the boys had to supply the paper. They waited in line anyway. After an hour or so, the youthful fans were allowed to file by his table. They smiled up at him. Clem looked down on them, extended his huge werewolf hand to theirs's, and quickly shook their hands—for free.

*

The annual "Local-Yocals-Vocal" contest began on Center Stage on the hillside in Pioneer Park at precisely 8:00 pm. According to the rules, each contestant must reside in Timberline County. Performances were restricted to singers only. The genre of music, the generation and gender of persons, and the number of residents who sang the music were unrestricted but must be family-friendly.The chosen music could be original, cover the songs of other singers, or be creatively arranged. Performers could play their music, use backup instrumentalists, or sing with pre-recorded accompaniment. Anything outside of the rules was usually performed at the HUB.

The winner of the contest would get a trophy, a personal interview on KYTC radio, and would have the chance to perform as the warm-up act for the climactic Saturday Night Concert; which featured "Legendary Ladies of the Grand Ole Opry." Could this exposure lead the winner to sing in Nashville? Answering that question was the motivation for most would-be singers who signed up for the annual event-- including Presley Jackson.

In the past, no one had succeeded in Nashville. After little Jeannie Belcher won in 1982 for her fully costumed rendition of "I Want to Be a Cowboy's Sweetheart," she was asked by the Timberline Chamber of Commerce to repeat her performance in their booth at the State Fair. She was so nervous in that venue that when she stepped up to sing, before her first lyric was sung, she vomited on a spectator's shoe in the front row. That spectator happened to be Timberline Mayor James T. Cunning.Little Jeannie went no further in her singing career.

After they won in 1981, the Douglas Dugger Clan Band continued to play their bluegrass around the region for special events, but only when Doug was sober or out of detention hall. Once, some high school students organized a gospel group, won the competition in 1982, and took it upon themselves to gather that year in Pigeon Forge to sing Christmas Carols, walking up and down the strip.After graduation, they disbanded.No Local-Yocal-Vocal Winner was ever fit for Nashville, but to their clans in Timberline County, it was more about celebrating family than acquiring fame.

The voice over the loudspeaker announced: "Folks! This is just a reminder that the LOCAL-YOCAL-VOCAL contest will begin at eight o'clock on the Center Stage near the war memorial. Be sure to bring your lawn chairs or blankets. Looks like a clear night, so come join in. That's in one half-hour from now. Thank you. Come cheer on your family, friends, and neighbors!"

Presley's part in the show drew near. The brothers were still at odds about Pres's entry into the competition. Presley insisted he sings *"Mystery Train."* The crowd being more estrogen than testosterone, he knew by using his pelvic gyrations, unbuttoned silk shirt down to his *outie,* and Romeo-eques brown eyes, he could triumph over the competition.He knew he could generate eruptions of volcanic applause from his more adoring female fans."I can *play* this, Hank!" Presley insisted. "I sing like Elvis, move like Tom Jones, and look like... ME. You just stand upstage, play the licks, and play 'em hard!My God, why do you want to change anything now?"

"It ain't real, Pres," Hank answered. "It ain't me."

Presley smirked, "Who gives a shit? It ain't you; they're look'in at! It's me—the *'Mystery Train' mooov'in on down the track.*You just pick a hot lick! Back me up!"

The introduction was made. Hank stood in the shadows upstage of his older brother. He was dressed down in his denim jacket, tee shirt, and jeans. As Presley stepped into the spotlight, Hank thumped, strummed, and clawed his guitar. Presley was enraptured by the spotlight, shifting his body to the rhythm of his younger brother's chick-a-boom tempo. He caressed the microphone, tilted it back and forth, dipped it down like a dancer in his arms. Then he fell on his knees and glared menacingly at the rather twitter-pated teenyboppers in the front row. He stood abruptly, rode the microphone between his legs, and jerked the microphone close to his lips. It became more than a competition composition; it was an exhibition of rock-a-billy copulation.

"Train I ride, sixteen coaches long

Train I ride, sixteen coaches long

Well, that long black train got my baby and gone." (Mystery Train, written by Sam Phillips and Junior Parker,1953)

The front row of pubescent females screamed their approval. With that, Pres *ultra*-crooned the song more passionately and perilously close to breaking family values. Girls from McGuffey High School clamored for more. So, he ripped open his shirt and exposed his sweaty chest. They screamed for even more! Presley unbuckled his belt. Onlookers were either aroused with gasps or agitated with gapping disbelief.Pastor Benny Peyton gathered his wife and two young daughters and ushered them away from the spectacle.

Hank stopped thumping the beat on his guitar! He was glad now that he was in the shadows behind his brother.Pres looked back menacingly at Hank. He demanded him to step up the beat to meet the frenzy of his performance.Hank knew that look. Reluctantly, he obeyed. He plucked faster at his guitar, feverishly, in an impulsive frenzy.This was not what they had rehearsed! Pres was out of bounds, not only with the rules of the competition but from all they had negotiated as brothers.

"What was Pres doing?""Presley seemed to be in his own world, doing what he thought was the right thing to do for the sake of his adulation and his renown as an "artist." But he was singing lyrics

172

out of sync with Hank's tempo. Hank tried to keep up, but he was losing his way. He was sweating drops down his back, and his hands were getting slick on the strings. Suddenly, a string on Hank's guitar snapped a string, slapping him on his cheek, barely missing his eye. Then another broke loose from the frame with an off-key "TWANG!" He stopped playing.Presley was in the middle of the last chorus and had to awkwardly conclude his entry acapella.Hank knew nothing else to do but exit the stage, abandoning his brother, whatever the consequences would be.

Presley stood sweating profusely before the audience, unsure of what would happen next. But whatever he did, it worked! There was a pensive pause of silence then a wave of laughter, but then came uproarious applause with feminine screams of approval! Presley looked over his shoulder for Hank, but he had disappeared. The applause surged and escalated to whistles, both cheers and jeers, and a few blatant proposals from the flirtatious girls in the front row. Not knowing what else to do, Presley Jackson conceded to the adulation. He stepped into the spotlight, pitched his shirt into the crowd, and nodded to the front row…*as come-hither as he could.*

Hank held on to the neck of his guitar, its string still dangling from the bridge, and exited the stage. He didn't know where he was running; he just had to get away. His cheek was still stinging from the slap of the broken string. He escaped into the shadows, touching gently the fat welt on his red face. He passed through the crowd into an alleyway to the creek that separated the Festival attractions from the backside of downtown. He waded through a shallow part of the creek and up a small embankment to the lot behind the HUB.

The noise inside the HUB was muffled, but even outside the joint, it was raucously deafening. One dim orange bulb from a lone light pole lit the back lot. He looked around to be sure he was not being seen or followed. Then, with one thrust, he raised his guitar by its neck over his head and slam-dunked it in a nearby dumpster. It rang with an echoing thud. He sat on the bottom step of the Hub's fire escape and exhaled his humiliation, his forehead in his hands, still feeling the sting on his cheek.

Roadkill was rock 'n and reverberating in the Hub. They finished 30 minutes of their gig with their infamous semi-hit, *"Retro-evolution."* The stringy-haired, ghoulish-looking, thirty somethings were screaming lyrics that, other than the expletives, were too frenzied to comprehend. The band mates included a lead guitarist who ad-libbed licks to suit his own fancy, a brooding bass guitarist who resembled the cartoon character, "Droopy Dog," an acrobatic drummer, a rhythmic contortionist of sorts who threw souvenir drum sticks into the crowd, and finally, the lead banshee, who looked to exploit himself as having *"de-evolved from a human being to a missing link."* They all looked as if they had been expelled from Sunday School decades ago. The musical menagerie was booked by the Hub sight-unseen with just their agent's promise of attracting a more *"progressive"* entourage of partiers. Their publicity man described them as a *"slum band, slamming down the highway and snubbing anything status quo that gets in their way."* Thus, *Roadkill,* progressive or not, was an acquired taste. They did attract and ignite an audience of their own kind. Hank was not a fan.

"Hank?" The boy was startled by both a familiar voice and a whiff of smoke from around the corner of the building. He looked up to see his Aunt Dolly sitting on the platform outside the HUB's backdoor. She had taken a cigarette break from *Roadkill* in the Hub when she noticed her nephew's lunacy. "You...chucked... your guitar! What the hell, Henry?"

Hank nodded. "I couldn't have shit any worse."

"Sorry, sweetie. So, you lost a hokey-pokey contest." Dolly puffed a smile. "Presley mad at you?"

"Prob'ly." Hank answered. "He's always mad at me."

"Did he do his thing?"

"He struts his butt around! All over the stage. Yeah."

She inhaled from her cigarette again. "Do you want one of these?" He glared at her incredulously. She exhaled, "course not."

"I didn't just lose, Aunt Dolly, *I bombed*! I bombed! Pres didn't. He never does! My string broke! He kept going on... I couldn't keep up with him. I can never keep up with Pres."

"Sorry, sweetie."

"The thing is, this time, I didn't *want* to keep up with him! He made me sick!"

Dolly descended the steps and sat next to her nephew. "So you slammed your guitar in the trash? 'Cause you didn't like what Presley did? Sorry again, Sweetie, but that's *your* shit. Everybody knows Presley's an ass. He ain't your fault. Shit, Henry! You take the blame for ever-thang! You gonna blame yerself for crucifying Jesus too?"

After a moment, Hank smiled, "Yeah, I guess."

She puffed. "Throwing your guitar away," she scoffed, "now *that* was your fault...and really stupid. If you don't like what Pres is do'in, don't cooperate with the asshole. But don't YOU quit play'in your guitar! Broken strings can be repaired." She tossed her cigarette to the side. Then his Aunt Dolly walked to the dumpster, lifted herself up, and crawled inside. "AWWWW! This is nasty!" she shrieked. "I can't believe I'm do'in this for you."

Hank stood up. "What are you doing?"

"I'm fetch'in your damned guitar!" She shouted from the midst of the trash bin. She held up the guitar and tilted it over the side of the bin. Just before her head appeared over the edge, she yelled, "Take it! TAKE IT!" He reached up, took it from her, and eased it down to the pavement in front of him. Dolly pulled herself up and climbed over the side. "Don't you tell nobody what I just done!" she gasped, swiping the grime off her blouse.

"You guys need to learn how to control yer testosterone," she replied. "Don't expect me to do anything like that again. It won't happen."

"It's useless! Look at the bridge…" Hank whined.

Dolly snapped, "Yeah, Sweetie, YOU did that! Yeah, it's cracked--look at the damned bridge! You pitched it-- I fetched it! Now, what're YOU gonna do with it? Not Presley or Senator Daddy or your momma… or God, *YOU* gotta deal with the strings and the bridge thing or whatever!"

Suddenly, the back door of the HUB swung open. "AUNT DOLLY!" yelled Wanda, "YOU OUT THERE?"

"YEAH, WANDA, I'M HERE!" Dolly yelled back, "I'M ON MY WAY!"

"HURRY IT UP. I CAN'T DO FEED *ROADKILL* BY MYSELF!" Wanda exclaimed, slamming the door behind her.

Dolly straightened her blouse and brushed some residue from her jeans. She climbed the stairs of the fire escape to the back door of the Hub. She sauntered over and punched the security code on the box outside the door. The light turned "green," and the door release clicked. She turned and glanced at her nephew. "Sweetheart, those balls God gave you. They ain't for decoration! Did you hear me, Henry?" She quickly entered the Hub. The door slammed securely behind her.

Hank stood silent. Then, he empathetically embraced his battered guitar.

*

"When I was a boy, of course, I had to go out and turn a man's work—at least what you might call a poor man's work—from the

176

age of ten, working in the fields and on the roads. It was good for me, for it strengthened my muscles and my body…It was a good thing for a boy to do some hard work, though I realize that it can be overdone." (Senator and Vice-President Alben W. Barkley, That Reminds Me, 1954)

Dorothy and Perry hosted Eva for the Local-Yokel-Vocal Contest. On their drive back to Eva's home, the Jacksons were ecstatic in celebrating Presley's win. Although there was some controversy regarding the boy's "family-friendly" performance, the judges were more impressed by the audience's reaction than with the protocol of the contest. Eva Kilbride too witnessed Presley's exhibition. Had he been a stranger, she would have walked out as soon as the boy flaunted his flesh. On her way home, she was polite. She congratulated Presley but was more worried about Hank. He just disappeared from the stage. "Where did he run off to?" she asked.

"Hank'll be fine, Eva." Perry insisted from behind the steering wheel. "He's just temperamental…prob'ly at home pout'in. He didn't do his best tonight. He gets temperamental."

"Tempered… mostly mental." Presley added, holding tightly to his trophy. "He 'bout messed ever-dang-thing. He's just out there lick'in his wounds."

Dorothy interrupted, "He was embarrassed when those strings popped."

"We should have waited for him, Dorothy." Eva scolded.

"He's seventeen. He knows the way home." Perry insisted. "He's prob'ly at the HUB with Dolly. You know how they are-- Wah! Wah! Wah!"

They drove up alongside Eva's house. Perry held the car in neutral and shined his headlights on the back porch. Presley escorted his Mamaw to the door, her hand in one hand and his trophy in the other. He kissed her on the cheek and retreated to the car. Before she stepped onto the porch, she called to her grandson, "Presley! You be careful what you're a-do'in up there on that stage! Sometimes I wonder if all that don't make Jesus mad?"

*

It was nearing midnight. Dolly was not yet at home from the HUB. Eva put on her gown, draped her shoulders with her fuzzy robe. She was weary but unable to sleep. It was the constant ringing in her ears from the noise at the contest; moreover, every time she closed her eyes, she envisioned Presley's shameless works of the flesh on stage, "bear 'in himself in front of everybody in the county." She was mindful too of Hank and Marcus, Dolly's position at the HUB; on and on her thoughts were in endless chatter.

Sominex was called for. She took two tablets and washed them down with a warm glass of buttermilk. (Aidan loved his warm buttermilk after difficult runs when he couldn't get to sleep.) She shuffled to the living room and eased herself into her well-worn recliner. The old Big Ben was *tick-tock'in* like a quickening heartbeat on the mantel. She looked around the room, surrounded by framed images, large and small, old and faded--her family history— concentric circles of Aidan. She began to dose off, drifting away into the space between slumber and sensibility. In her mindfulness, she was sure she heard the voices of those images in between the frames. Sometimes, when she was alone like this, she communed with those images, and they spoke back in whispers. Most of the voices she remembered clearly; others grew faint and fainter still.

Next to her glass was her favorite picture of Aidan. It was the only one depicting how she wanted to remember him. Viewing the photograph within the frame, she exaggerated the qualities about him she had loved the most. In the picture, he was taller than he really was, retained more wavy black hair than he did, owned broader shoulders than when he was alive, browner eyes, tanner skin, smoother hands, and a softer voice—that is how she chose to preserve him in her mind.

"Eva?" A masculine voice whispered. For Eva, it sounded seemingly like it was from inside the wooden frame.

"Aidan?" she whispered back. "…you talk'in to me again, Honey?"

"Yes." Returned the voice. The wispy tone seemed to surround her.

Eva tried to stand, but the dose of the pills weighed her down. She was groggy, but still had enough sensibility to discern the voice in the room.

"Aidan?" she called.

The voice sounded again. "Where is Marcus, Eva?"

"I don't know, Honey. I haven't seen him since Sunday…"

The picture in the frame grew silent. Then it growled, "He's wearisome."

"Lord, Lord, Lord…" Eva sighed.

"He's weary'in on me… again."

"He don't mean no harm, Aidan. He's try'in to be good…don't know why God allows for bad things to happen…and bad people in this world…"

Then the voice exclaimed in a voice unlike Aidan's, "There ain't no bad people, just lost ones. Bad things make things good. They wake up people to what's real."

"It's bad that you left me, Aidan." She was swooning now in her Sominex.

"Where is he, Eva?" came a more guttural whisper of the voice in the room. This time, the voice was behind her chair, hovering over her. "Where is Marcus? Hum? Where is Marcus?"

"Runn'in still, I reckon, runn'in still."

The voice became more pronounced, even threatening. "Where is he, Eva? Dammit, where is Marcus?"

"Honey, I don't know! Ever-body is look'in for him. I ain't seen him since Sunday." Eva held her hand over her eyes and forehead. She could barely hold her head up. She snuggled into her robe, hugging it close to her chest. She lay back in her recliner, dreaming she was being held in Aidan's arms. She closed her eyes and prayed, "Lord. Lord. Lord." (She never needsn't to pray anything more. She believed God always knew what she meant to pray without praying it.) Then she drifted to sleep. She slept so soundly in her recliner that she didn't notice the soft creaking of the floorboards behind her. Nor did she see the shadow man encircling her in her own living room.

The shadow man had peeped through every window, looking for his quarry. Confident that Dolly was not in any room, he managed to climb into the house through Marcus' faulty bedroom window. Now, In his frustration, he slipped through the back door and to the porch. Perhaps Marcus would return? He waited. The porch swing was comfortable. It seemed to sway backward and forward with the rhythm of his own heartbeat. He heard from somewhere in the woods the hooting of an owl. "Ah!" He pondered the sound. "I hear you, old friend." He loved the soft wooing of those tactical talons—those winged predators of prey.

*

The Thursday night festivities concluded. Behind the scenes, last minute preparations were being made for a good Friday. The booths were closed. The scent of pine was reclaiming the air. The music had ceased. The locals were dispersing to the hills and hollers. It was closing time at the HUB. Only Wanda and Dolly remained, cleaning up after *Roadkill.*

Dolly locked the front door and pulled down the blinds on the front window. Wanda yelled, "okay, Aunt Dolly, we're out'ta here!" She lifted a snoozing Dara from a nearby booth and headed toward the back door.

"Go on," Dolly yelled back, "get that girl to bed."

Dolly managed the rest. She tossed her cleaning cloth over the bar, put on her jacket, and headed toward the back door. It was late. She pictured Eva waiting impatiently, in her pajamas, sitting on the back porch or in her place in her recliner, staring at the Big Ben. It was after midnight when all good people were supposed to be home.

The day had been such a maudlin Thursday for Dolly. She was emotionally, as well as physically exhausted. She reached for the latch of the back door and pushed it open. The cool night air refreshed her face. She breathed it in as if newly born, breathing for the first time. Suddenly, the heavy metal door jolted open. Two men forced themselves inside. She was stunned for a moment, stepping backward with a gasp. It was Hank. Scurrying quickly behind him was Marcus.

"I'm hungry," Marcus said. He was trembling, partly due to the chill in the air.

Dolly wanted to slap him and embrace him at the same time. She was in no mood for pomp and circumstance. Once the agitating surprise wore off, she was startled by his appearance. He was disheveled, with a disfigured expression on his face. His eyes were squinting with the light of the HUB. He looked frail, alarmingly so, especially for one in his twenties.

"What the hell, Marcus?" Dolly asserted, quickly slamming and locking the door behind them. "What the shitty devil in hell?"

Hank and Marcus stepped quickly away from her and toward the bar. Marcus mumbled, "I'm hungry and thirsty."

Dolly stepped behind the bar. She cast a handful of stale vanilla wafers at him. Then she sat a half-empty bottle of beer in front of him. Hank sipped from the bottle and grasped a handful of cookie crumbs from the countertop. Dolly glared at her brother. The beer was still wet on his lips, so he wiped it away with the filthy sleeve of his shirt.

"Dammit, Marcus!" she scolded, "Where the hell have you been? They found Jasper's body up there, and now everybody's call'in you ever-damned-thing! A murder 'in maniac. You've nearly given Momma a stroke! What do you think you're do'in? You'd better talk to me NOW, brother! The last you said anything to me was 'bout going to fetch the damned truck!"

Marcus interrupted her tirade. "I'm be'in stalked, Dolly."

She grew silent. "Stalked?" she smirked. "What the hell does that mean?"

"I set out for the truck…. climbed up along the runoff ditch. When I got to the top of the ridge, I decided to just… get away… from everything. I was gonna take the highway *west*…out of the county. Y'all would never see me again."

"Shit, Marcus!" Dolly exclaimed.

182

"Shut up, Aunt Dolly!" Hank demanded, leaning his guitar against the bar. "I want to hear him! You said you want to know what's happened! Let him tell us."

"Hell, that was good, Hankie!" Dolly grinned, "Go on, Marcus. I'm listen'in."

Marcus continued. "… 'bout a mile down the road, I saw this man, a hermit or someth'in—worst ugly I've ever seen. He was on a rise in the curve. I kept walk'in toward him on the road…slow. He kept staring. Like he was dar'in me to take another step towards him…like I was wallk'in on his property. He didn't budge. I stopped…he took a step towards *me*…like he knew me…I took a step back. He took a step at me. He was between me and the county line! I started walk'in…I'd walk 'round him… 'cept he was head'in quicker toward me. He had a hunt'in knife—a big 'un, too. He was grin'in at me like knew me…clutch'in that knife…backwards… by the blade! His fingers were drip'in red! He started run'in at me!

I ran back down the road… slid down into the woods. He never stopped com'in for me. I hid…I found an opening in the rock…a cave. I barely fit, but I laid on my side and pushed backward –but first, so I could see in front of me… squeezed between the roof and the ground. I breathed only when I had to. Like bei'n buried alive. But I squeezed myself inside. All this runoff flushed from inside the cave behind me…kind of pushing me out of the hole. I stayed there as long as I could until the runoff got too much. He was out there somewhere, but he didn't find me. I stayed there til I knew he was gone. Then I pushed my way out. Got through the backwoods to the truck... found Casper's body. God! Casper's body! I couldn't go home, Dolly…that man with the knife…he's stalk'in me! I couldn't go home. Not with Mama there."

Dolly exclaimed. "Dammit Marcus! You've run too far! Where've you been all this time?"

"Found a hid'in place." he whispered.

"What the hell are you do'in here?" Dolly asked. "Go to Sheriff Keith! Tell him yer side of things."

Marcus shook his head. "Do you know what's go'in on? This ain't about run'in the truck anymore, Dolly! This is 'bout run'in for my life. Nobody's gonna believe me."

Dolly held her hand over her ears. "Stop that! Just stop that shit!" she shrieked. "Why does every man in Timberline County act like a bunch of pissants?Stop that self-pitiful, ever-body-pisses-on-me bullshit!You gotta face this! You gotta stop runn'in, Marcus!"

Marcus's sullen face glared at her now with a surge of deviance, "I didn't kill Casper!" Then he added, "I don't need the Sheriff! I'm gonna fix this…I've got to fix all of this. I was only run'in the shit. That was it. That guy and Casper… got in a fight 'bout something. I climbed out of the truck. Slid down the slope. Whoever killed Cas pushed the truck over the ridge and disappeared. Someth'in went bad! He killed Casper for it, now he's stalk'in me. It ain't safe for me to go home. Ain't safe for me to be anywhere!"

"You ought'a getaway, Uncle Marcus." Hank insisted. "Get out of the county!"

Marcus looked away and sighed, "Momma used to tell me there's go'in to be a reckon'in day. This is my reckon'in day. Holler law! That's why it's up to me to fix all this."

Dolly opened a can of beer and guzzled it down. With a guttural belch, she slammed her mug on the bar. "Well, I ain't reckon'on with you anymore, Marcus! It's too much: run'in with Daddy…run'in from the mine…run'in moonshine…run'in meth! Run'in from Momma for days without no word. You've been run'in…your whole life, from noth'in to noth'in to noth'in, hid'in away like some…some…"

"... *possum boy? Eh,* Dolly? Like Daddy used to call me? A *possum boy* play'in dead? Yeah! I always played dead a lot 'round Daddy..."

"Whoa, brother, don't be harp'in on our Daddy. He took care of all of us... did what he had to do. He didn't run from ever-thang when it got bad."

"SAINT DADDY! Daddy did ever-thang for everbody! Run'in from the mine, run'in shine...run'in in the morn'in, run'in when the sun don't shine! Yeah, Dolly, that was Daddy! Kept us all warm and cozy, full-fed, and faces rosy!"

Dolly erupted, "You selfish, ungrateful little bastard! He did all that run'in for all of us, including YOU!"

Marcus bit his upper lip with snarling teeth. His face flashed from ashen to crimson. "Dammit, Dolly! Didn't you all SEE anything?" Marcus shrieked. "Daddy was *run-in* ME! *HE WAS RUN'IN ME!* He took *ME* on *those runs*—not moonshine or marijuana or meth, dammit, Dolly, Daddy sold ME!"

Finally, Marcus wept.

*

"It was great to have freedom to roam the hills and run barefoot with your shirt tail flapp'in in the wind...getting chigger bites on your legs and skinning your knees. We kids would come home at night dirty and plum wore out...It didn't matter how much money you had." (Ricky Skaggs, Autobiography, 2013)

Aidan grabbed hold of Marcus for a truck run from the ridge to beyond the County line. "Across the county line," young Marcus thought. At eight years old, he had never seen anything outside of Timberline County. He rode shotgun next to his daddy and took in the unfamiliar sights. Aidan had never taken that route before run'in through thoroughfares Marcus had never seen. The night air was chilly, and the heater in the truck didn't offer much warmth. But

Marcus didn't mind. It was Marcus, not Rawley, who joined his daddy on this run.

The pick-up truck was loaded with jugs and jars. It skids along on gravel roads, more improved roads than thoroughfares that seemed to be improvised by his daddy's whims. Nonetheless, Marcus was delighted by his daddy's attention. "This is some'thin you can do for the clan. Not Rawley or anybody else. Just YOU." Aidan said. "You don't go in the mine no more if you just come run'in with me."

After an hour, the delivery run turned into a wooded and desolate place.It was within the outer perimeter of a state park. At this time of night, there were no sightseers, but as the truck slowed past the sign pointing to a disserted rest area, Marcus noticed beams from flashlights and lanterns waving back and forth a few yards ahead. The truck stopped in front of several men dressed in respective coats and low-brimmed hats or ball caps. Aidan leaped from the truck and confronted the entourage. Marcus sat motionless from the passenger seat. He watched his daddy work a crowd of darksome customers like a frontier medicine man selling his wares to men—incognito-- and in line for the merchandise. Aidan took their money and winked back at his son.

"Marcus!" he called, "Get outta the truck and help me pass out them jugs!" Marcus obeyed. He scrambled out of the door and climbed into the back of the truck.Upon handing a jug to his daddy, Aidan whispered under his breath to Marcus, "You're gonna help me buy your momma a winter coat for Christmas…just do what I tell you. There's more to gett'in money off'n these city boys than there is by cutt'in coal, *possum boy!*"

Aidan distributed the moonshine to each customer as they slapped cash into Aidan's hand. Then one by one, as quickly as they retrieved their jugs and jars, they got into their cars and drove out of the park. One customer remained. He held a dinky flashlight in one hand and a lantern in the other. From the back, looking over the top of the truck, Marcus observed the man talking with his daddy. After a few minutes of conversation, the man put a handful of cash in Aidan's hand. Together, the stranger and Aidan stepped to the back of the truck.

"This is possum boy," Aidan said to the man. He was dressed in an expensive overcoat, but his shoes were scummy with mud. The stranger was noticeably fidgety. He held his lantern up and around to peruse the boy. Then he raised and rested one foot on the bumper of the truck. He had no jugs or jars, only a lantern in his hand. His eyes were wildly wide as he lifted the brim of his hat (Marcus noticed it had a feather in it.) to gain a fuller view of the boy.

"Marcus," Aidan began, "this is a customer from the city." The man waved his fingers at the boy. "He wants to take your picture. Isn't that right...Sir?"

The man nodded and grinned in the glow of the lantern. Marcus took a step back.

Aidan continued, insisting the boy "...do what he says. He's a customer."

Marcus began to hyperventilate. He backed himself up to the edge of the truck bed.

The man set the lantern on the edge of the truck and stepped toward the boy. "Now, *possum boy*, I just want to take a photograph or two. It won't hurt, I promise. You're what we call 'photogenic,' a good look'in kid. I only want a couple o'pictures. See?" He reached into his pocket. "Here's my camera. It's instamatic. The flash doesn't work too well, but there's a light post down that path there. It'll only take a minute or two. Just a few...*poses* will do."

He paused for a moment, then grew foreboding, impatient. "I already paid your daddy for this...come on!"

Marcus looked down from the truck at Aidan. "Go on!" Aidan demanded, gesturing with his hand, dismissing the boy. "Let the man take yer picture, Marcus."

Marcus climbed out of the truck. He stood between Aidan and the customer, who was then focused on him from the eye of his camera lens.

"Come on, boy! It's getting late." The stranger groaned, then turned toward Aidan, "Your boy looks like he's balking! I don't have time for balking boys. You want this deal or not, Kilbride?"

Aidan growled and shoved Marcus toward the man. "Get on down the path with you, possum boy! Smile at the camera, Marcus! Go on. Go to the light post and give the man what he wants. We charged him a-plenty for this. Go along…we'll be down the road after…after…"

The customer in the feathered hat put a hand on the boy's shoulder and insisted Marcus follow him. "Come on, boy! Down this path…toward that old light post."

Marcus obeyed with shivering knees, stepping onto the path with the customer only a heated breath or two behind him. "That's it." The customer grinned, adjusting his lens on the boy. "Come on with me. I'm harmless."

Aidan turned and stepped away from Marcus and the man as they disappeared into the camouflage of the woods. In the stillness of the midnight hour, Aidan heard the man remark, "That's it, *possum boy*. I just like to take pictures of beautiful things."

On the way down the path, the customer led Marcus to a dimly lit lamp post. Bats were soaring and gliding above the lamp, snatching insects. The man stood only a few feet away from the boy. He aimed his camera and began his portfolio. It wasn't long before the man insisted that Marcus disrobe. Marcus removed his shirt. The man impulsively clicked the camera over and over, encircling the boy like the flying creatures hovering over them.

"So, what's your real name, possum boy? Matt? Whatever...Mark? Take off your boots and socks...(CLICK!) now, the jeans...(CLICK!) Don't move! Stand there in the little shorts!" (CLICK! CLICK!)

The camera lens hovered around the boy, who stood paralyzed and shivering. Marcus held his bare chest with crossed arms in front of him. "Now!" the man growled, "the shorts! Take off those whities." Hastily, the man aimed his camera once more at the trembling boy, who hesitated to comply. "DO IT!" the customer demanded. Terrified now, Marcus obeyed. He stood naked before the instamatic. (CLICK! CLICK! CLICK!)

After the clicking stopped, Marcus reached for his shorts, but the customer was unrelenting. "NO! Possum boy! We aren't done yet. I paid your daddy FULL PRICE!" With that, he set his camera to the ground and sauntered toward Marcus. Then for the boy, all went silent.

Aidan heard Marcus' whimpers echoing through the woods; he heard his muffled cries. Aidan reasoned he was only doing *business* with whatever resources he had. He could invest Marcus by cheating the customer as he did. Imagine wanting to take a few pictures of a boy for five hundred dollars with a bonus of six months' worth of food stamps! In Aidan's mind, it was all about revenge. In cheating this customer with such a commodity as Marcus, he took revenge on what outsiders had taken from the hollers. "Imagine cheat'in 'em outta five hundred bucks like this! With six months of food stamps to boot! City boys are just damned stupid!"

None of the three in this seclusion knew how much time had elapsed. The customer approached Aidan at his truck and handed him his cash and the stash of food stamps he had promised him.

Then, as quickly as he had appeared, the man in the feathered hat drove away into the dark.

Aidan called Marcus. There was no reply until Marcus emerged, half-dressed, shuffling slowly from the path. He came to the truck and climbed into the passenger seat without saying a word. There he sat, holding his tee shirt and staring blankly at the floor. Aidan opened the door and sat behind the steering wheel. "Here." he said, tossing a few dollar bills to him. "Here's what you earned tonight just for 'him tak'in a couple of damned pictures of you, *possum boy!*"

Marcus wiped his eyes with his shirt and tugged up his pants over his belly. He left his socks and ruined shorts at the lamppost. He managed to slip in his gym shoes on without tying them.

"No need to pout." Aidan repeated, starting up the truck. "Yew did what you had to do. We made a fortune tonight."

The darkened clouds drizzled-down rain. It trickled like tears through the leaves. The truck turned sharply and headed toward the highway. "Get yerself propered, 'fore yer momma sees yew. Put on yer tee shirt and line up them britches!"

Marcus stared blankly ahead of him. He put on his tee shirt. He held his skinny arms around his chest and kept Aidan Kilbride out of his sight. The road home was agonizingly long. All Marcus could see along the way were the lens, the bats hovering over him, and the lingering odor of the disgusting breath of his daddy's "customer" on his "britches."

"You earned us five hundred dollars, *possum boy*. Got us some food stamps too!" Aidan gloated. "That'll take us through a month of pangs. Remember now: don't tell, don't tell, don't tell *anyone!* This is our secret 'tween you and me. 'tween you and me. This is how we cheat city boys---by God, it's holler law!"

*

191

The three were silent in the light of Marcus' discourse. Dolly turned away to pour herself a dram of something strong. Hank stood motionless, staring at the floor.

"You believe me, Dolly?" Marcus asked.

Dolly gulped her gin. "It'll take me a while to answer you." She poured herself another. "Why didn't you tell somebody?"

"Who was I to tell? Momma? Rawley? Hell, I just told you, and it got YOU to guzzl'in gin. This wasn't someth'in that a possum boy could go tell … anybody."

"How many times?"

"Off and on, 'til I was go'in on twelve."

Dolly slammed down her shot glass on the bar. "You should have told somebody! Momma!"

"How do you tell Momma that the person she worshipped all her life wasn't Jesus?"

"God have mercy…"

Marcus scoffed, "He never did."

"Bullshit. You could've gone to anybody in this clan, any neighbor in this county, but instead, YOU take to the Emporium and Carl Jaspers!Now look at you! You're on the run again! Hid'in this and ever-thang else you've done in your life! Well, you damn well can't live out there alone. Not with this Jaspers thing!"Dolly managed to mutter amidst her unbelief. "You gotta go to the Sheriff."

"I ain't alone." Marcus replied, "I got… shelter."

Dolly was adamant, "Go to the Sheriff!"

Marcus erupted, "I ain't gonna trust nobody. Sheriff Boswell is like everybody else… bound to the buyer. That's how it works. It's about the payoff."

Finally, Hank spoke up. "What're you gonna do?"

He sighed heartily, "I'm gonna fix this, my own way, by holler law. It's my 'reckon'in time'. I'm not 'possum boy' anymore. It's payback! All the bastards in the world who abuse poor people ain't gonna do it no more! I'm gonna find the guy who did this to Casper by myself! It's MY justice now—MARCUS Law!" Marcus's eyes were determined yet squinted with exhaustion.

"Henry," Dolly began, "I want you to go home. Don't talk about any of this. But go home 'fore Perry comes look'in for you."

Marcus instructed his nephew not to divulge what he had heard to anyone. "Swear to me, Henry."

Hank nodded.

Hank walked to the front door. He and his crippled guitar slipped out onto the deserted street. Dolly locked the door securely behind him. As the boy stepped onto the sidewalk, Perry Jackson had just made his way driving down Main Street. When he caught sight of his son standing outside the front door of the HUB, he stopped the car at the curb and called, "I had to drive all the way back to find you. Have you quit pouting?"

Hank climbed into the car.

"That your guitar?" Perry asked, keeping his agitation in check. "What happened to it?"

"I dropped it." Hank replied.

"How the hell are you going to play for your brother on Saturday night with that beat-up guitar? Well, you are not lugging that thing home!"

He angrily accelerated down Main Street to the alley behind the Hub. He slammed on the brakes and shifted the car in neutral. Then he got out and opened Hank's door. He snatched the guitar from his son's hands. "You don't want to be seen with this mess!" With one thrust, he pitched Hank's guitar into the dumpster.

"You can borrow your Uncle's. He won't be around much anymore." Perry asserted.

He climbed back behind the wheel and drove around the block to Main Street. As he passed the front door of the Hub, Perry noticed two shadows in a dim light on the blinds covering the front window.

"Who's in there with Dolly now?" his father asked.

"None of our business?" Hank replied.

"Another innocent bystander, I suppose. A HUB-BUM! He doesn't know what he's getting into."He scoffed.

Hank hesitated for a moment. "Yeah. Aunt Dolly and just some other guy."

They drove up Main Street. As they turned onto the highway to their house, Perry told his son, "By the way, Presley won the trophy tonight. You should have stayed around to see it.That would've been the correct thing to do."

Chapter Nine:
The Fifth Day After Sunday

A Gaudy Friday

"Together we are bringing a new way of life to the coal-producing and coal impact areas and a better life for all Kentuckians." (Governor Brereton C. Jones, Public Papers, 1993)

Friday.

The forecast called for rain with a "pending possibility of severe stormy weather." But the traditional fervency for the Festival with the promise of cash flow overcame the threat. While the clouds grew foreboding, nothing would nix the festive spirit in the hollers, storm clouds notwithstanding.

By noon, tourists infiltrated Timberline County. There were designated areas for them to park both in town and in the median strips of the highways coming into the county. Most of the tourists obeyed the respective parking regulations; others ignored them.Still, as those regulations were not well-enforced, no parking area for the Festival was truly reserved for anyone. It was the open season for "Ya'll come!"

The booths were *up and at 'em* by lunchtime. Tents became shelters for any potential downpour. Chuck wagons and grills enraptured the air with succulence—the sweet and savory incense of Appalachian cuisine.Local musicians were merely rehearsing, but even their tuning up was virtuosic ecstasy. Woodcarvers were whittling. Weavers were inspecting their delicate threads and yarn. The sorghum press had been rounding about since before dawn. The rich liquid readied to flow and stirred into steaming vats, transformed into a thick black syrupy delight!

A truck arrived, hauling the hot air balloon for the tethered rides. It parked less than a mile away on the McGuffey High School football field. It would take some time to unravel the monstrosity, align the cables, straighten the canvas, attach the oversized wicker basket, and ultimately inflate the balloon. By 3 pm, it would be aloft, ready to ascend—depending on the whims of the atmosphere. (In Timberline County, much depended on the velocity and direction of the wind.) It would be tethered to the ground, lifted and suspended between the sky and the earth, offering a glimpse of the panorama of the mountains. The balloon inhales its warmed breath and rises— rises to reach the length of its tether. There it lingers, swaying lazily- -hovering above the frets and frenzies in the marketplace. In that space, suspended between earth and heaven, one can realize the dilemma of humanity: beings of both flesh and soul, of woe and wonder-- and discover what we are to believe and how we are to live well.

*

Eva was still wearied from the contest the night before. This morning, she was content to follow her daily routine with little thought of attending the weekend festivities. Eva was sitting at the table, sipping her tea and reading the *Annotated Book of Psalms*.

Just after sunrise, there came a pounding on Eva's porch door. Before she could answer it, the door creaked open. "Eva! You in here?" bellowed the call. It was Aidan's sister, Grace Kilbride, but by the tone of the voice, she was more *Sister Dazzlingstar,* who barged into the kitchen, with Emmanuel sheepishly tagging behind her.

"Sister Eva!" she bellowed. "Are you alright?"

Grace gallantly approached her sister-in-law. She caressed an alabaster cup of virgin olive oil in her hand. She dipped her finger into the oil, dabbed Eva's wrinkled forehead with a touch of *"blessing,"* then recited a homily: "' Is anyone among you sick? Let them call the elders of the church to pray over them and anoint them with oil in the name of the LORD.'

196

I anoint you, Sister Eva! For you and ALL who might dwell in this house! Amen." Then she handed the cup to Emmanuel and motioned him with a nod. He turned and resolutely proceeded to walk about the house, anointing each doorframe.

Grace began again, "I just heard about Marcus. Very sad. He is such a troubled boy. So...lost. But God told me to share a word of hope with you. You know, *'all things work together for good...'* Not all things are good, but if you trust in the Lord... (She began to sing:)

"There is a balm in Gilead

To make the wounded whole

There is a balm in Gilead

To heal the sin-sick soul."

Abruptly, Sister Dazzlingstar continued with a theological tirade. "Oh, Eva, a balm is a medicinal oil derived from plants. Gilead is east of the Jordan River in Israel. It's known for scented ointments. This *'balm from Gilead'* is for you're the healing of this house! I brought some with me. Emmanuel is anointing every threshold with its healing power."

Dolly came to the kitchen in a noticeable huff. "Aunt Grace, your little angel is smear'in grease all over our bedroom doors!"

"Dolly," said Eva, "It is too early to be difficult."

"Dolly Kilbride, don't be sassing me!" Grace returned. "You could use some anoint 'in yourself, deary."

Dolly rolled her eyes at her aunt. "I get my lay'in on of hands my own way." She smirked.

Then, in a moment of euphoria, the prophetess emerged again. This time, she directed her homily to her niece. "You can't possibly understand things of the Spirit. *'The wind blows wherever it pleases. You hear its sound, but you cannot tell where it comes from or where it is going. So, it is with everyone born of the Spirit.'* John chapter three."

Emmanuel Kilbride meandered in and sat at the table. He was only a few months older than Marcus. They had been chummy growing up with one another as cousins. At times, Manny was more like a brother to Marcus than Rawley.Emmanuel's birth was mysterious to the clan. Suspicions were raised in the clan that the boy was conceived during one of Grace's mission trips by a transient migrant worker named Manuel. But Grace insisted that one way or another, her son was immaculately conceived. Most in the family didn't believe her story, but few were ever brave or bothered enough to question it. He was given the surname *Kilbride* when there was a father to claim the child's birth.

Emmanuel was solidly handsome, in his twenties, with a guileless smile and a hint of 'help me' in his sullen, brown eyes. He had a tanned farmer's frame and a delicate demeanor that was truly indicative of a child still untarnished by the whims of the outside world. He was home-schooled, church-ruled, socially deprived, and destructively curious. He had a passion for learning, but he rarely facilitated a conversation outside his mother's congregation, contented to question things when he was given permission.

Grace sat down and, without a word to him, pulled out a chair for Emmanuel to do the same. She turned to Eva. "Tell me 'bout poor Marcus. I heard the news uptown, but I want to hear your side of things, Darl'in."

Eva sighed, "We don't know much. He hasn't been home. Out there hid'in, they think."

"What news have YOU heard, Aunt Grace?" Dolly smirked.

"It's all over town. That Jaspers man…dead. Aidan's truck was at the scene. Drug do'ins in the back of the truck. Looks to me like my nephew needs to turn himself into the Sheriff and plea for God's help. Jail could turn him around to a good."

"We all need Jesus." Emmanuel added.

I ain't got a problem with Jesus." agreed Dolly.

"We haven't seen Marcus since Monday morning," Eva muttered.

"Marcus has a polluted soul. I knew him as a boy, pure like Adam in Eden. But now he's punctured with poison by some...serpent!" proclaimed Dazzlingstar. Her plump bosoms were shrouded in a gingham gown printed with petunias. She leaned over the table. Her herculean hands clutched the edges like a pulpit. "He needs to repent and turn himself in. God's justice will work itself out. We can pray for his soul. He must stop run'in away and face the face of God and Sheriff Boswell.God can do miracles with Marcus! God can change ever-thang for His glory! But Marcus has to have the 'want to' in his heart. He can use anything He wants to make things right."

"He even used a jawbone of an ass," Dolly whispered into her coffee cup. (Emmanuel chuckled, but not so much as anyone noticed.)

Grace continued, "I want to help Marcus. He's heard the gospel preached all his life. He's like the prodigal son, 'cept he's never come home from the hog squalor. He *should* know better! He *should* pick himself up and march down there to the jail and confess whatever he has to confess...and then he *should* profess what he needs to profess to Almighty God!"

Dolly spouted suddenly, "Quit s*hould'in* on him!" She slammed some silverware into the sink. "You got no idea what you're talk'in about! Quit *should'in* on him! You *should* on ever-body, they *should* do this and *should* do that! You don't know anything 'bout Marcus! Ever-body in this damned county got him hog-tied, hung, and hell-bound without even knowing who Marcus Kilbride really is!"

"He's perverted the plumbline of God!" Dazzlingstar proclaimed. "What else do I need to know? Ain't noth'in he's done that's justifiable! The prophet, Isaiah saith 'the LORD is a God of justice.' He judges the evildoer."The word of God is all we need to know 'bout people! It is our filter for what people SHOULD be do'in or not be do'in—thus saith the Lord."

Eva spoke up softly, *"'This is what the LORD Almighty said: 'Administer true justice; show mercy and compassion to one another.'* Zechariah 7:9. There comes a time of reckon'in. That's all I have to say about it all, Grace. That's Bible."

"It's good to be speak'in Jesus?" Emmanuel asserted suddenly. "Reckon'in?" he asked, "Maybe reckon'in means like a reconcil'in? Maybe Marcus needs reconcil'in? Maybe people should be reconcil'in?"

Dolly caught her cousin's submissive demeanor and winked at him. He nodded back at her.

Grace glanced at the clock. It was nearing 9:00 am. She had a Festival booth to operate. She gathered herself and her son behind her and headed toward the door. "Thank you, Sister Eva. I pray for salvation all around this house." Then she glanced at Dolly. "Marcus? God KNOWS him, Dolly. I'll pray for him. And If I find him, I will—I *shall,* by God's grace, turn him in."

Grace and Emmanuel gestured their "farewells" and took their leave.Dolly followed them as far as the door, closed it, and locked it securely behind them. Then she strolled back to the kitchen and opened a drawer of cleaning rags.

"What are you do'in?" Eva asked.

"I'm gonna wipe her Holiness from the door frames!"

"Let it be." Eva insisted. "It ain't hurt'in nothing!"

"But Momma…"

"Leave it…I said!" Eva ordered.

Dolly put the rags back in the drawer. Reluctantly, she left alone the anointed smudges of Sister Dazzlingstar.

*

The Autumn Echoes Celebration of Appalachia commenced with its annual opening day agenda. City Officials gave their opening remarks highlighting pioneers of Timberline County. Typically, the current mayor would try connecting himself to the lineage of the more notable pioneers. For generations, being Mayor meant one of two rivals that alternated terms in office; it was a rotating system of political savvy, a hostile tag team of sorts. This year's opening ceremony was inaugurated by Mayor James T. Cunning. Cunning was an annual candidate in Timberline County.His dowdy, buldog appearance, dress shirt and tie with rolled-up sleeves, and gruff demeanor convinced many that he was a strong leader. Those who were his classmates in high school years ago knew he was more into public relations than public service. He was as astute with the content of his speeches (respective of his audiences) as he was clever in their delivery (aware of his meter).His Opening Day oration was a recycle of pomp and circumstance with a litany of his accomplishments and challenges yet to be solved:

"We are making great strides in Timberline County. But we still have challenges with our post-coal generation. Poverty is unacceptable, and initiatives for income are essential. We must attract new businesses for jobs, adequate coal pension payments, drug running, and our over-reliance on government aid. My challenge to you is to recognize that the choices we make today will affect our lives for generations to come. In the meantime, let's get the Festival started! Welcome, one and all!"

The message resonated every election year with those who heard it. Like the Festival itself, it became a traditional political diatribe hoping to spark the devotion of both the clans in the present and impress outsiders for the future. The shops along Main Street were enticing. The Isaiah Boone Memorial Library created an extended entrance on the sidewalk and offered free library cards to first-timers. Scheduled every two hours on the portico of the library was a dramatic presentation featuring Leland McCreary. Out of character, the dramatist favored the looks and demeanor of Harry S. Truman without the tendency toward earthy language. McCreary was an undisputed hero in Timberline County. He served as a medic in the Korean War. Afterward, he returned to Timberline County in a surplus Army Jeep to care for the woe-begotten clans he knew so well. He was not only a licensed physician but also a true MD-- Mountain Doctor, who dispensed both homemade and medically approved remedies to folks in the hollers. Although he had an examination room in his home, Doc Mac was most content making house calls in the hollers.

Dr. Leland McCreary was a lifeline to the hollers in Timberline County, a constant and consistent presence. Rarely could anything keep Doc Mac for his appointed rounds. He knew the terrain and could maneuver his Jeep through the most precarious situation, except in the case of the flash flood of 1962. Josephine Jaspers, up the holler and across Fallen Timber Creek, was due with child any minute. Her midwife, Lettie Rawlings couldn't ford the creek. The call came through the hollers to Doc Mac. When he reached the end of the road where the creek had swollen over its banks, the Jeep became useless. McCreary had to park his Jeep nearly a half mile from the swollen Creek bank. The current was too swift to risk his Jeep being swept away.

McCreary had the foresight to devise a way to reach the clans (when necessary) by tying lifelines of thick rope from tree to tree, from one side of the creek to the other. Thus, when the bridge over the creek was out and the water overflowing its banks, Doc Mac could pull himself across the stream from one side to the other side. Rarely did he ever falter in reaching his patients. He was present for those taking their last gasps with black lung; as well as, to welcome the arrival of new life. Although that day, the undertow was daunting, Doc Mac arrived in time to care for both Josephine Jaspers and deliver her newborn son, Casper.

Besides his expertise as a physician, McCreary was also a passionate historian and amateur actor who celebrated both during the Appalachian Festival.Doc Mac wrote the script and masterfully portrayed *Daniel Boone* on the library portico every year. It was a first-person, one-man, melodramatic narrative of Boone's exploits with hostile Indians in the exploration of new settlements in the West.Through the years, he was an inspiration, especially to the school children. In his later years, when he donned a rummage-sale, coon-skin cap on his bald head, he prompted some chuckles in the crowd. Although he remained passionate about Boone, he did get confused, at times calling himself Davy Crockett rather than Daniel Boone. As a physician, Doc Mac was able to portray the tale in graphic detail. This event was most popular with the out-of-town tourists.

Leland McCreary understood this tragedy in the life of Daniel Boone. Through his practice in a Korean war zone and in the untimely death of both his son and his beloved wife, the MD learned to "rejoice with those who rejoice, and weep with those who weep." He was not just a formally educated physician; he was a humanely empathetic Mountain Doctor. His own firstborn, Vernon, was swept away in a mine explosion many years before. His wife, Gladys grieved so deeply there was nothing even Doc Mac could do to prevent her downward spiral into an incurable depression. It was a painful journey for Leland and his daughter, Leah.

His original script depicted the slaughter of Boone's young son, Isaiah, by a band of rogue Indians. It was a well-memorized excerpt from the memoirs of Peter Houston, an original settler of Boone Station. Again, this year, the event took place on the portico outside the Isaiah Boone Memorial Library. Typically, McCreary's rendition of Daniel Boone's closing soliloquy always brought him to tears:

"It was the 15th day of August in 1782. A brood of Indians were stealthily appearing in various locations, attacking settlements they claimed were encroachments upon their territory. Having secured that intelligence, I set out to the very seat of war to defend our settlements and our forts from any indigenous conflagration. We had to be wide-eyed and of silent foot-fall, of our advance would be detected by the some forty or fifty Indians making havoc in our pilgrimage. After they would assault an area, they would retreat, knowing that once the news reached the outer perimeter, they would be pursued by as many as one hundred and eighty-two men, young and old, myself among them. With my arsenal of men, I would trail and track them.

I tracked them beyond Blue Lick to the River. It was hard to know just when they saw us, for Indians were good at concealing themselves for ambush in the underbrush and ravines. But we had force enough to whip all the Indians we would find. Still, there were those who were a-feared of Indian attack at any moment. I had my son, Israel, and my nephew, Samuel with me. They were afraid as well, but they kept faith that I would keep them out of harm.

Suddenly there was in front of us the "whoooop!" of a terrific war. A body of Indians was making an attack between us and the river we were intending to cross. The Indians were surrounding us, and there were some who desperately cried for our retreat. Many scattered. "Hold them at bay!" I called, "Cross the river!" The men emptied their guns, but the Indians were swarming from the woods in front, and having no time to reload, over a third of the men, sweltering in blood, retreated. I continued toward the river with those who were brave enough to follow.

Indians were now in pursuit of us. We reached a ridge overlooking our pursuers. "Stand and fire!" I shouted, then gave the command for those who remained to make it across the river to better ground.

The Indians must have exhausted their ammunition, now using their spears and tomahawks in the fray. Undauntedly, we kept advancing and eventually made it across the river and unclaimed territory. The Indians fled. Later, we re-crossed the river to bury our dead. Samuel was wounded in the leg. He told me that my son, Israel, had been shot from his horse…shot in the neck. I saw him fall and so I leaped from my horse and tried to retrieve him. I called for my fleeing men to help me, but they heeded me not; whereupon I took my boy on my shoulder, and with the gun in my hand, I hastened to the bushes on the bluff. Three Indians discovered me and with a hideous yell, pursued me into the bushes. They were advancing, and with my son on my shoulder, I knew I would be overtaken and was forced to abandon my son…I let him to the ground and eluded pursuit of the other Indians.

Here I am now…safe, thank God, but it is still painful to think that my poor boy fell prey to the scalping knife." (from the autobiography of Squire Boone)

(Business: DANIEL BOONE weeps bitterly as the story concludes)

*

Perry Jackson broadcasted *live* from his KYTC-am radio booth. His PA speakers dominated Pioneer Park. He sat at the microphone as the host for the "Country Gospel Hour…the best in music celebrating that 'ole time religion…that makes you love everybody!" Later, as the festival crowd was roused, he hosted his call-in show by interviewing people who stopped by his microphone or happened by his roving through Pioneer Park. Perry Jackson was "live and in-person."

In and outside the KYTC booth, Dorothy was present to toss out complimentary Frisbees inscribed with: *"Perry Jackson: He's One* of Us" on the front. His campaign posters were scattered on posts and poles within the visual perimeter of his booth. Presley distributed buttons with his father's slogan while at the same time displaying his "Local Yocal Vocal" trophy. It was shining under a track light, celebrating his achievement and popularity.

Not far from the radio booth was the *canvass tabernacle* of Sister Grace Dazzlingstar. The flaps to its entrance raised as a proscenium, sacramentally folded, high, and lifted up with white poles, like pillars. The entrance was adorned with three flags: an American flag on one side, a flag of Timberline County on the other, and a Christian flag draped prominently in the center. Displayed on her table were various gospel tracts answering ultimate questions like *"Where Will You Spend Eternity?"* and *"What Does it Mean to Tithe?"* There were also cassette tapes of the sister's most popular sermons, record albums of her favorite gospel quartets, and various books she consigned from other evangelists; colleagues who affirmed her fancy and faith.

Prominently appendaged to her tent was her popular dunking booth: *"Dunk the Devil!"* For a contribution of just two dollars, you could "SEND THE DEVIL INTO THE ABYSS!" Moreover, for that same $2 if you threw the ball that hit the bull's eye, you won either a free pocket New Testament, a cassette, or a gospel record album of your choice.

The devil who hovered over the pool was her son (reputedly conceived by immaculate conception), Emmanuel. He disguised himself with thick, slicked-backed black hair that he twirled into horns, a painted-on mustache, and red-dyed long johns. He held a garden hoe in his hand. Rather than teasing passers-by with "I dare you," he taunted them with "I TEMPT you!" It was all concocted to somehow "save the lost in the highways and byways of Timberline County and throughout the uttermost parts of the world" at only two dollars per throw.

*

"Out in the cold world and far away from home
Some mother's boy is wandering all alone
No one to guide him or keep his footsteps right
Some mother's boy is homeless tonight.
Oh, bring back to me, my wandering boy
For there is no other that's left to give me joy
Tell him his mother, with faded cheeks and hair
Is at the old home, awaiting him there." (A. P. Carter, "The
Wandering Boy," 1963)

"But when he came to himself, he said…'I will arise and go to my father…'" (Luke 15:18/ ESV)

Sudden storms were not uncommon during Autumn in Timberline County. By midday, the clouds gathered dark and menacing. The wind arose, ebbed, and flowed, swooping down from the mountains, swirling around Pioneer Park, and sweeping through Main Street. Most local vendors secured their booths in case of a serious deluge, keeping their patrons and products safe until the storm passed by. The rain began. Tent flaps were tied, securely closed. Chuck wagons were temporarily shut down their concessions. Band members cowered with their banjos and guitars in their trucks and vans. The hot air balloon rides were canceled for the afternoon. Center Stage was barren.Common in the threat of the approaching storm, locals and tourists alike found shelter in the shops along Main Street or in the halls of the nearby churches.

The HUB was standing room only.That was where Dorothy and Perry Jackson, along with Rawley, Fern, and Dean chose to wait out the storm.So close were the tables within earshot of one another; as well as near to those who were eavesdropping, that the conversation between the Kilbride kin that the news *"maniac on the loose"* was sparked and set ablaze in the crowd.

Rampages have been known to arise through rumors gone ablaze. Second and third-hand rumors evolve into living and breathing entities, and lies often ignite raging holocausts. In the

HUB, customers demanded factual rumors.Many inquired of Deputy Hudson, wanting specifics about the murder in the mountains. He tried to keep the patrons from panicking, but they demanded immediate answers. "I better deal with this," Hudson told the Kilbrides. He held up his nightstick to part the crowd and ascended to Center Stage.

"Ladies and gentlemen!I am Deputy Travis Hudson. We are in the process of tracking a suspect of interest in a murder. That suspect is currently in hiding or on the run. State Police have been notified and are in the area. I will give you further instructions as the situation unfolds. There is no reason to panic as we are in control of the situation. In the meantime, there is no reason to let this disrupt your time at the festival. Thank you."

The patrons gasped. Hudson detected an emerging pandemonium. He tried again to console them. "We have State Troopers stationed throughout the County. You are completely safe. Please do not panic. We are in control of the situation. However, we prefer that no one leave Timberline County until the suspect is properly apprehended. Thank you."

The patrons were agitated and terrified, sweating and sweltering with fright and fret. Impulsively, Perry Jackson put a quarter in the pay phone. "Any publicity is good publicity," he thought to himself as he reported the news to the State News agency. Rawley was incited by the turn of events. He gave Wanda his car keys and instructed her to gather his grandchildren and slip out the back door. "Get the kids home."

Fern was outraged with the Deputy's premature dispatch. She intended to speak her mind to Sheriff Keith about it when he arrived. "Why is this rookie in charge of *anything*?" Fern exclaimed to Dean. "Everything he said was so damned contrived!"

Sheriff Boswell arrived. He was immediately briefed by Deputy Hudson and the Kilbrides. He took their statements and anyone else in the HUB who might have seen or heard anything. All their statements seemed to implicate Marcus Kilbride.

Fern stepped to his side. "Keith, Marcus can be a moron, but he isn't capable of killing anybody!"

"Dammit, Fern!" Sheriff Boswell began, "I've seen a lot of things I thought human beings weren't capable of. At this point, I don't know anything for sure. All I do know is Marcus has disappeared…may be on the run! He ain't above suspicion just 'cause he's a Kilbride! I've seen kin around here do desperate, unspeakable things. Marcus ain't any immune from noth'in. The country folk are scared. When that happens? They're call'in for a *reckoning*. They want it NOW! This ain't like run'in shine or shoot'in a neighbor's dog! What I saw on that mountain was heinous. I WILL find Marcus eventually.Now…do you all want to tell me where he is?"

Rawley answered for the rest of the clan, "We don't know, Keith. He can't drive the truck. If he's out there at all, he's probably hiding in a cave or on the run. Believe me, my friend, we all want to find Marcus!"

Boswell quickly retrieved his radio and dispatched an APB to the State Troopers: "Track down Marcus Kilbride for suspicion of murder. He's on foot or in hiding.Knows the mountains. Check the caves. Description:mid-twenties, stringy red hair, maybe a beard. Stocky built. I've not known him to be dangerous, but proceed with caution. If meth is involved, who knows? I'm headed out to patrol 'round town. Then, up to the old county highway. Alert me first when you find him. REPEAT: I want to be there when you find him!"

There were out-of-towners who fled the festival. But as the bulk of the storm subsided and the presence of the Troopers made known, the fear waned. The braver bystanders were content to wait out the storm, observe the police action around them, and continue their

Festival frolic. For the locals, the danger of a murder suspect was minimal. They had known feuds between clans before. If you didn't get in the way of gunfire or take sides, you would be fine. For most who lived in Timberline County, this was regarded as just another drug deal gone bad or some domestic dispute. It had nothing to do with them or the festival. Besides, if the State Troopers were in pursuit of the suspect, there was, in their festive folly, nothing to fear. For a few bystanders, Casper Jaspers reached his inevitable end.

*

Marcus knew by-ways and backroads well enough to elude State Patrol cars. He took to the wooded paths to reach his sanctuary: a misbegotten storage shed camouflaged by dean vines and piles of debris. It was secretly provided for Marcus by his cousin, Emmanuel. Marcus arrived at the shed, creaked open the door, and carefully stepped inside. Out of the backpack of provisions, Emmanuel had gathered for him, he took a match and lit a small coal oil lantern that sat on a nearby crate. The wick was extended, so when he lit it, its flame took fast and lit the room quickly and brightly.

"Marcus!" whispered a voice. It was Emmanuel, sitting in a broken lounge chair with his knees crossed in front of him like a sage in the Himalayas. He was wet to the bone and still in the devilishly red long johns from the festival dunking booth.

Marcus was startled and gave out a yawp.

"Quiet!" Emmanuel frowned, "Mom doesn't know you're here." Marcus was given this shelter from Emmanuel to help him in his quest for *justice*. The posse of patrolmen would certainly keep watch for Marcus at his mother's home. None would imagine he would find a sheltering hand within the hallowed perimeter of Sister Dazzlingstar.

Marcus sighed in relief, "Manny."

Emmanuel stood up and handed his cousin a bread-and-butter sandwich wrapped in foil and a thermos of hot chicken soup. "Here," he said, "You need the soup. Momma made it for friends in need."

Marcus opened the thermos and guzzled down the soup. "Thanks, Manny. You're a good friend."

"'A friend lays down his life for a friend.'" Emmanuel recited. "Or just give him a bread-and-butter sandwich and some Campbell's chicken soup."

Marcus bit into the sandwich. He looked at Emmanuel, staring at the sandwich, "Here." Marcus tore the sandwich in two, "take half." Then he offeredthe thermos of soup to him. "You take the first swig." Marcus insisted.

Emmanuel nibbled at the bread and then took a sip of the warm soup.He looked up at Marcus as if tasting bread and soup for the first time.

"They're after you, the guards," Emmanuel murmured. "What are you doing to do?"

"Find the guy who killed Casper." he answered. "I'll keep after him 'til I fix all this."

"Who is he? How ya gonna know when you find him?"

"'Cause he's stalk'in me too. I just have to let him find me…and be ready." I've seen him on the service road, but I don't know who he is."

"Does God know who he is?"

Marcus shrugged. His cousin's question didn't matter.

Emmanuel replied, "God can fix all this."

"Wonder why He ain't fixed anything yet, Manny?"

"Don't know. Mom knows. But there's a lot of questions, ain't there?"

Marcus nodded, sipped from the thermos, and handed it again to Manny.

Emmanuel took a longer sip then continued, "I ask Sister Dazzlingstar, but sometimes she doesn't answer me. But when she does, she's powerful sure."

"Uh huh."

"She talks a lot 'bout Heaven…I think it's 'cause she's get'in closer to it."

"Maybe."

"I asked her why God put us here if we're go'in to Heaven anyway? Seems like the long way 'round to me. And why did He give ever-body life when he just takes it back? And why do we learn more when we get old, 'cause we then, when we know it, we just die? After we know more, we live less."

Marcus grinned. "Sometimes God don't make natural sense."

Suddenly, Emmanuel caught himself in mid-inquiry, "I'm sorry to Jesus. I don't mean to be *blasphemious*. (I know the right word, I just can't spell it.) Anyway, I think sometimes we can ask God questions, and it don't make Him mad."

"It's okay, Manny." Marcus assured him, "We're in the shed. We're safe here."

Manny nodded.He handed the empty thermos back to Marcus.

"EMMANUEL!" Grace called from her back door, "EMMANUEL! YOU OUT THERE?"

Emmanuel leaped to the floor and scrambled to the outside of the shed. He closed the door carefully behind him. "YES Momma! I'm out here by myself!"

She drew nearer the shed. "What are you hanker'in 'round in the shed for? The storm stopped. We gotta get back to the booth!"

"I'm com'in!" Manny yelled back.

"Go ahead, Manny." Marcus whispered, "I'll be fine."

" EMMANUEL!" Grace yelled.

Emmanuel ran in his red-devil long johns toward the house. Customers were waiting, primed at their Dazzlingstar Festival booth, ready to "Dunk the Devil."

*

Earlier in the afternoon, *Roadkill* fled their gig, leaving an empty stage for the evening festivities. Although the festival had been dampened by the storm and the scuttlebutt, there were still customers who remained and demanded to be titillated for their dollars. With *Roadkill* gone, Dolly phoned Hank to step up to the crisis. She instructed him to retrieve Marcus's guitar at Eva's house. "You're play'in your songs tonight. Get that guitar! Get here, now!" Dolly hung up the phone before her nephew had any chance to argue.

*

Friday night at the HUB.

The HUB is filled mostly with local patrons, including the Kilbride clan. Some who came to hear *Roadkill* were disappointed but remained to hear what the local kid had to sing. They didn't expect too much more than a good chuckle or, at most, polite applause out of devotion to one of their own.

Hank did as Dolly instructed. He retrieved Marcus's guitar and dressed himself simply in a faded tee shirt and blue jeans. That evening, he pulled a stool to centerstage and sat behind one lone microphone on a wobbly bandstand. A spotlight caressed his frame as he wrangled the guitar strap tightly around his shoulders. The leather strap was engraved: *"Emporium."*

"Sing yer songs...HENRY!" Dolly yelled from the bar.

At that, the audience politely applauded.

Hank began his set. It was a soothing departure from the frenzy of *Roadkill*. Somehow, the folksy tunes *Henry* Jackson performed lulled the crowd to a romantic sigh from the fray of the day. Hank offered a presence with his music. It was not a performance of testosterone like his older brother, but a simple troubadour unveiling his soul in the glow of one lovely spotlight. After he sang a few satisfactory tunes, it was when he sang his *"Ode to a Singer"* that he floated adrift away from the stage. Somehow, he was singing to angels, not an audience. He dedicated the moment to anyone who ached for someone to hear his song:

"It's raining on the streets of nowhere
From the barrooms to Music Row
With tears of the singers who never arrived
Before they had to go back home.
Behind the hard licks in lounges
In a shadowy band
Stands a singer anonymously known
Out of reach is the spotlight of somebody else,
He keeps looking for a light of his own.
(Chorus) Here's a song for the singer
Who never arrived
Who's heart's been long'in too long
In'spite of midnight rejections
Just string'in him on
He will never abandon his song.
Fumbl'in with chords in smokey old rooms
And dream'in of steal'in the show
Kissing up to roadies, and camping in bars
Meeting has-beens he never will know.

214

Just the Good Lord and he, an old Gibson makes three
The star-path to heaven unknown
Tread'in demos, bussing tables,
Pray'in to God when he's able
While Mamaw's faith still burns bright back home.
Yeah, here's a song for the singer
Who never arrived
Who's heart's been long'in too long
In'spite of midnight rejections
Just string'n him on
He will never abandon his song...
No, he will never abandon his song."

Hank finished the last chord. He tilted his head low. There was ample and lively response, but he didn't care so much about hearing the applause. He just hoped the heart of his song had been heard.

*

It was Leah McCreary with whom Marcus Kilbride imagined his escape from Timberline County. As a child, Jesus may have saved his soul, but it was Leah McCreary who saved his sensibilities. Many times, Marcus pleaded with her to explore the West with him. But her devotion to her father, Dr. McCreary, with *his* devotion to the clans in Timberline County, precluded any impulsive invitation from Marcus Kilbride.

It was after midnight. But he had to see Leah one more time. The night of the storm, he stood in the rain, in the garden of her father's home. As was his custom, he selected tiny pebbles in the garden outside her bedroom window and tossed them gently at the pane. After being away for so long, "Would she remember?" he thought to himself. Suddenly, she appeared at her window. A bit startled by the once-familiar sight, she motioned him to wait.

The rain became a soft mist. The garden was untidy. All their leaves had fallen. Flowers had gone to seed.Sullen wisteria and

215

honeysuckle vines were bending low about a small gazebo wherein Marcus found shelter. One thinly lit porch lantern illumined the gazebo. From their baptisms, the two had owned a devotion to God and one another. Here, in her garden, they would meet—whenever Marcus had a mind to see her. She never turned him away.But after Marcus became more and more devoted to the Emporium, and without her compliance to escape Timberline County, Leah saw less and less of Marcus.

Leah came through the door.Her brownish hair sparkled with raindrops.She wore her father's raincoat over wool pajamas. On her feet were socks covered by rubber slippers. She wasted no time to reach Marcus in the gazebo. "What are you doing here? It's almost midnight, for God's sake."

"…had to talk to you…don't know why." he muttered, "…had to see you."

"What's happened to you, Marc? I've heard terrible things."

"Leah. I need *you* to know I didn't do what they're say'in."

"I know that!' she insisted. "But that's all I know. What else do you want to tell me?"

Marcus shrugged and looked away.

Leah grew agitated. "You need to tell the truth to somebody. My father? The Sheriff? ME? Quit this stupid running around and tell me the truth!"

"I don't know what the truth is anymore."

"Yes, you do! You just run from it all the time! God is the truth! You are the truth! I am the truth! You accepted that once. Remember? That's what our baptisms were all about."

"I think I must have gotten a defective baptism. Don't think I believe it anymore."

She took a step to him and looked at Marcus in the dim light."Why are you here, Marc?" she asked. "What do you want from me?"

Marcus reached his fingers to her and brushed drops of rain from her brow.He smiled. "I just want you to know," he gasped, "that I always…wanted *to run awa… with you.*"

"I know that."

"No, I mean, really. More than *run away…FLY away.*"

"Yes, you told me that a long time ago. I didn't understand it then, and I don't know. That's old news, Marc. This is my home. I was always here. Where were you? OUT THERE somewhere! Always OUT THERE!"

He nodded and stepped off the gazebo.

"NO! You got me out of bed in the pouring rain to tell me something. So, tell me. Talk to me, Marcus!"

"I always wanted to just … fly…away with you, Leah. Out of Timberline County." He stopped for a moment. She stared at him as if he was "high" already. "I'm not drunk. I'm just think'in 'bout you. I ruined ever-thang 'tween you and me. I just want… to fix…US…somehow… before anything else happens…I'm sorry, Leah."

He wasn't sure if it was the rain or tears dripping down her face.He picked up his backpack and started down the steps again. She held his arm, pulled him to her, and kissed him on the cheek. "Marc, I don't know what this is all about. But you have never *ruined* my love for you. You never believed that anyone really loved you, even me. I hope someday you can believe…*know* that someone *really does* love you, Marcus."

Marcus nodded and stepped away, silently—reverently, as if leaving behind some sort of sacred ground. Leah watched him disappear into the soft mist of midnight.

*

In the shadows and the furor of the Festival, the shadow man lurked unnoticed. He peered and poked about as a predator in pursuit of his prey, with a deep, foreboding snarl of vengeance. He kept mostly to the alleyways. He kept his head low, his meandering eyes concealed behind a ratty profusion of thick black hair. He was the stick figure—a dot on a graph—anonymous, unnoticed, and unaccounted for.As the night progressed, he could only think of Marcus. His stomach burned in anticipation.He moved stealthily, slithering without pomp but much circumstance.

He was assumed by tourists to be one of the Appalachian *unfortunates*, a poverty-stricken sluggard. He risked being seen at the festival for the sake of shadowing Marcus, but the festival was in his DNA. He had rarely missed the Timberline event. He wouldn't miss the merriment, even if he stayed secluded in the alleyways to do it.Every now and then, when something caught his sight, he lingered—lending an ear to the laughter and play. He saw young boys rambling on with Country Boy Clem, smaller children were bouncing in the inflatables, and one girl was even riding on the back of a mule that was circling the sorghum press. He stopped tentatively at the storefront window of a dress boutique. Inside, he saw a pre-teen girl shopping for dresses. The sights nearly made him forget about Marcus, but as the storm arose, so did a resurgence of his holler law.

The storm had pelted him. His filthy flannel shirt was drenched and soaked him, cold to the bone. He moaned that, for some Divine reason, it fell steadily only on him. That night, he searched the alleyways for refuge. He was lured by the rancor of the crowd and the band at the HUB. There was his refuge for the night. He climbed into the dumpster, closed the lid, and snuggled beneath discarded trash bags, layers of cardboard, and broken bottles. A small mouse scampered across his leg. He grabbed it sternly. "I'll call you Marcus." It squealed in the man's tightening grip--until it stopped. Then he tossed it aside. He would continue his search again before daylight. For the moment, the shadow man was content.

Chapter Ten:
The Day Before Sunday

The Outings

"These mountaineers are rugged people…"(Governor Albert B. "Happy" Chandler, Autobiography, 1989)

Saturday.

Dawn. Marcus crawled out from the mildewy sleeping bag Emmanuel had provided for him. He sorted the provisions from his backpack. Dolly was quite resourceful with the supplies he needed: a canteen, a flashlight, a compass, a knife, rope, a tarp, matches, several packs of jerky, and a small woolen blanket. He reviewed the items in front of him on the floor of the shed. He noticed the backpack was bulging on one side. From an accessory pocket, he pulled a revolver with a note attached: "Thinking of you. Love, Dolly."

He hoisted the pack of essentials over his shoulders and creaked open the door of the shed. The morning was damp, cold, and murky. Relentlessly, he set forth to begin the search for his stalker at the top of the ridge, the God-rock, from where his troubles began. The air was filled with the aroma of coal-burning stoves. Smoky residue flew in the breeze like tiny darksome fairies. He rambled out away from the shed, scaling up and down the hollers. His own fortitude for *fixing things* through holler-law overcame his fear. His Momma's faith that "all things will be well…eventually" kept him moving forward and upward.Dolly's provision in the pouch of his backpack reminded him of young David's stone-in-the-sling when he faced Goliath. He had confronted Goliaths before and cowered before them. This time, he would prevail. He would fix this; all things would be well—for if necessary, like the shepherd boy in the Bible, he could not hesitate to *cast the stone.*

*

The Appalachian Festival Parade began at 9 am with a rendition of *'O say can you see'* sung by Sandy Alcorn, the McGuffey High School Homecoming Queen. She was followed in the program by Mayor James T. Cunning's introduction of the Grand Marshall, Country Boy Clem. (Clem, whose real name was Clarence Clemson, was born and bred in Newark, New Jersey. He was only marketed as kin from Stinking Creek, Tennessee, to fit his image.) He became a folk hero in Timberline County when he retained his *Smoky Mountain Wrestling Championship* belt by defeating the Iranian Sheik in the best out of two falls. The two unlikely dignitaries climbed aboard the back of an ornated open-bed pickup truck that led the parade down Main Street, waving to the crowd that lined the sidewalks along the festive thoroughfare.

Convertibles from Philip Hayne's Budget Used Cars taxied county shakers and shuckers who were strategically interspersed within the lineup. Presley Jackson drove his father down Main Street in a hot-red convertible. Perry Jackson reclined in the backseat, waving to every individual he could make eye contact with and tossing candy to the kids. The senior embalmer and funeral director, Rosalee Wiley drove a hearse adorned with tissue paper lilies and a banner with the slogan, "Dignified Departures."

There were floats and flat-bed clunkers hauling bluegrass combos and cloggers-on-trailers. The school bands paved their way wearing high-featured crowns, in-tempo with the bass drums, and in-time with the bombastic brass. Girls in scanty garb waved their pom-poms at the crown, did somersaults, and led patriotic cheers. The "princess darlings" from Norma Nobel's School of Dance pirouetted down the street dressed in Halloween leotards and tutus, twirling about like ghosts and goblins.

Horse-drawn carriages clip-clopped down Main Street, followed by riders on palominos and quarter horses. The horses were immediately followed by a couple of hapless volunteers with shovels. Tractors from great-great grandpa's era meandered down the festive lane. Truck-drawn floats intermingled in the flow to catch the attention of the crowd. Baptists, Methodists, Presbyterian, and non-descript denominations constructed ornate mobile sanctuaries and rode aboard them singing hymns. McGuffey High School football and basketball athletes caused an uproar of cheering from the spectators as their float passed by along the way.

Everyone applauded for the float carrying their VFW veterans. Those war heroes who still could march triumphantly in full uniform beside their float, waving the colors for which so many from Timberline gave their lives. The County Fife and Drum Corp followed behind, pitching well the high notes of the fifes with the heartbeat of the drums.

The finale of the parade came with the Timberline County Fire and Rescue Vehicle. The squad of volunteers was cheered for being a constant presence—especially during mining emergencies, ecological crises, and domestic disputes. The TCFRV was an expensive investment, but it represented and proved to be a vessel of hope in the hollers.

*

The manhunt for her son took its toll on Eva Kilbride. Hastily, she called her clan together. Her heart was ready to implode. She had allowed the rumors and accusations to go on too long. Aidan Kilbride would never have allowed all of this "damnable talk" about Marcus, especially outside his household. She evoked his name in calling all her brood to the house. After the parade had scattered, all arrived for their reckonings: Fern and Dean, Rawley, Wanda and her children, Dorothy and Perry, Presley, Hank, and Dolly.

Eva dismissed Wanda's children to play outside. Denise and Dusty, Donny, Donna, and Dara were delighted to oblige their Great Mamaw's command. It was an unusually warm Autumn afternoon, so the children were happy to strip to their wading shorts and run to a channel of Fallen Timber Creek. As they scurried passed Eva, she warned them, "Watch fer snakes!" as they scampered to the Creek.

Eva's offspring sat in the living room, staring at one another. In a maternal huff, Eva sat on the edge of her recliner. She would not recline. She eyed each one sternly as if taking inventory of each one's Kilbride legacy.

Fern broke the silence, "Do you want some tea, Momma?"

"No!" Eva snapped, "I don't want no damned tea!"

Perry subtly glanced at his watch, "The station can't be on auto too long."

Eva spoke up again, "Perry, darl'in, I can say I want to say to *you* first, then you can get right out that door!"

Before Perry could spark a word, Eva continued. "You ain't nobody in *this* house but little Perry Jackson. The little snot kid I've known since you were born! You ain't no big radio star or government high-'n- mighty! You shit like ever'body else in this county! You married my Dorothy, and dad died of my grandsons. You got yerself big do'ins and such. That's fine, you always were a big shot. But if you think you can get somewhere by...criminiz'in Marcus, you're gonna reckon with ME! I want your bad-mouth'in stopped! You might be a high government man but ain't my boy's judge and jury; you ain't noth'in but a damned, conniv'in carpetbagger!"

She inhaled a breath, still glaring at him eye-to-eye. Then she demurred. "You can go now, Perry. Go get elected or erected or whatever you're gonna do with yerself!" Perry was a bit aghast, but he politely nodded, tried to grin, and then slipped out the back door.

Those who remained in the room were stunned. They were blinking, wide-eyed at each other. Eva never lost eyeshots of any of them. Fern was sure her mother was having a seizure or a fit of dementia. Rawley thought she was suffering from some dose of under or over-medication. Dorothy was completely dumbfounded and sat an inch or two in front of her boys, Hank and Presley, shielding them from any fallout. Dolly braced herself. She hungered for a cigarette, but she wouldn't risk any impulsive movement. She knew what had been bubbling inside her mother was about to *spew* out upon them all.

Rawley asked, "Momma? Are you alright? I'm worried about you."

"Fine." Eva glared at him, "Let's put aside your worry'in, Rawley. Are you yer *brother's keeper*?" She paused for an answer. Rawley shrugged off the question. "Are you?"

He didn't answer.

"Well, you ain't been so far, Rawley! You've been noth'in but yer brother's pain-in-the-ass for years. Now, you got 'im hogtied and hung 'fore you know anything 'bout anything!"

"Momma, he wrecked Daddy's truck!" Rawley argued, "God knows what else he's done. He's violated the law! May have even killed a man."

"What law, Rawley? YOUR law?" Eva snapped again. "Mr. Big Gold Cuff Links! Do you think you can judge people before they even have a damned chance to defend themselves? YOUR law! *You* don't even measure up to YOUR law! Marcus always flew between the lines of your law, so you swat him away like a gnat! Now you want to squash him underfoot like some slug. Stop it!"

"But Momma…"

"Stop it, Rawley!" she demanded.

Then she twitched her head to Dean. "Dean, I don't know what you're think'in 'bout Marcus. Don't care. All you ever know is what you read in the papers or watch on yer favorite news show. Mostly what you want to agree with anyway. But 'bout Marcus? Do yer homework, Dean 'fore you *think for yerself.*"

"Momma," Fern argued, "Marcus has been a thorn in everybody's flesh all his life. You know that better than anyone. He's *the runt of litter.* Nobody could make sense of him!"

Eva grimaced a glance now at her firstborn. "Well, Lucy-Fern," Eva answered, "What *YOU* don't see is what ever-body has to do to get along with YOU! You're the rude of my litter! *How did Almighty God create ever-thang in creation without consult'in YOU first?* You see ever-thang, even Marcus, through the filter of Fern's close-minded point of view. Believe it or not, you can be a thorn in ever-body's flesh too. Stop it!"

Then she turned on Dorothy. "YOU, my dear Dorothy, need more Kilbride *in you*! Perry Jackson is your husband; he ain't your God! You better speak your Kilbride mind! Your brother is your kin. Perry needs to quite try'in to get votes by castrat'in Marcus! YOU better tell 'im so!"

Dorothy sat motionless. "I love my husband, Momma. I will support him as much as I can."

Eva replied, "Good. You love him, Dorothy... *'Cleeeeeave to the man!'*-- as the Bible says. But likewise, the man's supposed to *cleave* to the woman he's *married*, not to some concubine he's *trained* to do his bidd'in."

Eva then looked directly at Wanda, Presley, and Hank. "I don't know what you all've come to think 'bout your Uncle Marcus. But you better see for yerself. Someday, you may runn'in and need someone to see you too. When it comes reckon'in time, all you got is God and kin."

Fern grimaced. "Momma, you skipped Dolly!"

"Dolly's protect'in Marcus...and hid'in her damned cigarettes in her dresser!" came the answer.

Eva eased back into her chair and leaned her head back with a sigh. "Someth'ins destroy 'in love 'round here. Whatever it is, I want it stopped." They were silent, more in awe of her stature than her words. "Now you all go on--let me be. There's ham in the fridge if you all want any of it. Beans in the pot. Fend for yourselves, I'm tired...tired of ever-one of yew."

Rawley, Dorothy, and Presley followed Fern and Dean into the kitchen. "I guess she told you," Dean remarked under his breath to his disgruntled wife.

Wanda owned none of it. She slighted the kitchen and vigilantly stomped out the back door. She wanted to take a long walk in the woods...alone. Hank was most empathetic with his Mamaw's routing. He had no appetite just then. His thoughts were in a quagmire when thinking about Marcus. He kissed his Mamaw on the forehead, told her he needed space, and so slipped away to join his cousins at the creek.

"Watch for snakes!" she called to Hank. "They're out there! Under the leaves! They hide ever-where... 'specially where you ain't look'in!"

*

"There's an old swimming hole about a half mile away

We used to tell stories, and some of them true...

But they can't remember, and I ain't gonna tell them...

Back when the old homeplace was new." (Tom T. Hall, "The Old Homeplace," 1997)

"Black waters, black waters, run down through my land." (Jean Ritchie, "Black Waters," 1977)

Marcus meandered along a middling trail between the old service road and a distant ravine. He was sure if he re-traced his steps from the wreckage to the edge of the county line, his stalker

226

would find him. It was a treacherous upward climb, negotiating a less-traveled, arduous terrain; steep and rocky. It weighed heavy on his knees upward, then downward with sharp descents that tested his youthful agility.

The thickets, laden with fallen timber, gave him some leverage. Thorn bushes and prickly branches scratched his flesh despite the heavy jacket and blue jeans he wore. He ignored the wounds. He kept thinking about how he would fix everything, make all things new. Afterward, in the afterglow, he would rest in his father's house, in his own quiet room, under his tattered quilt---home. But It was too soon to contemplate the afterglow. He took another deep breath and adjusted his backpack. Another steep climb was just ahead of him.

"Everything works together for good…eventually," Marcus repeated. But somehow, her words grew faint. This was *his* journey. This was a journey he had to map with his own faith, not his momma's. It was time he faced the reckon'in in the hollers with his own beliefs-- perhaps even in a God who was more realistic than the One in whom he had been proselytized to believe. That God of his childhood had disappeared with both a disillusionment and an awakening. That god became irrelevant and impudent. Now, in the soul he hoped was still there, Marcus strangely experienced a blossoming belief in a better God, a *real One,* whom he could trust with his life… and hopefully, his death.

After three hours or so, he crossed over the Timberline County line. It was near where he had once seen the stranger with the knife. He traveled so far, that the surroundings were unfamiliar. He had never been this far before. The rough terrain dissipated to a well-trodden path ahead of him. He smelled the aroma of the encampment before he saw its smoke rising, commingling with the falling leaves. He quickened his pace carefully so as not to attract anyone to his approach. A slab of meat was roasting on a spit over a primitive campfire. Its alluring aroma was peaty and raw, tantalizing Marcus' appetite. Impulsively, he hastened his pace toward the scent. Still a distance away, the smoke grew dense and burned his eyes. Carefully, he unzipped the hidden pocket of his backpack and tip-toed forward toward the encampment.

The campfire was burning low just outside the mouth of a cavern. It was a secluded settlement, a makeshift residence, hewn upon a cliff overlooking a sharp slope of jagged rock and a swift channel of whitewater rushing far below. As the mist from the stream swirled high to the top of the cliff, every now and then, as sunlight pierced through the trees, mystical rainbow clouds appeared and disappeared in the air encircling the cavern. Marcus drew closer to the fire. Suddenly, a stranger (more a *stickman*) emerged from the cave. Marcus was stunned by the man's ghastly appearance. The man was taller than Marcus. His clothes were drab and hanging loosely on him. His bare feet were grimy, with mud caked between his toes. He was emaciated, pale as to be nearly translucent. He waved claw-like fingers at Marcus, then slithered methodically closer and closer to his visitor.

"Marcussss Kilbride." Hissed the stranger, "Come to share of my bounty?" he inquired.

Marcus stood his ground. He held firmly to the backpack. "Who are you?" he asked.

"Come closer." the stickman replied. He tried to smile, but he found it a difficult thing to do. He had obviously not smiled for a long time. His lips cracked in the effort, and his rancid teeth smeared with blood.

Then, the stickman came out of the shadows into sight. He looked more like a brittle skeleton than a brutal stalker. He sauntered confidently out of his cavern and sat on a tree stump near the smoldering fire. With his long-honed fingernails, he poked at the lump of meat hovering over the spit. The fear in Marcus waned in mounting curiosity. Marcus cautiously accepted the stick man's invitation to "come closer."

Marcus drew near. The entity's appearance was of nightmarish proportions. His eyes were wide and dull, illumined only by the blaze in front of him. He peered up at Marcus through a dense mass of hair and offered him a bloody grin. What teeth he had were like random stalactites, fangs of solidified residue, dangling, seeping moisture from his gums. His sporadic beard could not cover his distorted face. He looked old, but there was no gray in his thick black hair. He trembled as if perpetually chilled to the bone. He squinted as Marcus, then reached forward, picked off a scab of meat, and beckoned it to his guest.

"Come on, Marcus." He beckoned.

Marcus refused the man's cuisine."Who the hell are you?" he demanded.

The shadowy stickman impulsively leaned into a slight beam of sunlight that revealed his face. When he tilted his head slightly and looked up at Marcus, he made himself known. Marcus knew him now, but only as a facsimile of his former self.

"Bucky?"Marcus's stared incredulously, "Bucky Sorley?"

Bucky nodded."OOOOO!"He waved and wafted his elongated fingers at his quarry. "Yew thinks you've seen a ghost, huh, Cousin Markie?" He jabbed his finger deep into the meat and thrust out a fatty sliver. It held it in front of them, turning it around like it was still on the spit. It dripped with grease down his filthy hand. He looked at the sliver with a lowered brow. "It's a bunny, I think. An innocent, little bunny that tried to cross the road. After a while, all roadkill looks alike." he looked up at Marcus and grinned, "Come on!" he giggled and hissed at the same time, "I really didn't scrape it off the road! Don't be sssstupid."

Marcus recoiled and took a step back.

"Nah?" Bucky erupted, "not to your taste?"

Bucky stuffed the sliver of fat into his mouth and chewed and chewed some more until he realized it was not to be consumed. Then he grabbed the rest of the carcass by the spit and flung it over the edge of the precipice.Bucky watched as it splattered on the rocks below.He looked back at Marcus and chuckled, "Hummm" he concluded, "it *was* roadkill. But it was *rare roadkill*. I prefer medium raw." He grinned with a snarl.

Marcus watched without speaking. Bucky paced back and forth between mania and melancholy in front of him. At once, Bucky boldly preached his convictions about wickedness in the world, then after a pause, he calmly whispered in solemn contemplation of the majesty of the universe. Then, he exploded in a catharsis regarding all the injustices that bedeviled him. The overlook of his settlement became his natural pulpit.

"Do you sleep?" he asked Marcus, but he didn't wait for an answer. "I don't. People waste lifetime sleep'in. I've overcome sleep… found a solution to life: don't sleep. You get more lifetime if you don't sleep. Do you sleep?"

"Yes." Marcus replied.

"I know you do! I've seen you sleep'in! I watched you sleep'in!You miss a lot that goes on 'round you when you sleep. I was gonna wake you once. But I didn't. I don't sleep. You sleep, but Marcus, I see more than you!" Then he growled, "I *know* more than you!"

"What do you *know,* Bucky?" Marcus inquired in a sarcastic tone. His stomach was nauseous, and his knees trembled. He fondled the pocket of his backpack.

Bucky twitched his eyes back at Marcus. "I know there ain't no gold cannon!" he began. "What else do I know? I know how to cook stuff and send it off with you and Casper. I know you and Casper've been cheat'in me from what was owed me. Let me see, what else do I know? From now to backwards, here's what I know, Marcus Kilbride, that you DON'T know: I know you got a gun in yer pack. I know you thought you were safe in Ricky Retardo's shed. I know nobody knew I was sleep'in in the dumpster behind the Hub. I know you cried like a damned baby when you ran 'way from Leah McCreary last night…I know your Momma talks in her sleep. You think I don't know anythang, but it's YOU who don't know anything, Marcus Kilbride!"

His eyes widened to a deeper red. His gestures more erratic. "Shit me hell-fire, Marcus! I knowed all the time you was in your daddy's truck that night. That's why I flung it over the edge.I knowed it was you! But you never knowed it was *me!*

Ever-body cheated me! There was no damned gold cannon like Casper promised. Spent my lifetime looking for a cannon made of gold! But I did find someth'in better. Silver crystals more damned precious than gold. And you assholes would take it away from me. You sold me out for your own cut. So, here I am. I found my gold with true friends. Friends I can trust. This is what I am now. THEY helped me find my way."

Marcus slowly inched his hand into the backpack.

Bucky erupted again, his eyes swirling menacingly at his prey. "I'm run'in too, Marcus! I purify the stuff! I fire it pure! All you did was run the damned truck! But I made it! I pured it up! You sold me out down the road, Marcus! You and Casper did this to me! But my true friends offer a rightful cut. Like you said, you're 'done.'"

Tears were dripping down his crimson face. "You cheated me out of my rightful portion. You ain't treated me fair! But I know better now. Me and my new friends, we all know better."

Bucky stopped short his tantrum and rousted matter-of-factly, "Jaspers cheated me. So, I cut *HIM*…and cut him…and cut him. It was the right thing to do. Cut my losses."

Bucky bolted at Marcus with his hunting knife, crisscrossing the space between them with the jagged edge, wielding the blade wildly like some maniacal warrior. Marcus retreated along the ledge of the precipice and scrambled for the gun, but it was lodged inside the walls of the backpack. He struggled to loosen it from the pocket. Bucky lunged at him again and again, poking at Marcus's belly with the tip of the blade, then sweeping it erratically back and forth. Marcus dodged his advances, thinking the emaciated man would tire. But with every sweep of his knife, Bucky became more invigorated, drifting closer and closer to his prey.

Suddenly, Bucky stopped and caught his breath.

"Oh!" Bucky exhaled with a grisley smile, "And I knowed you would come here. Do YOU want to know *how*?"

Marcus was silent, still subtlety grappling with his backpack for Dolly's gun.

"WANDA! She was my *angel!* Just like the rock says, *'God visits for sin.'* 'Course it is *your* sin. God brought her to me so I could visit *your* sin."

Bucky pricked his thumb on the point of the knife. He began to bleed. He put the knife in his other hand and rubbed the spurt of blood between his wounded thumb and his index finger.

"I apologized to her for mess'in up things 'tween us and the kids. She forgave me. I told her I couldn't find the cannon. I follered the map Jaspers sold me. But all I found was bats and copperheads, coons and possums, bears scratch'ins on trees. I learnt to live with 'em all. Gave me a kind of peace in the wilderness. I even pissed on things to mark off my turf. You can live with things if you don't tromp on their turf, Marcus. Wanda wants the gold now too."

Bucky jolted the knife at Marcus again. This time, it punctured deep into his side.

Bolstered by a rush of self-preservation, Marcus managed to pull the trigger inside the backpack. It fired. The bullet grazed the shadow man's chest. Bucky's body jolted back and forth, shaking in an unrelenting seizure of giggles. He wouldn't believe *Uncle* Marcus would shoot him.

Bucky's giggling accelerated into uncontrollably maniacal guffaws! He threw his hands up over his head, twirling about like a crazed dancer until he dizzied himself. Suddenly, lost in his frenzy, he leaned backward and over the edge of the cliff, descending, flapping his outstretched arms into the open air. Down—down—down he plummeted, erratically twisting and turning; his head and body were thrashed by jagged protrusions of rock and roots until the shadow man finally met his fate, battered and broken in the unrelenting tributary below.

Marcus pulled the gun from the backpack. He peered over the edge of the cliff.All he could see was a ravaged deformation of flesh, fetal-like, shrouded in a reddish ooze, undulating in the current, flailing his arms from the rocks. Marcus seemed out of his own body, hovering over a scene as surreal as a sudden apocalypse.

He had little time to think. The wound on his side was severe. He took the First Aid Kit from the backpack and grabbed all the gauze and ace bandages he could find. He took off his shirt, stuffed the gauze into the wound, and stretched the bandage around it. Then he wrapped his shirt tightly around the bandage and tied it with the sleeves.

He fell to his knees. From the depths of him, Marcus unleashed a primal wail!His outcry was so emboldened, reverberating, it resounded between the gates of heaven and the threshold of hell. With one hand fisted to the sky and the other holding his bleeding side, he lifted his eyes and howled in agony. The bitter cries went on until fatigue overwhelmed him.Marcus unclenched his fists and opened his palms. With his bloodstained fingers outstretched to the sky, he pleaded for whatsoever Holiness or Heinousness there may be to usher him home.

*

"The water coming down Yellow Creek out of the mines will eat the fenders of your truck. What do you figure it will do to your belly?" (James Still, The Wolfpen Notebooks, 1991.)

The primary source of Fallen Timber Creek emerges from a pristine underground spring. It flows through a narrow mountain ravine. Its current trickled unceasingly under the crimson and yellowish-brown Autumn foliage. The channels wide and narrow throughout the region were usually surging with its sustainability for creation and re-creation. To abide alongside or near its banks was a multi-sensory delight; its dance, never the same choreography; the fragrance of the seasons carried aloft with the breeze; the melodious sound of its rippling, resonating refrain; the taste of the edibles it nourishes along its way; and, as one wades into its depths, its swirling caress which soothes the soul and detoxes the flesh.

The runoff from the roads high above the natural streams often cascaded down from the mountains and mingled with the fountains of numerous underground springs. When the heavy storms came, the tranquil trickling became a devastating intermingling of the streams with an onslaught of runoff, waste rock from the coal camps, and the erosion of saturated, acidic soil. But by the time the pristine stream reached the channel of Fallen Timber Creek, the water had become tainted by the sooty runoff from the strip-mining operation further up the mountain. What was once pure by natural standards had become poisoned by the primitive regulations of industry.

When the outcries of the clans in the hollers were finally heard about the inclement effects of the mining economy on their water, most to whom they pleaded just termed it an "act of God" and deferred any solutions to Him.

"With any new infrastructure, like new roads, there is always a risk of harm," remarked Mayor James T. Cunning. "But the payoff is worth the harm or the inconveniences it may cause. Realistically, the benefits to our economy in Timberline County make it a Godsend and charm'in."

*

Wanda's children were delighted to have been freed from the chatter of their elders. They raced through the harvested field, through the woods toward Kilbride's *sacred space*—a swimming hole adjacent to a channel of Fallen Timber Creek. Although there was no well-defined path, Denise and Dusty knew-by-heart the route to their glorious destination: a deep reservoir fed by the endless palpitations of an uncharted underground spring. The secluded pool was shrouded in a kaleidoscope of amber-brown and various shades of olive green. The sun trickled through the remaining autumn leaves of birch and oak. The pines enveloped the bank around them, still holding firm the needles on their limbs to conceal this haven of innocence and frolicsome play.

Saturday afternoon. Wanda's children didn't care about any clan rules. They reached the stream and unashamedly forsook any proscribed garb that was unnecessary for the occasion. Dusty was the first to leap into the pond. Clad in only his undershorts, he treads the bubbling water, swishing and swaying as the undertow tickled his toes. Denise was content to wade only to her knees. She waded to a floating mass of residue a few feet away. She thought perhaps the black-speckled, yellow foam a-top the water might have a natural mineral property, like she had seen in tv commercials: *good for her adolescent complexion.* She dipped her fingertips in the mixture and spread it gently over her face. Donna held little Dara close to her side. They stepped cautiously from the bank to the edge of the stream. They sat with their toes in the water. Donny followed Dusty's lead. He catapulted himself into the pool like an otter that had been grounded for years and was now set free. He floated a while, then kicked his feet erratically, diving deeper into the more fanciful currents of Fallen Timber Creek.

Donna called to Denise from the shore. "It smells yucky!"

"It's the vitamins in the water, Donna!" Denise yelled back. "It's good for your skin!"

Dusty took to the land and climbed up a boulder overlooking the stream. He flexed his thirteen-year-old brawn and yelled, "Watch me!" as he cannonballed into the pool. Donny tried to follow his lead. Instead, he clumsily slipped down the slick, muddy boulder and fell backward into the water. The sloppy dive didn't matter to him. He merely immersed himself under the current again, as if he had planned his own unique "backward flip."

"The water's all black!" Donna called Denise. "The boys are gett'in all yucky."

Dusty rubbed his chest and yelled, "You're stupid, Donna! Just splash around! The black stuff goes away!" He dived into the pool again. When he emerged, he noticed something making its way from the hill, through the thickets, and down to the stream. He climbed out of the stream and atop the boulder for a better view. The "something" (maybe a dog or hog?) was falling, sliding quickly down the slope. The boy reached over the rock and grabbed a long branch that was leaning against the boulder. He could use it for a club or a spear if necessary. He stood up again and held the limb firmly in front of his chest. Like Country Boy Clem, he would not allow the whatsoever-it-was to advance toward Denise or his half-siblings. He was the oldest son; he took his stand on the boulder between the sloping bank and the stream!

Abruptly, the "something" slid uncontrollably down the hillside, tumbling and rolling through the thickets. It was halted by the boulder. Dusty held up his staff and looked over his feet. The "something" was Marcus! He lay wincing in the impact of the fall. His shoulder was out of place again. His face was pale, but his torso was darksome-red. He turned his head upward. His eyes were dim for a moment, widened in recognition of Dusty.

The son of Wanda and Bucky Sorley hovered over him and then leaped off the boulder to his side. Marcus looked up at Dusty. The sight of the boy both comforted and grieved him. His adolescent face and frame were smudged from nose-to-toes with soot from the creek. His once-white briefs were coal-dust gray. Dusty Sorely leaped from the rock and knelt beside Marcus, holding the limb for leverage.

"M-M-Marcus?" Dusty asked.

Marcus nodded. "Give me that stick, Dusty." He gasped. Dusty handed it to him. Marcus grasped the staff, secured it into the mud, and pulled himself up. As he did raise himself, his stricken shoulder lodged back into place. He tried to stand, relying on the staff as a crutch. Mud, blood, dried leaves, and twigs stuck to his chest. Denise and the others were horrified by the sight of the "forest beast" and quickly retreated to the other side of the stream.

"What happened to you?" Dusty frowned, "You smell like a dead possum."

Marcus ignored the boy's critique. He was dizzy, lost in a convoluted labyrinth of puzzled pieces. He limped to the edge of the stream. He looked across to the other side of the stream. There, Marcus saw Wanda's other children, their skin and skivvies blackened by the excess drainage and eroded runoff that infiltrated Fallen Timber Creek from the abandoned strip-mining operation further up the mountain. He had to find a way to ford the stream before he fell unconscious. In his weakened condition, he knew he couldn't swim through the unrelenting current alone.

He looked at Dusty. "You gotta help me get home. I can't swim this…you gotta pull me to the other side."

"How?" asked Dusty.

"I'll float…holding the limb…you swim ahead of me…pull the limb and pull me over." Marcus answered. "You can do this, Dusty."

Dusty stepped off the bank, floating backward into the stream. Marcus removed his boots and socks and waded in. He gasped sharply in the sudden chill of the frigid rushing water. A cloud of crimson oozed from his wound. He held fast to one side of the limb with his hands and floated forward, surrendering himself to the current, relying on the limb and the boy. Dusty grabbed firmly the opposite end of the limb with one hand, floated backward, and then frantically kicked his feet. With his other arm, he pulled and navigated them through the stream, wafting above the undertow to the other side.

Marcus's flesh was aflame with fever but was soothed for the moment in the cold water. Dusty climbed on the bank and then reached for Marcus's hand. When Denise and Donny saw what was happening, they joined their brother as he strained to pull him ashore. Marcus was breathing heavier now. He was exhausted. His knife wound was deep. He looked at the children that surrounded

238

him on the bank, Bucky's children. They surely couldn't carry him the rest of the way home. His "reckon'in time?" Marcus saw the pathway to home just ahead of him, but his stamina left him. He had no strength to finish the journey. Then Hank's hand reached down to Marcus. "Come on, Uncle Marcus," Hank exclaimed. "I'll get you home." Hank put his arms under his uncle's shoulders and lifted him up. Marcus winced with the extreme pain in his torso.

The children rallied around and helped raise Marcus to his feet. Dusty handed the staff to Marcus for leverage, and both Hank and Dusty supported him from under each armpit. Together, they all led him forward to the path toward Mamaw's house. Denise and the others scurried on ahead.

As the girls neared Great Mamaw's house, they ran faster yelling, "We found Uncle Marcus!" Donna and Donny ran through the harvested field, racing each other to see who could bring the news to the back porch first. Little Dara struggled to keep up with them. Denise tripped over a low pile of fodder stalks but caught her footing and raced on behind the other three. But her trip awakened a den of small copperheads underneath. By the time Marcus, Hank, and Dusty reached the field, the young copperheads were prowling, slithering surreptitiously through the disarrayed field.

Marcus was burning with fever. He mumbled erratically about his daddy hoeing the field when "a copperhead bit him." Marcus rambled on and on. "He was a bit real bad. It stuck on his leg …wouldn't let go. He cried all the way to the house. Momma rubbed on the poultice. Have you ever had the poultice, Henry?

Momma had a poultice in the pantry. It was charcoal and lavender oil, marigolds and echinacea oil, and the root of cohosh. Momma said, *'Poultice and prayer stop the poison.'* But it don't. I think the poultice is just another legend, like Daddy. Some things you can't fix…even with the poultice."

Home was in sight. Hank hurried his pace. Dusty tried hard to keep up. Marcus dragged his crutch, limping and swooning, missing steps along their way. The blood was caked on his shirt, the bandage dangling at his side. Hank held him tighter.

"Come on, Uncle Marcus, you have to help me. If you want to live, you've got to cooperate."

In the distance at Eva's house stood the Kilbride clan poised in formation. Rawley and Wanda, Fern and Dean, Dorothy and Presley, Aunt Grace and Emmanuel gathered there.Parked nearby was a patrol car with a red flashing light. Deputy Travis Hudson was in the driver's seat, conversing on the radio. Marcus glanced at them and cringed. He wished he had an ingenuous escape plan, but he knew in his condition, such an attempt would be futile. "The reckoning..." he resigned, "no more run'in, Hank. It's 'bout finished."

"What did you say, Uncle Marcus?" Hank asked, straining to keep him aloft.

"Wish I could fly." Marcus surrendered."Always just wished I could FLY. Ever wish *you* could fly outta here, Henry?"

From the middle of the clan emerged Dolly holding Eva's hand with Leah McCreary beside them.iWhile the clan stood their ground, the three women broke their huddle and rushed toward Marcus. In his swooning state of mind, Marcus envisioned them, angels, crossing o'er a turbulent sea, bidding him to safe harbor, or at least into their arms. He was reminded of the only words he ever memorized from Vacation Bible School: *"Come unto me...I will give you rest."* For the first time in his life, he somehow trusted those words. He was convinced now that "unto *Him*" was the ONLY place in the hollers he could find "rest."

The women were only a few feet away when suddenly Hank lost his grip on Marcus. Hank faltered and fell on the field and yelled in agony. A small, coiled copperhead tagged him! Its fangs stuck, loosened itself to hit the ground, then struck him again! Dusty screamed and ran toward the house. "Snakes!" the boy screamed, "Snakes!"

Marcus eased him away and lifted the staff near where Hank had fallen. "NO MORE!" Marcus screamed. With a rush of adrenaline, he raised the staff and pummeled the serpent—over and over--until it was rendered dormant. Then, with one final thrust, he lifted high the limb, directed the edge of the staff, and sunk into the serpent's head. Marcus scooped up its wobbling body with the stick and flung it far off into the field, away from his nephew. Hank writhed on the ground, holding the sudden incision on his leg. With what strength he could muster, Marcus picked Hank up in his own aching arms and carried him across the field, yelling to the clan, "Help me!" he cried breathlessly, "Help…HIM!"

The clan commenced to action. Eva retreated to Dorothy and ordered her to prepare the poultice. Grace closed her eyes in prayer-- her joints cracked as she bent down to one knee. Rawley waved a gesture, alerting Deputy Hudson from his patrol car. Fern watched for random snakes—to keep the predators at bay while Dean and Presley ran to retrieve Hank. Emmanuel inconspicuously disappeared.

Dolly and Leah ran to Marcus, lifted him up over their shoulders, and guided him across the field. Marcus collapsed, surrendering to their care. Rawley and Hudson stood intransigent between the field and the house. Dolly and Leah noticed them but continued guiding Marcus, diverted on a path *away from them.*

She yelled at the lawmen, "Move out of my way! I'm gett'in him to the hospital!"

They maneuvered themselves to halt the women's advance, but the women ignored them.

"Dolly!" Deputy Hudson demanded, "I have to cuff him!"

241

But she directed her way passed the melodramatic deputy.

"He has to be cuffed, Dolly!" insisted Rawley.

"He's going to the hospital!" she demanded. With Leah's help, she quickened their pace.

"Dolly!" Hudson ordered, "I have to cuff him!"

Leah bolted sharply, "CUFF YOU!" she yelled. "Cuff both of you!"

The lawmen reached to apprehend Marcus from the two women. Then, a van came screeching and squealing into the field. Dust was spreading everywhere. Emmanuel catapulted his mother's "van of salvation" toward the three, with the side door wide open to Marcus, Leah, and Dolly. He stopped the van, and the three climbed inside. Leah embraced Marcus in her arms. Dolly slammed shut the door. Emmanuel turned the van around to the driveway and accelerated away.

Emmanuel was at the wheel. Dolly sat in the front seat. Leah was in the back seat, straddling Marcus's head in her lap, caressing his face with one hand and holding firmly his open wound with the other. Marcus was aware of his circumstances but barely conscious. His breathing grew erratic and strained. He looked up at Leah, and his eyes grew wide in recognition. "Leah?" he whispered. The blood on his side was blackening. "Dusty told me I smelled like a dead possum…Do I smell like a possum to you?"

"You were never a possum, Marcus." Leah smiled with tears in her eyes.

"Marcus?" Dolly called back to him from the front seat, "Are you still with us?"

Marcus moaned, "I don't know, Dolly. Where are you?"

"Shit!" she replied, "I'm taking you to the damned hospital!"

There was silence for a moment. "NO!" Marcus demanded, "I want you to take me somewhere else."

"I'm taking you to the hospital!" Dolly argued. "You ain't run'in anymore!"

"I ain't *run'n* to nowhere." Marcus insisted, then he pleaded, "Dolly, do this for me! It's all done."

He decided he was in no condition to *run* anymore nor face the lawful rights of Hudson or his brother, Rawley. He could barely whisper his demand to his faithful companions. They were conflicted, but there was little time to argue. They agreed to honor his directive.

Emmanuel shifted the van toward the football field at McGuffey High School. The tethered hot air balloon was stationed on the ground with only a short line of patrons. Emmanuel stopped the van just behind the waiting line and carried Marcus in his arms toward the balloon. Dolly and Leah wildly heralded those in line to clear their path. The owner of the rig stood dumbfounded, but Dolly assured him they meant no harm to him or his balloon. When they reached the empty basket, Emmanuel placed Marcus gingerly inside. He was barely breathing. The women climbed in next to him. Dolly waved her signal to Manny. Leah knelt next to Marcus. Emmanuel ran to the owner of the balloon and explained what was happening: "his cousin was dying. He wants to 'fly away before he dies.'" The owner stepped back and allowed Emmanuel to navigate the tether.

Deputy Hudson's raging patrol car screeched around the bend of the school parking lot, ablaze with sirens and strobes.Other State Patrol vehicles followed and encircled the field. When Hudson caught on to what was happening, he alerted all the bystanders to "disperse and stand clear!" Troopers got out of their vehicles. Emmanuel released the tether. The balloon arose!

Deputy Hudson pulled his gun, pointed it at the rising entity, and ordered them to halt. But Dolly pulled the dangling cord to free a surge of fire—and the balloon lifted quickly into the air. "Halt!" ordered Deputy Hudson. Then he ran to Emmanuel. "Pull that thing back down here!"

Emmanuel refused. "That can't be done without help." Manny replied, "That cable is stronger than me. If that fire is burn'in hot, it's gonna go up. I can't pull it down. It's gonna keep on ris'in, Sir."

Not to be outdone, Travis Hudson ran to the State Troopers, calling for their assistance. Six or so officials came to the Deputy's rescue. They surrounded the base and grabbed hold of the cables. They pulled together with all their might, but the thick steal stung their hands in an exasperating tug-of-war. Dolly grew more relentless with fueling the flame. As the tug-of-war continued between the ground and the sky, Marcus was suspended between earth and heaven. All the Troopers could do was to secure the cables that kept it grounded by four heavy clasps stationed precariously in concrete blocks. But even that was a daunting task as long as the rushing fuel and rushing, up-lifting wind grew more dominant.

The Troopers pulled harder. Hudson grew so exasperated that he drew his gun, ready to fire at the balloon. "That'll bring the damned thing down!" he asserted.But at the sight of the Sheriff's patrol car nearing his, he quickly placed his gun back in his holster.

Dolly saw the Deputy's gun and impulsively pulled hard the rope to the fuel one more time. A monstrous surge of fiery hot air jolted the inside of the balloon so abruptly that the Troopers lost their grip on the cables, and the lifelines snapped from their locks.The balloon was torn aloft. It arose without restraint. It glided away from the field with the wild Appalachian breeze. The balloon arose above the town in a drifting westward. Leah managed to raise Marcus safely to see the panoramic purview just over the rim of the basket. The wind navigated their way. Marcus was finally flying!

The October afternoon was cresting, a crescendo of the wonders of Autumn. There was in this skyward realm a silence and the wonder of a soul ascending into serenity. As the balloon drifted over the Festival, the three in the basket could faintly hear an echo of voices on the city square, the interdenominational choir singing in harmony:

"I will arise and go to Jesus

He will embrace me in his arms…"

Marcus was weak, but as the balloon arose, he found a resurgence of strength. He held on to the edge of the basket and to Leah, and he managed to stand. He released his hold on the edge of the basket and raised his hands above his head. Blood was dripping from his outstretched arms, and he set his sights on the horizon.

Marcus Kilbride was aloft, drifting high over mountain peaks and valleys, ridges and ravines, rivers winding through the flatlands and meadows wild and green. He was no longer run'in; he was soaring into a dimension of a sacred space between Earth and the Universe. It was a place he had heard of and never really believed existed. But as his life was fleeting, it became the Greater Reality he had always hoped he would find.

245

Chapter Eleven:
"All will be well…eventually."

"In the arms of my dear Savior

You can rest forever more." (Joseph Hart, 1765)

The Appalachian Celebration continued amidst all the hollering gossip, rumors, innuendos, and blame. The community was at ease that the suspect had been apprehended one way or another. Thus, the festivities continued without interruption or inconvenience.

Presley was a solo hit on Center Stage as the warm-up act for *the Legendary Ladies of the Opry*. But in a last-minute contractual agreement, he was only allowed to sing one song. He did, and that was that. (No talent scouts were present. The only offers he got were propositions from his rambunctious adolescent fans.)

Dorothy was in the audience to cheer on her son. While waiting for his performance, she distributed campaign brochures to the audience. Perry royally presented himself to the crowd, although he was campaigning for an uncontested election.

Fern and Dean decided to lock up their home and take a trip away from all the falderals. They had enough drama and inquisitive phone calls from long-forgotten friends who had heard about their family crisis in the newspapers. They packed their bags and made a getaway to Pigeon Forge, at least until the spectacle of Marcus's escapades subsided.

Rawley had his daddy's truck dislodged from the ravine and delivered to his momma's land. There it rested in a clump of stalks, in a sort of monument to his daddy and a reminder of better days. Wanda worked more hours at the Hub with a plan to purchase her own trailer further up the holler in a more discreet location. Having her own place would care for her children better.She could decorate her own place as she wanted. She could purchase her own furniture and even display any photographs she wanted to hang on her walls, like the 8X10 of Bucky Sorely she had hidden under her bed at her daddy's house. Although her wayward husband had disappeared again, that photograph reminded her that one day, as before, Bucky would return to her for good and with their fortune.

Wanda's children grew within the environment their Papaw provided. One day, Rawley invited Dusty and Donny to the mine. He introduced them to the corporation and gave them an executive tour of the last working mine in Timberline County. He instructed them that one day, the coal would flow again through a worldwide market. The boys were bored with the talk, but they were enthralled with the adventure underground.

While visiting her great Mamaw Denise wandered to the truck to inspect it for herself.She was euphoric when she discovered a stash of coins under the front seat. "Easy pick'ins!" she thought.She told no one about the cash. Instead, she discriminately, over time, invested the buried treasure in fanciful fashions she found from Mary Turley's Boutique. She hoped in being a McGuffey High School fashion statement, she would eventually land a handsome teen idol all her own. Perhaps one who would sweep her off to Hollywood.

Donna and Dara were most content when they were visiting Eva. From all they had seen around them, they found more comfort with Eva than with anyone else. They became her emotional caregivers, a Godsend to the aging woman. More and more, Eva Kilbride was aching, ailing in body and temper of soul. She never complained openly, although her health her well-being, had deteriorated rapidly since the ordeal with Marcus. She couldn't come to any conclusion about the causes of her dis-ease. Nor could she discern a cure. "It's sad when know'in for sure gets lost in things." she would say, "…forgett'in what *you know* makes you feel hollow inside."

Much of what she remembered about Marcus, she refused to speak. In her lonelier hours, as she reclined in her chair, she pondered those things but never dared share those "*ponder 'ins*" with Aidan's picture. Every now and then, when there came an *Autumn* "*reckon'in*" of her own, a seasonal sum of things, she could only hope to forget some unsettlingly true things.

Dolly worked part-time hours at the Hub. Eva needed her more and more at home. Timberline folks were divided in their opinions of her. Some say she aided and abetted a known murderer to flee. Others thought her a devoted sister (and "living legend") for attempting such an ingenious escape. After over an hour of flight in the hot air balloon, Marcus died. The fuel in the rig dropped low. Dolly erratically but safely landed the balloon and basket in a remote area mile outside of Timberline County. By the time Sheriff Keith Boswell arrived, Dolly and Leah had pulled him from the basket. They cradled him in a meadow of wildflowers.

Hank was rushed to the hospital. The poultice his mother applied notwithstanding, he survived the venomous bite of the copperhead when Dr. Leland McCreary postponed his role-play as *Daniel Boone* to tend to the boy. Hank recovered from the venom, but he incurred a deep bruise that left an indistinguishable scar on his leg. He grew fond of the scar. When he wore his cross-country shorts, he flaunted it as unique, a personal rite of passage, defeating the sting of the copperhead.

Eva awarded Marcus's guitar to Hank. She thought Marcus would have done the same. Hank continued to compose his songs. Now and then, he was invited to sing at the HUB for his respective groupies. Hank had a natural inclination toward the music in the mountains. In his mind, he called himself "a romantic realist." His music blended both soul and flesh. His compositions recognized and reflected cooperation with a Composer undergirding the wonder of all things around him. In a strange way, Marcus' life and untimely death became a moment for Hank to be seemingly born again. The scar on his leg and the new songs he composed transformed Hank into *HENRY*. The tragedy of his Uncle Marcus awakened him toward a hope in something Holy; seeking the wonders (rather than the woes) of Timberline County, and running beyond the boundaries of restrictive holler law.

Chapter Twelve:
Awake

"I shall behold your face in righteousness; when I awake, I shall be satisfied beholding your likeness." (Psalm 15:15)

"When you lie down, your sleep will be sweet." (Proverbs 3:24)

It was well into the month of November, just a few days before Thanksgiving, when the Kilbride clan held a memorial wake for Marcus. It was decided among the siblings, under the circumstances, that a private service for family alone seemed more appropriate than one that would make a public spectacle of things. Marcus had already been buried unceremoniously in the clan cemetery on a hillside in the upper bottom. Fern and Rawley chose a small, gray granite stone with black specks that sparkled in the sunlight for a marker. It was left marked until Dolly insisted on adding the engraving:

Loving Son and Brother: 1955-1983

"He mounted up with wings as an eagle" Isaiah 40:31

By holler law, a memorial service was held in the parlor of the Wiley Funeral Home. Pastor Benny Peyton of the Baptist Church officiated. He had known Marcus as a child through his attendance at Vacation Bible School many summers ago but knew little of him in later years. Pastor Benny remembered how anxious Marcus was to be baptized when the boy was only eight years old and how he forgot to wear his long johns under his baptism gown.

"He wanted to be saved." Preacher Peyton recalled. "I remember, he was probably 'bout twelve, he made so many trips down the aisle for repentance, I thought maybe God was call'in him to be a missionary. I imagine he was struggl'in back then with deeper struggles we will never know about.

"Marcus just couldn't grasp a'hold of 'the peace that surpasses all human understand'in.' But now, due to his profession of faith as a child, he knows it well."

That was all Pastor Benny said about Marcus. From his eulogy, Peyton launched into a sermon for those who had yet to be *saved*, for whoever wanted to see Marcus again, specifically, to go to Heaven. The scripture flew unrestrained about the room from the heart, soul, and will power of the preacher:

"For all have sinned and the wages of sin is death, but the free gift of God is eternal life through Jesus Christ our Lord! It is a free gift! Where sin increased, grace abounds all the more! It is a free gift! If you confess with your mouth the Lord Jesus and believe in your heart that God raised him from the dead, you shall be saved...Everyone who calls upon the name of the Lord shall be saved! Romans 3:23.

God's grace is all sufficient! In his gospel, John said, "we have all received grace upon grace... Everyone who calls upon the Lord shall be saved! It is a free gift, not of works lest any man should boast! It is all sufficient grace given to us by faith!"

Pastor Benny sighed for a heavy burden, wiped his brow with his forearm, and then continued. "I hope that as that child in our VBS, Marcus received the free gift. *You* can receive the free gift today. All you must DO is recite the sinner's prayer, follow the ordinance of baptism, join a gospel-preaching church, and then witness to others 'bout salvation in Jesus. It is a free gift of God. Will you receive it today?" Finally, to seal the deal, the preacher added, "Per chance to see Marcus again in the glory of Heaven, you must accept this free gift of God!"

The organ played the anthem of all altar calls: *"Just as I Am, without one plea...I come..."* Preacher Benny stood before the gathering, hoping for the awakening of at least one soul. When no one responded publicly to his plea, he closed the service in prayer.

He thanked God for the life of Marcus Kilbride and for the prospect of reuniting with him in…eventually.

*

The tone of the memorial service was ritually somber but sufficient. (Sister Dazzlingstar critiqued the sermon, but Aunt Grace was comforted by his sincerity.) The undertone in the conversations afterward in the reception hall was more personally beguiling. The fallout of Marcus's existence trickled lazily throughout the room.Post-funeral conversations often become teachable moments.While few would remember the verbiage in the sermon most would recall the conversations in the aftermath of a clan awakened to communion by tragedy that was Marcus Kilbride.

The clan filed by the table of the funeral faire prepared with care by Grace Dazzlingstar's congregation and supplemented by the Woman's Missionary Association of the host church. It was a feast fit for the grieving:ham and tuna salad sandwiches, chips and dip, mac 'n cheese, baked beans, a bucket of fried chicken, and a variety of assorted pies, cakes, and cookies. Wanda's kids were the first in line, bumping into mourners, running around a few distant relatives, and skipping the entrees for the assortment of sweets.

The hall was small and congested with the clan. Each had a chosen space for their respective chit-chat. Dolly brought her mother a cup of coffee from the kitchen. Eva was sitting alone at a table, glancing out the window at the prayer garden outside. "Momma, here's your coffee." Dolly whispered, "Do you want a sandwich? It'd be good for you to eat someth'in."

Just then, Deputy Travis Hudson sauntered through the threshold of the hall. He didn't speak to anyone, just nodded to anyone with whom he could make eye contact…especially Wanda. Curiously, he was not interested in making trivial conversation but was more concerned with being an official uniformed presence for the event. He passed by Wanda and smirked in a whisper to her, "Timberline's fines--always at your service, Mam."

Eva sipped the coffee and shook her head. "Don't feel like eat'in right now...feel'in a bit poorly."

"Want to go home?" Dolly asked.

Eva shook her head. Dolly sat beside her.

Keith Boswell entered the hall. He was not wearing his uniform but instead was adorned in a fine black suit, white shirt, and deep crimson tie. His demeanor was unofficial, more chivalrous than ceremonial. Even in his proper attire, there was nothing stuffed shirt about him. His street shoes were worn, laden with the dust and soot of the hollers. He nodded to those around him but stepped directly to Eva. The plainclothesman sat down and gently placed his hand over hers.

"Eva," he sighed, "Are you all right?"

She answered, "...cept'in for that old coitus, I'm fine."

"*Colitis*, Momma!" Dolly exclaimed, "*Colitis*, not coitus. Gawd!"

"Well, whatever they call it." Eva frowned, removing her hand from under his. "You know what I meant. Dolly, I changed my mind! Go get me a sandwich or someth'in."

Dolly left them alone. She walked back into the kitchen to fetch herself something to drink and quietly exited into the garden for a cigarette or two.

Keith Boswell continued, "You know, I'm sorry for all of this, Eva. There wasn't much I could do to save Marcus."

"I reckon you did the best you could, Keith." Eva said.

He nodded.

Then Eva added, "What 'bout Dolly? What you gonna do 'bout her?"

He thought for a moment, then whispered, "The record officially records her as a *hostage,* not an accomplice. She's…safe."

No words came between them for a moment. Then Eva gasped to break the awkward silence between them. "We sowed unholy seed. We're reap'in what we sowed."

"Don't say that."

"I broke my holy vow with Aidan. He never said anythang, but Lord, somehow, he knew Marcus weren't his. He kept it to hisself, but he knew…took to him anyway."

"Marcus was conceived *in love*, Eva. That's all that mattered."

"Hush!" Eva gasped, turning her head away to the window again. "Leave me be, Keith. You did what you could to save Marcus. He's gone. There ain't noth'in more 'tween us. Leave me be."

"I'm sorry, Eva." He stood over her and warmly grasped her hand. "I won't be 'round…less you need me."

She glanced at him one last time, "Thank you…Sheriff."

Boswell walked away. He passed Travis Hudson, standing unassumingly nearby. He ignored his deputy and departed the reception.

Travis overheard their clandestine conversation. He was conflicted between loyalty to his superior and the knowledge of a miscarriage of protocol by an elected but now-benighted servant of the people. Then it occurred to him. Perhaps he could devise a more intriguing strategy through which to address this infraction; a way to bring stricter law enforcement to Timberline County. It was at that moment when Travis Hudson decided to position himself to revolution: to become the new sheriff.

He scanned the hall for potential movers and shakers, influential persons he could groom for future leverage. In Timberline County, everyone with grit could influence the political tide. He merely had to find those who lived behind gated egos and convince them there was something for them in his replacing Keith Boswell with the likes of Travis Hudson.

It was a strategic move to start with whomever he could elicit trust: Pastor Peyton, Dr. McCreary, business owners like Mary Turley and Rosalee Wiley, Senator-to-be Perry Jackson, and the patriarchal older brother, Rawley Kilbride. If he could groom support from those respected in Timberline County, he would undoubtedly merit votes from the other clans in the hollers as well.

There was Wanda Kilbride! Sparking with Wanda was an uncomfortable thought for Travis, especially considering the complication of her many offspring. But she was a threshold to the radar of Rawley Kilbride. Wanda was leaning against the kitchen doorway, sipping punch from a paper cup. She seemed coy, but Travis read her poised body language as an invitation. He sauntered up to her, his spine erect, his hands gripping the leather belt that confined his protruding pistol.

"All these kids run 'in 'round here belong to you?" he asked. "They're quite a brood."

"Mostly." she answered, "They all got daddies somewhere."

"Those 'daddies' 'round much?"

"Yeah. They're 'round all right...'round and 'round and 'round....and where they stop... nobody knows."

"Want to sit down?" he asked.

She poured her punch in the sink, then pulled two chairs together against the wall. She tilted them toward each other, then sat down. "This one is yours," she said with a grin.

"I'm Deputy Hudson." he said, adjusting his pistol.

"I know your title. " Wanda replied. "But I'd like to know who you are."

"I'm Travis." He smiled.

"That's better." She smiled back. "I'm Wanda Kilbride...um...Sorley."

"Rawley Kilbride's daughter. He's a big man in Timberline."

"Uh huh." she sighed heavily, "That's my daddy."

"So, you're...married?"

"Barely....sometimes. Hopeful."

"What does that mean?"

Wanda tilted her head like a puppy, hearing a shrill noise for the first time. "Come on, Travis. You're a cop. You've already done a *make* on me. You know I got five kids. Two of 'em from Bucky Sorley. He's-- in and out. You know. The other two daddies? Took advantage of a good thang, that's all. But you know all that, you got a badge...and a bulge: a big, dangl'in pistol under your belt. You did a make on me.What is it you *really* want, Deputy Travis Hudson?"

Hudson removed his cap. "I reckon I want to know more than facts."

At that moment, Dusty ran up beside him. "Hey!" the boy yelled, "Can I see your gun?"

"This is my son, Dusty. If he's bother'in you, I can..."

"No!" the Deputy exclaimed. "I need kids to respect the law."

Hudson donned his hat. Then, he slowly removed his pistol from its holster. "Guns ain't toys, kid. But don't let this thing scare you..."

Dusty was mesmerized by the .357. He exclaimed, "That's a Smith and Wesson!"

Hudson lifted the pistol in front of him and scoffed, "Um--yeah, it is. How did you know that?"

"My daddy taught me." The boy smiled. " 'fore he run away on his *mission*."

Wanda added, "His daddy taught him lots of thangs-- 'fore he run off."

"That's exactly what this is, Dusty. You have a good eye." Hudson began, "But if you want to keep that eye, you have to treat guns with respect." He glanced over the boy's shoulder at Dusty's mother, "like you would a real woman."

"What's it feel like?" inquired the boy breathlessly. "Can I hold it?"

"It's iron. Hard and heavy. You've got to learn how to balance it properly. The sites are perfect, so you can pick off whatever you're aiming at. I learned to shoot it. A lot of experience. I'm a certified marksman."

"Can I hold it?" he asked.

"Come here." With one arm, he lifted Dusty to sit on his knee. "You can hold it with me holding on to your hand."

Hudson locked the safety in place, then, guided by the Deputy's grip, Dusty held the gun, turning it from side to side, squinting his eyes down the barrel through the sites, and mimicking gunshot blasts.

"What're you shoot'in at?" asked Deputy Hudson.

Dusty grit his teeth, "Whatever gets in my way."

While they were squinting through the sites, Rawley Kilbride approached them. "And what is in your way, Dustin?" Rawley asked.

Dusty released his grip on the gun and slid himself off the deputy's knee. "Look at his gun, Papaw! It's a Lugar! Smith and Wesson! Deputy Travis, let me hold it! He's a perfect shooter—a marked man!"

"A marksman." Travis smiled.

"I see." Rawley answered. "I guess we need marksmen in the Sheriff's office these days, huh?"

Hudson smiled, "In times like these, yessir. It's good to have an Academy-trained officer nearby. Someone sharp, you know, alert 24/7."

Wanda added, "A man who can handle his pistol—nearby."

"Nearby in town, yes." Rawley began, "But not near my grandsons. Keep your weapon in your holster, Deputy."

He left Wanda and Travis alone, then ushered Dusty away to join Denise, Donny, Donna, and Dara at another table. Rawley had prepared a decent plate of food for them, but those plates were still full. Not a nibble had they taken. Instead, while their Papaw was distracted, they had prepared their plates stacked with cookies and chips.

Rawley sat Dustin at the table with his siblings. Papaw squeezed himself into one of the kiddie chairs next to him.

"I want to talk to you all." Papaw insisted. They continued munching on the sweets while he spoke. "I want to tell you about an adventure I had with your momma. This was when your momma was small, like Dara. Your Mamaw Alma and I took her to a wonderland called Coney Island."

"You went on an island?" Donny asked with wide eyes. "On a boat?"

"No stupid." remarked Denise, "It's a park with rides and stuff."

Rawley smiled, "More than a 'park,' Denise. We floated in canoes on a lake, climbed aboard a Coney Island steam-paddler called 'Princess,' and ate corn dogs and funnel cakes. We slid down a giant slide and rode 'round a Ferris wheel so high we could see the hills across the river. We rode a *Shooting Star* coaster! Walked through a spook house! There were whirley-birds and bumper cars, giant swirling swings, and snow cone bars. We flew in the breeze on a sky lift and sang 'round-the-rosy on the lighted-up merry-go-round. That night, we shared the best Bar B Q chicken you ever ate at the Moonlite Gardens. And when the day was over, we sat on a hillside by the river and watched the fireworks exploding all over the sky! No, Denise, it was more than just a park."

Donny yelled, "Can we go there? I want to ride the Shoot'in Star!"

"A whirley-bird for me?" Donna asked.

"I would go in the spook house!" declared Dusty.

Rawley lifted Dara and put her on his knee. "What about you, Dara? What would you like to see?"

Dara tilted her head sheepishly toward her Papaw, "a purple snow cone."

Denise responded, agitated with skepticism. "But it ain't there no more! Why are you telling 'em all this? GOD! I hate it when old people tell you things, and then they let you down. Coney Island is what you remember--it ain't real!"

"It WAS real, Denise." Rawley answered, "More than Coney Island. It was the love we had, the moments we shared."

"So?" Denise replied, "We ain't got those 'moments.'"

259

"You will. When your Mamaw Alma died, I didn't want anything but those moments to last. So, I stopped making new ones. But that's not how it's going to be anymore. I want moments with you all—memories you can hold on to."

They looked at him a bit confounded. They stared at him as if he were an alien from outer space.

"So?" Dusty began, "Does that mean we're go'in to Coney or not?"

"I'm planning an adventure for all of us—you, me, and your momma. Not Coney Island. But it will be *our* place, *our adventure,* just for us."

"Really?" asked Denise.

"I promise." answered their papaw.

Donny noticed Emmanuel, sitting alone, noticeably uncomfortable in his ill-fitting sports coat, shirt buttoned to the neck and tightly knotted tie. He was munching on a chicken leg and sipping a cup of iced tea without any ice. Manny's thoughts were adrift to how he rescued Marcus. In his mind, he had done "good." He sheltered Marcus in the shed, gave him bread and soup, whisked him away in the van, and even helped him fly in the balloon. Even if Grace Dazzlingstar chided him for "breaking the law," he couldn't believe he did "bad."

Donny stepped over to Manny. The two decided to fix Marcus's hiding place into a shelter for stragglers rather than a shed for storage. The backyard they could cultivate into a community garden.

Donny could help Manny landscape the area into a garden with good seeds, planted in fertile soil and nourished in a better environment. They would build an oil-anointed wood fence around the yard to protect the garden from menacing critters. Donny ran to share their idea with his Papaw.

Whenever Manny thought about the shelter in the garden, the theological conundrums of Sister Dazzlingstar faded away. Many a time after the tragedy of Marcus Kilbride, his mother transposed from Sister Dazzlingstar in her pulpit to Grace Kilbride on the front porch in her rocking chair. It was at those times that he recalled his childhood. He remembered himself sharing her rocking chair and being held in the embrace, not by Dazzlingstar, but of Grace; her fingertips stroked his hair while she sang softly:

"I'll fly away, O Glory

I'll fly away...

Some glad morning when this life is o'er

I'll fly away..."

Rawley left his grandchildren and walked over to Emmanuel. He always approached at the young man with apprehension and a pinch of pity.

"Emmanuel," he began, "I'm taking my grandkids on an adventure soon. An amusement park. They're pretty rowdy. I need some help. Would you be brave enough to go with us? Help me out?"

"Me?" Manny asked with some disbelief.

"Go ask your momma, Manny." he said. "Ask HER, not the *prophet*!"

Grace Kilbride had enlisted the help of her niece, Fern to keep the hall kitchen tidy. Being a co-matriarch (with Eva) of the Kilbride clan, she felt it her duty to do such things. While Fern was replenishing the table, Grace was in the kitchen scrubbing residue from the counter tops and scouring whatever needed to be scoured. She believed that keeping busy, especially for the Lord, kept her from earthly distractions.

261

Emmanuel was quick about his quest for his mother's permission. "Momma?"

"Emmanuel," Grace quipped. She was in midstream, dusting the sink with Comet cleanser. "Tie that trash bag of mess and take it to the dumpster!"

He stepped to the trash can and began to tie the bag tightly so as not to allow any refuse to escape. He continued, "Rawley is taking the kids on an adventure. He needs me to go with them."

Grace put on her gloves, grabbed a sponge, and began to rub circles of the cleanser in the sink. "An adventure? What kind of adventure?"

He shrugged. "A park."

She rubbed the cleanser harder in circles. "You have to get that shed repaired and that fence built; that's your adventure!"

"Good God, Grace!" exclaimed Fern from across the kitchen, "Let the man go! He's with Rawley and Wanda's kids. What the hell are you afraid of?"

Then she stomped over to the older woman and took the sponge from her hand. " And you don't need to scrub so hard. That residue will come clean with just a little prodding. Prodding is better than scrubbing! You don't get scratches do'in that way!"

Fern gathered the last morsels of the meal and left Grace and Manny in the kitchen. She stepped over to Dean and laid a platter of chicken on the table in front of him.

"Here, Dean," she ordered, "Finish this off." Then she scurried away to find a broom from the janitor's closet down the hall.

Presley spied the delivery of chicken and sat next to his Uncle Dean. Dean leaned back and chuckled, "Go ahead, Pres. I can't eat all o'this. Get yourself a breast or a wing." Presley grinned and grabbed a piece of chicken.

262

Dean asked, "So, Pres? Are you Army bound?"

Presley shrugged, licking a piece of chicken from his lips. "Don't know yet."

"Elvis joined."

Presley sat back in his chair. "I got to work for my dad at the State Capitol."

"Yeah, your mom told me. What's he been appointed to again?"

"Family Health and Welfare Committee."

"What is that exactly?"

"He's on a committee that takes care of family health and welfare."

"Oh." Dean grinned, shaking his head in agreement. "Of course. What will you do exactly at the State Capitol? To support your dad?"

"Odd jobs, I reckon. Run'in for him...whatever he needs me to do."

Dean watched him devour the rest of the chicken, then asked, "What does Presley Jackson want?"

Presley stopped short, "To see the world, I reckon."

His uncle, Sergeant Dean, put his arm around his nephew's shoulder. "Let's talk." he smiled.

*

The seed of some pine will not yield to the soil of the earth unless the cone has been in some way experienced intense heat. After a wildfire has swept through the forest, while there is the charred devastation that occurs for many years thereafter, there is also the miracle of new life that emerges from the fledgling seeds that lie deep in the inner core of the cone. What is deepest and concealed is often protected by the strength of the shell that surrounds it. When nurtured by the light, fertile soil, and a healthy environment, there grows a root with a gentle shoot arising from the ground, stretching forth to the sky, until a stronger seedling stands, weathering the elements thereafter with a determination to live…and grow.

*

Henry Jackson: The End of the Parable as a Beginning

Hank periodically visited the graveside of Marcus Kilbride for two reasons. The first because it was a steep, uphill climb to the family cemetery. The exercise was good for training his legs in preparation for the high school cross-country team.

The second reason was to play new songs for Marcus on his old guitar. He discovered surges of inspiration on the secluded hillside, what Hank claimed as "sacred space."Here, Henry could breathe

264

deeply, listen to the orchestration of the woodlands, and watch the pristine choreography of life around him. Henry was growing through a multi-sensory phenomenon he couldn't express through either scientific theory or religious rhetoric. He had to compose the music in the wonder he experienced; then he had to sing it. He was running with the Wind and soaring in his awe of creation.

Hank changed his name evermore to *Henry*. This was befitting his desire to refine himself rather than to be defined by others, particularly those in his own clan. As he conditioned himself for cross country competition, his legs grew stronger. He learned to breathe like a runner. He could soon climb up the rocky heights in the hollers without the pain he felt before. He ran with unyielding momentum on a course that he was convinced he could win.

The boy ran well now, having outgrown the snake bite. He ran at his own pace, sometimes swiftly, with the momentum of the woodland breeze. At other times, he sprinted in a rather sauntering stride so as not to miss the majesty of the forest. All the while, he breathed deeply in wondrous syncopation with the beating of his heart. His legs were growing stronger, responding brazenly and boldly to meet the terrain in the hollers. Most every morning, he would run, setting his course through unbeaten paths he had blazoned, trails that challenged even the boundaries of Timberline County. Perhaps that was a lesson, a prompt, he learned, gained from the traumas and tragedies of the past?

By early Spring, at Eastertide, Henry Jackson was scaling high and pristine trails. Such mindfulness dispelled the primitive wantonness he saw around him in the hollers.He ran freely through the woodlands, splashing through shallow streams, down rugged slopes and up perilous ridges, bounding over fallen timber and galloping around dens and ditches. He was mesmerized with holy adrenaline yet quite cognizant of those creatures that could be coiled in the shadows. Sometimes, he would sprint, but mostly, he chose to gallop lightheartedly in longer stretches. His heart desired to run well, with agility, stamina, and with the perseverance of a long-distance runner.

Into the warmth of a new Spring morning, Henry ran to the God-rock, where he always paused to catch his breath. Effortlessly, he ascended, climbing upon the rock that overlooked the places where so many horrible things had happened. The damaged trees and brush around where the wreckage occurred were recovered. By late Spring, new green vines and seedlings would overgrow the obscure landmark.Henry removed his tee shirt and wiped the sweat from his face and chest. He removed his running shoes and socks and laid back on the rock, his hands behind his head. He stretched his long-distance runner legs, stood atop the God rock, and reached his open palms toward the sun. It was at that moment atop the God-rock that *Hank* released a reservoir of bittersweet tears-- both for the demise of Marcus, and for the new birth of *Henry*.

*

That evening, alone in his room, he picked up the refurbished guitar and composed a psalm dedicated to whom he discovered to be the *real Marcus Kilbride*:

To Marcus…and others like him
"What wonder have you sensed?
What Presence have you discerned?
By holy contemplation
What renderings have you learned?
Have you heard a mystic melody?
Savored sacred incense in the air?
Been mesmerized by life in motion?
Or lulled in the Breeze's compassionate care?
Have you scaled a towering summit?
Or strolled softly in submission to the sea?
What mindfulness has ascended beyond
Pious rhetoric or heady capacity?
Wonder woos me to awareness

and surrender to vulnerability.
Through parables of living: a guiding Word of poetry
"' Never fear, never fear... to come and see."

Acknowledgments:

My gratitude to the following:

Brian Shoemaker,aka; the real author

Rhonda Leah Shoemaker

Jim Curry

Keith Ward

The clan, McBride

Debbie Miles Lester

Wolfgang Gunnar Miles

Matt Moore

Mac Keiffer

and

 (Those who ignited my respect for good literature)

Ruth Edgington

Arlene Akerman

Joan Leary

All photos used in this novel were used with permission by the photographers, subjects, and iStock by Getty Images